THE AIRMAN'S
E-MAIL ORDER BRIDE

BY CORA SETON

AUTHOR'S NOTE

The Airman's E-Mail Order Bride is the fifth in the five volume series, **The Heroes of Chance Creek**. To find out more about Mason, Regan, Austin, Zane, Colt and other Chance Creek inhabitants, look for the rest of the books in the series, including:

Find out where it all began with **The Cowboys of Chance Creek** Series:

THE SEALS OF CHANCE CREEK

A SEAL's Oath
A SEAL's Vow
A SEAL's Pledge
A SEAL's Consent

Visit www.coraseton.com for more titles and release dates.

Sign up for my newsletter here.

www.coraseton.com/sign-up-for-my-newsletter

PROLOGUE

July

STAFF SERGEANT COLT Hall squatted in the darkness on a rocky outcrop high in the mountains on the border between Afghanistan and Pakistan. His father, Aaron, crouched silently beside him. Dawn would come soon, but for now the valley was full of shadows where anything could hide.

"Tough country."

"Got that right," Colt said. He knew his father shouldn't stand watch with him while the rest of his team slept; he knew something was odd about Aaron's presence there at all, but he couldn't quite work it out. Colt had served with this small band of Navy SEALs for the past year in his position as an Air Force combat controller, and he needed to stay alert and not be distracted by conversation—or conundrums. This hour of the night was lonely, though, and he appreciated his father's company, even if they were breaking the rules.

"Hard to make a living from that land."

"They grow 'em tough as nails around here," Colt

agreed. He didn't know how the Afghans eked sustenance out of these hills year after year, lifetime after lifetime.

"You've got some good land waiting for you back in Montana."

Colt shifted. He knew that. He could just about taste summer in Chance Creek, but he chased all memories of Crescent Hall, his family's ranch, from his mind. "I've got a job to do here."

"I think your stint here's about finished, son."

Finished? His job was never finished. If it wasn't the Taliban in Afghanistan, it was drug lords in Central America, or an earthquake in Haiti. "I don't think so."

"Someone's waiting for you. Don't let them down."

Waiting for him? Colt turned his head to look at his father, all the time knowing he had to keep watch on the valley below. They could be ambushed at any time, especially in these hushed moments between night and sunrise.

His father's expression held love, compassion and something else—something... wistful. He set his hand on Colt's shoulder.

"Time to go home."

Colt reared up from sleep with a gasp so loud he woke his three companions and sent their lookout scrambling for cover under the nearby trees. His father's voice rang so clearly in his mind he jerked around to find him, but all he saw was the rocky escarpment on which they'd made camp. A hint of the coming dawn eased the dark grays into lighter shades in the east. Otherwise, all was as bleak and grim as it had been when he'd gone to bed.

"What the fuck, Colt?" Tanner Hudson hissed close by his side.

"Just a dream," Colt managed to say. But what a dream. He still couldn't believe he'd been sleeping instead of standing guard. It had felt so real—especially Aaron's hand on his shoulder. *Time to go home.*

Colt eased back to rest on his elbows. Aaron had been dead for over a decade and Colt had never had a visitation like this. *Not a visitation*, he reminded himself. *Just a dream.* Just his mind playing tricks on him.

He hadn't wanted to go home since Aaron had died and his family had been forced to leave Chance Creek and go to live with his aunt in Florida. Even now that his brothers had begun to move back to claim their family's old ranch, there were too many memories he didn't want to face, especially the ones that had to do with his father.

Colt had joined the Air Force just as soon as he'd turned seventeen. His brother, Austin, had already decided to enter the military and the rest of them had joined up when it became clear their mother, in her grief over their father's death, couldn't support them. Colt had worked his way up the ranks and now his job was to aid this advance party behind enemy lines by calling in airstrikes and relaying coordinates to the pilots and rear crews.

Time to go home.

Why had his father been so insistent? And who could be waiting for him? *Don't let them down.* Colt settled back and pulled his covers around him, his heart rate slowing. He'd already let his father down the day Aaron died. The last time he'd seen his father alive, he'd been in too much of a hurry to slow down and talk to him. His family had still owned Crescent Hall back then, the old three-story mansion and the ranch that shared its name. Colt, just sixteen and on fire for Heather Ward—his new girlfriend and his brother Austin's ex—had met Aaron on the path between the house and the barn.

"Hold up a minute," Aaron had called out. "You off to cause trouble?"

"No." But he hadn't met his father's eyes as he raced on by.

"You know what you're doing isn't right!" his father had shouted after him.

Colt hadn't answered. Hopped up on adrenaline and hormones, he'd done exactly what his father had feared he'd do: slept with the girl who only weeks ago had dated his brother. He'd regretted every last illicit minute with Heather ever since. Before he'd even reached the woods and his meeting place with her, his father had died from an aneurysm. Colt didn't learn of it for hours. His tryst with Heather marked the last few moments of what he now knew was a glorious childhood, and introduced him to the wonders of making love. But the nightmare he'd come home to had wiped any joyful memory from his mind. He couldn't think of that day with anything but horror.

He'd killed his father while betraying his brother. Aaron must have worried so much about the rift he knew was coming between his sons that a vein in his brain had burst and felled him instantly.

Colt swallowed against the nausea that rose in his throat. His older brother, Zane, was the only one who knew that he'd been with Heather at all, and no one knew about the words he'd exchanged with Aaron on the track between the house and barn. No one would ever know. He'd never been with Heather again. Had broken off all contact with her as soon as he learned his father was dead—even before his family was forced to leave the ranch a scant two weeks later. It was the hardest thing he'd ever done, especially since none of it was Heather's fault. All the blame was his. He was the one so caught up in lust and love that he hadn't heard the sense in his father's words.

Heather Ward. Colt turned over, knowing soon it would be time to get up. Around him the others settled in again to try to glean a few last moments of rest. Once he thought he'd marry Heather and live out his days on the family's ranch, but that was so long ago it didn't matter anymore. Four months ago, he and his brothers had been given another chance to win it back. He'd scoffed at Mason, Austin and Zane when they'd agreed to his Aunt Heloise's crazy conditions for inheriting the place, but when they'd pressured him he'd agreed to do his part. Heloise had insisted they fix up the buildings and stock the ranch with cattle. In addition, all four of them had to marry, and one had to have a child.

"I won't leave the Air Force," he'd told his brothers, and they'd agreed it wasn't necessary. All they needed was for him to find a wife.

The dream about Aaron had cracked a fault line through his resolution to stay away. The truth was he'd never felt worthy to go home—not after what he'd done. Maybe the aneurysm would have struck whether he raced by or stopped to talk to his dad. Still, he couldn't help think that losing his father and the ranch all in one blow was divine retribution for his sins.

But if his father wanted him home...

It was just a dream, he reminded himself.

"It's time," Brian Leyton whispered from several feet away. The others began to stir and prepare to move out for another day's reconnaissance. As Colt got to his feet and silently stowed his gear in his backpack, he felt again the pressure of his father's hand on his shoulder.

Time to go home. He stood still amidst his team's activity, and took a long look around him. Mountains stretched in every direction. He'd never been in such a starkly beautiful, empty place. For a moment, the sounds of his companions fell away and Colt stood alone under a sky so large it seemed to recede from him. The details of his mission emptied from his mind and he gave himself up to the beauty of the sunrise in a strange land so far from home.

Someone's waiting for you. Don't let them down. The words were only an echo from his earlier dream, but the message sliced through all Colt's defenses straight to his heart. He missed Chance Creek with an ache he'd lived with so long it had become part of him. Maybe his father was right; maybe it was time. Time to confess to his brothers what had happened the day of their father's death. Time to apologize to Austin for his tryst with Heather. Time to find a wife, get married, and take his place on the ranch with the rest of his family.

Colt let out a breath and the world came rushing back in. Small birds peeped in the brush around them. His teammates, as quiet as they could be, still rustled as they moved. Tanner edged up to him. "Ready?" he asked, voice low.

"Yeah," Colt said, taking one last look around. "Yeah, I'm ready."

CHAPTER ONE

December

"ARE YOU REALLY going home to Montana to marry some stranger?" Tanner said, lounging in the doorway of Colt's room at Eglin Air Force Base.

"Yep." Colt focused on the laptop screen in front of him. "As long as I can find a stranger who wants to marry me. How's this for a title: *Get Paid to be My Wife.*"

"Catchy." Tanner rolled his eyes. "You'll reel in some high quality girls with that one."

"You got a better idea?" Colt had already spent way too much time on this damn ad. Each time he tried to write it, his gut tightened with an anxious feeling he was setting a lethal trap for himself. It was one thing to go home. It was another to get married, especially when you had a deadline. Back in the spring when Mason first told him about Heloise's conditions, he'd thought it would be funny to advertise for a fake wife. Now it wasn't quite as amusing. He would have to live with the woman for months and he'd have to convince his aunt he actually loved her, which wouldn't be simple. Heloise was wily.

The process had made him face the fact that he'd never given marriage a serious thought. He wasn't a man to ruminate over the reasons behind his actions, but it was too clear to miss that he'd avoided any kind of commitment with a woman.

He knew why, too.

"How about *Airman Seeks Bride*? They'll line up to get you."

"No way. I don't want them lining up. I want one woman who gets the drill and won't try to hang around when it's time for her to hit the highway."

"Always the romantic."

"To hell with romance."

Tanner watched him type. When his scrutiny got irritating, Colt locked eyes with him. "You got something to say, say it."

"You could approach this differently."

"Differently how?"

"Like there's a chance you'll actually fall for one of the women who answer your ad."

"There isn't any chance of that." He might be ready to go home and patch things up with his family—if that was possible—but he wasn't ready to fall in love. Certainly not with someone he met from an online ad.

He'd fallen in love once. It hadn't worked out.

"Why not? Each of your brothers has, right?"

He didn't know why Tanner kept trying to make the situation more than it was. "Here's the rest of it," he pressed on. *"Wife needed for four to six months. Room, board and expenses plus generous salary. Must act the part under intense scrutiny and be willing to sign a pre-nup.*"

Tanner sighed. "You're missing an opportunity here, Hall."

"Yeah? What's that?" He filled in his payment information and prepared to place the ad.

"What about that girl—Heather? Why not see if she's still around?"

Colt stilled. He should have never told Tanner anything about Heather. Unfortunately Tanner had snuck up on him earlier this year and saw her photograph on his laptop screen. It hadn't meant anything. When Mason sent Colt an invitation to his wedding last June, Colt had looked her up to see if she was still in town. Pure curiosity, nothing more.

She was still in town as far as he could tell, but her Internet presence was decidedly lacking. She featured in photos taken by a few of her friends. Once he got over his surprise that she'd dyed her dark hair blonde, he decided she hadn't changed all that much. The few photos he found showed a mature version of the girl he'd lusted after all those years ago. She was still beautiful, but something in her eyes told him her life hadn't been easy.

His curiosity was far from satisfied, but he didn't plan to pursue his search. He hadn't seen Heather when he attended Mason's wedding, and he told himself he was relieved about that.

He wouldn't look her up when he got home, either, and even if he saw her he wouldn't try to renew their relationship. Heather belonged to the past—to the life he'd had before Aaron's death.

As a teenager she'd meant everything to him. He'd wanted her from the first time Austin brought her to the ranch, and he'd done everything he could think of to show her he was the one she should be with, but in all the months she'd dated Austin she'd never noticed him. The day she and his brother had split up, however, he knew his chance had finally come. He'd waited three more weeks to make his move—three weeks that felt like three years to a sixteen-year-old boy. When he'd finally asked her out and she'd said yes, he'd felt faint for the first time in his life. He'd taken it slow and minded his manners on the first date, kissed her good-night on the second, and made out with her until neither of them could breathe on the third.

"I want to be with you," he'd whispered into her hair as they stood on her front porch late that night.

"I want to be with you, too." Her soft words had sent shivers of desire down his spine.

"When?"

"Tomorrow. I'll borrow Mom's car. Meet me at the obstacle course."

He had, but after that Colt had never been with Heather again.

Heather had been proud, happy, intelligent, and going places. He wondered why she'd never left Chance Creek.

Did she ever think of him?

"You should at least meet up with her. Go have a drink or two. What harm could come of it?" Tanner interrupted his memories.

"Not going to happen." Colt scanned his ad one last time and checked the image he'd added, a photo of himself in uniform that was several years old. He wondered what kind of woman would be attracted to the serious man with close cropped hair and blue eyes the photo depicted.

It didn't matter; he'd take whomever he could get.

"But, you—"

"I said, it's not going to happen. Why are you so set on this, anyway?"

Tanner looked sheepish. "Because… that day you had her photo up on your screen? I don't know, man. I've never seen you look like that. You're still in love with her."

Colt clicked to publish his ad and waited for confirmation that it would post soon. He was not in love with Heather. Or even the memory of her. "This marriage will be a business deal, plain and simple. Once it's over, it's over."

"And you still haven't let your family know you're coming home, either?"

"Nope."

"That's fucked up."

"I want to surprise them."

"More like you want an out in case you can't go through with it. What kind of ghosts are you running from, Hall?"

He wasn't running from a ghost. If anything, he was running *to* one. Colt remembered the words he'd thought he'd heard his father say on that ridge in Afghanistan. *Time to go home.* As much as he thought he'd made the right choice by terminating his career in the Air Force, he was beginning to have doubts about his father's message. He wasn't sure his brothers would actually welcome him home once they heard all he had to say. Austin in particular might hate him when he learned that Colt had dated Heather, and the others might blame him for not stopping to talk to Aaron the day their father died. What if his brothers sent him packing again?

"If you don't go home you won't have the military, you won't have a ranch, you won't have a real wife." Tanner ticked each item off on a finger. "What the hell will you have?"

Colt had no idea.

And that scared the hell out of him.

"IF YOU TRY to refinish that dresser inside you're going to make yourself sick," Heather Ward said, tucking a strand of hair behind her ear.

"I don't want to wait until spring. I wanted to get it done before New Year's." Camila Torres bent over the display of wood stains. They stood in the third aisle of Renfree's Home Décor, which Heather had purchased only a few months ago with the help of a hefty loan from her mother to cover the down payment. She still couldn't believe the place was hers. Hers and the bank's and her mother's, that is, with the bank and her mother owning the lion's share. She appreciated her friend's desire to make a purchase, but it was late December—not the ideal time to stain a dresser.

Heather had learned over the last few months though that once Camila had an idea in her head she ran with it. A vivacious woman with thick, dark curls and sparkling brown eyes, Camila was more fun than just about anyone else Heather knew. She had a seemingly unlimited supply of energy and a can-do attitude Heather could relate to. She'd left Texas due to a family fight and now co-owned one of the most popular restaurants in town.

"Isn't there a workshop you could use—?"

"There you are!"

Heather turned to see Regan Hall walking toward her down the aisle, her long dark hair caught up in an artfully messy bun and her pregnant belly protruding in front of her. Regan was married to Colt's older brother, Mason, and Heather had gotten to know her over the last few months when she took her son, Richard, to see his uncles. Regan held out a cell phone and waved it at her. "I found it!"

"Found what?"

"Colt's ad." She reached them and shoved the phone into Heather's hands. "It took forever, but I did it."

Camila looked from one to the other. "What's going on?"

"Nothing," Heather said, shooting Regan a signifi-cant look.

"Colt finally put up his wife-wanted ad," Regan said. "Now Heather has to answer it and win him back!"

"Keep it down!" Heather stood on tip-toes to make

sure her employee, Susan Beecham, still manned the till at the front of the store and no one else was close enough to hear their conversation. "For heaven's sake, Regan—are you going to tell everyone?"

"No." Regan looked contrite. "I'm sorry, I thought Camila knew."

"I know Colt has to marry within the next three months. I didn't know Heather wanted the job."

"Of course she does. Colt is Richard's father."

"But I haven't seen him in years," Heather said. "Who knows what he's like now."

"He's sweet and kind..." Regan caught Heather's expression and laughed. "Okay, he's a handful, but he's a good guy at heart. And he's cute, too. Not as cute as Mason, mind you, but not too shabby." She poked through the contents of Camila's basket. "What are you working on?"

"A dresser," Camila said.

Heather looked down at Regan's phone, but the screen had gone dark. Regan took it back, fiddled with it and handed it to her again. Now a photo of Colt filled the screen and Heather bit back a sigh. He looked so good. All those years in the Air Force had turned him into a hell of a man. He'd already had the height when she'd known him, but now he had the broad shoulders and powerful musculature of a seasoned warrior. Looking closer, she frowned. Colt had always been happy-go-lucky when they were young. In this photo his expression was serious and his eyes haunted her. What had he seen that had changed him so much?

"Colt was the one to spill the beans about Heloise's requirements to me when Mason had hoped to keep them a secret." Regan's lips turned up in a wry smile. "I was pretty pissed off then, but now it's kind of funny."

"Better you should know about Heloise before your wedding than afterward," Camila said. "Can you imagine how mad you would have been if you came home from your honeymoon and then found out she'd forced Mason to marry you and get you pregnant?"

"That would have been a mess. Not that anyone had to force him to do anything once we fell for each other." Regan lifted up the can of stain Camila had chosen. "Ooh, this is nice. Anyway, all's well that ends well, right Heather?"

"Nothing's ended well for me yet." She kept looking at Colt's photograph, but asked absently, "Do you have a drop cloth, Camila?"

"No."

Heather pointed down the aisle. "Down there. Get a big one."

Regan moved to her side. "Scroll down and read the ad."

"*Get paid to be my wife*," Heather read. "Ugh, that's awful!"

"Keep going."

"*Wife needed for four to six months. Room, board and expenses plus generous salary. Must act the part under intense scrutiny and be willing to sign a pre-nup.* Oh my God, it gets worse and worse! Who on earth is going to marry him?"

"It sounds to me like he's just being practical," Camila said, coming back with a drop cloth. "Didn't you say he plans to stick with the Air Force until he retires?"

Camila was right. Heather knew from his brothers that Colt planned to make the Air Force his life. It hadn't always been that way. Back when she'd dated him—briefly—he'd talked only of the ranch. He'd outlined a future for them in which they would build their own house somewhere on the property and he'd take his place by his father's side running the cattle operation. That was before Aaron died, however, and all their dreams died with him. Colt's Uncle Zeke had kicked his family off the ranch after the funeral and Colt hadn't spoken to her once before they left. She had been sure he'd come to say good-bye, but he hadn't, and to this day she regretted waiting for him to make the first move.

"Maybe he'll change his mind and quit," Regan said. "Once he knows about Richard…"

Heather had no idea what Colt would do when he learned he had a son. Would he want to be involved in Richard's life? Or would he be too angry with her to want anything to do with either of them? Richard was so ready to love his father. Now that three of the Hall brothers were home, he was desperate for Colt to come home, too. If Colt hurt their son's feelings, she didn't know what she'd do.

"Maybe," she said. "But remember, he hasn't gotten in touch in all these years. After his father died, he never talked to me again."

"I don't understand that," Regan said. "He couldn't have blamed you for Aaron's death."

"No," Heather said softly. "But I think he felt guilty about being with me when he knew Austin would hate it, and I think that guilt got all wrapped up with his sorrow over Aaron's aneurysm. Whatever the reason, he never got in touch with me again." She wondered what her life would have been like if Aaron hadn't died. Would Colt have stayed on the ranch? Would he have asked her to marry him?

She would have said yes.

She understood his guilt, though. She'd wrestled with her own after Aaron died and the Halls left Chance Creek. If she was honest, she'd begun to be attracted to Colt long before she broke up with Austin. His passion for life and his utter lack of concern for authority echoed her own inclinations. Austin, on the other hand, lived for order and long-term plans. The more Austin talked about enlisting in the Army—and what their future might hold—the more Heather understood that soon he would ask her to be his wife. At seventeen she wasn't ready for marriage—especially not to Austin. Not when she secretly wanted Colt.

Back then her guilt had nearly overwhelmed her. How could she cast off one brother for another? Austin had always been loyal to her and she didn't know how to break up with him in a way that wouldn't hurt his feelings, but when he took her out for a special dinner and announced that he'd filled in the paperwork to start the enlistment process, Heather knew she'd waited too long.

"I don't want to go out with you anymore," she'd

blurted.

Austin had turned pale. Neither of them had known what to say next. Fifteen minutes later he dropped her off at her home and she'd cried all night. Heather had never found out whether Austin had brought a ring to that dinner, but her gut told her he did. It still made her wince to think about it. Afterwards, she resolved to have nothing to do with the Hall men.

Her resolve only lasted three weeks. Without Austin's daily presence in her life, Colt consumed her thoughts and dreams. She'd hadn't told any of her friends what she was feeling because she'd known it was wrong. So wrong.

Still, when Colt came calling and asked her out, she said yes.

"And you didn't get in touch with Colt when you figured out you were pregnant?" Camila asked.

"I was going to. Then I thought about what that would do to him and his brothers. They'd just lost their father. How could I turn Austin against Colt? What would Mason and Zane do, choose sides? I couldn't bear the thought of them fighting about what Colt and I had done. I felt guilty enough already."

"I understand. I'm sure Colt will too," Regan said.

"Really? Would you understand if you were him? If you found you'd missed the first twelve years of your child's life?" Thirteen, now. Richard had recently had a birthday. Heather's heart squeezed. She knew Colt too well to even hope for understanding. He was proud and stubborn and he took things to heart, no matter the tough exterior he turned to the world.

Regan considered this. "I don't know," she admitted, "but you promised to answer his ad. It's the only reason Mason and the others haven't told him about Richard."

Colt's brothers had been shocked and angry when they found out she'd hidden Richard from all of them so long. She'd had to beg them to let her tell Colt about his son in her own way. "Maybe this is a huge mistake."

"It's not a mistake," Regan said. Heather scanned the store again, glad it was nearly empty, although that reflected problems of a different kind. If sales didn't pick up quickly she was going to be in trouble.

"He was here in June. It would have been easy for him to look me up."

She was careful to hide how much it hurt that he hadn't. It was for the best, after all. She'd known the minute Mason had returned to Chance Creek last April she was in trouble and she'd been grateful for the reprieve, although it only lasted a few months. When Mason and Regan set their wedding for June, Heather knew the rest of the family would come and she wasn't sure what to do. She remembered the way she'd been torn between hope and fear the entire time Colt was in town for the wedding. Hope that he would come and find her. Fear that when he realized she'd hidden Richard he'd hate her and leave again.

She needn't have worried; he hadn't come after her at all and before she knew it he was gone again. Once again she'd waited too long for him to make the first move and bitterly regretted it later. It was Richard who finally spilled the beans to Austin when Austin left the Army and came back to Chance Creek to stay in the summer. She'd never told her son who his father was, but he'd looked through her scrapbooks from when she was younger, seen all the photos of her and Austin together, and come to his own conclusions. He'd confronted Austin and Austin had confronted Heather. She hadn't known what to do. Paralyzed by what would happen if the truth was known, she'd said nothing at first. Austin had thought Richard was right—that Richard was his—and she'd managed to make things even worse than before.

When the truth had finally come out both Richard and Austin were devastated, but time had begun to heal those wounds, thank goodness. All of the Halls had agreed to let her tell Colt in her own way as soon as she was able to contact him. Unfortunately he'd left on a mission last summer that didn't allow for any communication. She knew Colt's brothers were worried; it wasn't normal for him to be off the grid so long. She'd been worried, too, and she'd prayed for his safety every night before she went to sleep. Now that he'd put up an ad, at least she knew he was still alive.

She wanted another chance with Colt, and Richard was dying to meet his father. Meanwhile, Austin had stepped up in his role as uncle, as had Mason and Zane.

"He didn't know about Richard in June," Regan pointed out.

"He still doesn't, and I don't want him to be with me because he feels like he has to be. I probably don't want to be with him at all. I'm not the same person. Why should I assume he is?"

Camila picked out several brushes and added them to her basket. "You think you've changed that much since he's been gone?"

"I know I have." She heard the bitterness in her voice. "Look at me—I'm an old, boring woman who owns a home décor store."

Camila stopped. "First of all, you're not old. Second of all, if you feel that way it's your own fault. Look at you! I have no idea why you think that owning this store means you have to dress like Renfree used to. I mean, when you worked at the bar you dressed hot!"

"I dressed like a bartender is supposed to dress. Now I own a store. I have to look the part."

"You have to look like a cat lady?"

"She doesn't look like a cat lady!" Regan, ever the peace-maker, intervened.

"Yes she does. You're veering awfully close to polyester pantsuits, woman. Please don't tell me you threw out your real people clothes."

"These are real people clothes!" She looked down at the no-nonsense pants and blue sweater she wore. Camila was right: she'd adopted Renfree's style when she took over the store. And it wasn't attractive.

"I'm going to pretend you didn't say that." Camila pointed at Heather's pants. "If you have any self-respect you'll burn those tonight and tomorrow you'll wear something from the twenty-first century."

"If you need to update your wardrobe, go to Willow's. Storm's got a great selection of new clothes in. We could go together," Regan said. Storm was Zane's wife and she lived at Crescent Hall, too. The same aunt who'd come up with all the crazy conditions for Colt and his brothers to inherit the ranch had also given Storm an old store she'd bought for a song, along with the money to fix it up. It was her attempt to anchor Storm to Montana when it seemed likely Storm would want to return to California. The women of Chance Creek were thrilled to have a new clothing store, especially since Storm had a keen eye for up-to-date fashions. Heather knew Regan liked to drum up business for her whenever she could.

"I'll definitely do that soon. After New Year's when I get home from Colorado, maybe."

"Owning Renfree's is supposed to be your dream," Camila said. "Why are you acting like it's a prison sentence?"

Heather was grateful for the change of topic. Even if her store was floundering, it was safer to talk about than Colt. "I think I'm afraid of it," she admitted, plucking a piece of lint from her sweater in an attempt to hide her embarrassment. "What if I crash and burn?"

"Why would you? You know how to run this place," Regan said.

Heather bit her lip. She lowered her voice. "I haven't wanted to tell anyone. Sales are down from last year. I don't know what I'm doing wrong."

Camila narrowed her eyes. "Are you sure Renfree didn't inflate his books when he showed them to you? Maybe he sold the store because it was going under."

Heather couldn't pretend the idea hadn't occurred to her. "No, I don't think that's it. I worked here, remember? The store was much busier last year. I think it's me. I think the contractors are traveling to Silver Falls instead of buying from me because I'm a woman."

"Seriously? In this day and age?" Camila looked skeptical. "I guess that explains why you're trying to look like a man."

"Camila! I'm not joking. Look around you. Do you see any men in the store?"

Camila scanned the aisles that were all too empty. "I don't see much of anyone in the store. Are you advertising?"

"Yes, I am. I don't know what I'm doing wrong and something's got to give or I'm in trouble. Maybe I'm not a businesswoman at all." She caught Regan's worried look and rushed to add, "Oh, I'm probably over-dramatizing things. I'm sure I'll be fine." She didn't want her friends to worry.

"If your sales are down, you aren't over-dramatizing." Regan was all business. "You know I do consulting on the side. Why didn't you come to me?"

"I didn't want anyone to know I was having trouble."

"Ignoring the problem won't make it go away. Let's meet up for coffee when you get home from your trip and brainstorm some ideas."

"Fila and I could help, too," Camila said. Fila was Camila's business partner. Their fusion Afghan and Mexican restaurant in town was so successful they'd had to hire extra help.

"That would be great." Heather felt a rush of gratitude toward both of them. She'd been so excited when she first bought the store, but now the adrenaline had worn off and the hard work of running the business for years to come pressed down on her. If anyone could help her brainstorm, they could.

"Don't think you're off the hook on answering Colt's ad," Regan said. "Do it. Tonight."

CHAPTER TWO

C OLT STOOD UP from his cramped seat and pulled his carry-on bag from the rack overhead. Twenty-four hours ago he'd completed the process that separated him from the Air Force and he'd hopped on a plane early this morning. It took several flights to reach the tiny Chance Creek Regional Airport, but he'd made his connections easily. It felt strange to know that the US military no longer directed his life. He'd jumped out of plenty of aircraft in his time, but always with a parachute—now he was free falling into civilian life and the sensation unnerved him.

He still hadn't told his brothers he was coming home. In fact, he hadn't answered any of their messages since the beginning of his last mission—that wild ride on the Afghan border that ended in an extended jaunt behind enemy lines. He'd meant to reconnect with his brothers and mother after he'd been shipped back stateside, but he hadn't been able to make himself reach out to them, and they were used to him dropping out of view. He simply wasn't ready to face the past yet and he knew he had to do so before he could build a new future.

He'd pretended he was still on a mission—out of reach of any phone or Internet connection—and borrowed himself some more time.

He'd missed Christmas, but it was still two days until New Year's—at least he'd get to celebrate that holiday in Chance Creek. As he stepped off the plane he took a deep breath and filled his lungs with cold, crisp Montana air.

Inside the airport, renting a car was a hassle as usual, but when he'd loaded his gear and pulled out of the parking lot, traffic thinned out and he had plenty of time to think. He knew he should call ahead and warn his brothers of his arrival, but he couldn't seem to pick up the phone. Tanner was right; he wasn't ready to go through with this. When he reached the turn off for Crescent Hall, he hit the gas instead of the brakes.

For miles he tried to force himself to turn around, but his fingers clutched the wheel like a flotation device as he tossed in the stormy seas of his guilt. Colt drove all the way to Billings to try to outrace the pain of his memories. Finally he gave up pretending he would turn back.

He needed more time.

He pulled into the parking lot of the Four Spruces motel off the main strip of Billings, hoping to find a safe haven within the anonymity of its walls. After booking himself in and taking a quick trip down the street to stock up on basic provisions, he returned to the room, took off his coat, sat down heavily on the end of the bed and pulled out his cell phone. Maybe it was best to ease back into civilian existence. He'd start with the messages that had piled up for months.

Most were junk and easily dealt with, although their sheer number meant more than an hour passed while he trashed them. With those cleared away, he started with the messages his family had sent. Some of the news surprised him. He'd known before he left on his mission that Austin had met a woman, but now he found out that they'd married and were expecting a child. Zane had married, too—to a woman named Storm, who was also expecting. He had notes from several of his brothers reminding him it was his turn next.

There was a sweet note from Regan, Mason's wife, wishing him well and saying she hoped he came home soon. She didn't nag him to find a wife, and he thought she honestly meant she'd be pleased to see him. Regan was one of the good ones.

After the batch of messages that had come around the time of Zane's wedding in November the notes thinned out even more, although nearly everyone wrote in early December that they hoped he'd be home for the holidays. Everyone except Austin, that is. He hadn't written once since August, Colt noted with a frown. Zane, however, wrote frequently throughout the period Colt was incommunicado and some of his messages were downright unnerving.

Take the next leave you can get and come home. Don't worry about a wife. You're needed here. That one was from September. *You're needed here.* What was that supposed to mean?

Zane had written again in October: *I know your career*

means everything, but there's something else that needs your attention. Come home.

Was someone sick? His mom? She'd written him just a couple of weeks ago and her note was cheerful, full of news from Florida and wishes to see him soon. Julie was the type to hide an illness, though.

In November: *Wherever you are, get the job done and come home.*

But it was his latest note that had Colt tense with worry.

Too much time is passing. You're going to lose your chance to make this right. I mean it, Colt. Do whatever it takes, but get back to Chance Creek.

His chance to make this right? Make what right? His mind flashed to his father's death and his heartrate picked up. Colt bitterly regretted ever confessing to Zane that he'd been with Heather. Maybe Zane blamed him for Aaron's death now too. Had he told their brothers? Were they angry at him?

He surged up from the bed and grabbed a beer out of the small refrigerator across the room, thankful he'd thought to pick up a six-pack. He needed it.

His fingers itched to call home, but at the same time that was the last thing he wanted to do. Instead of placing the call he thumbed through more messages, but stopped when he realized what they were.

Answers to his wife-wanted ad.

Dear Colt,

A cowboy stole my heart once, but he walked out my door when I was only seventeen and I've missed his brand of loving ever since. Could you be the cowboy who will bring my heart back to me? I could use a man like that right now.

I'm a strong, independent, loyal and loving country girl who is ready to live the ranch life with you for as long as you'll have me. I don't need diamonds or a fancy wedding, and I've always liked the back seat of an old Impala better than a soft bed in a four-star hotel. You're looking for something simple and temporary. I can be simple and temporary. I can be complicated and permanent, too. It's up to you.

How about you toss your hat in the ring and give us a try? You might be surprised what you find out about yourself.

Helena Warner

Heather sat back and took a deep breath as she scanned her answer to Colt's ad. It had taken a lot of trial and error—and a lot of swearing—to set up the fake persona she was using to hide her tracks. She'd bought a stock photo to send to him of a woman who bore her a slight resemblance, picked a name with the same initials as hers, then set up a new e-mail account to match.

If her plan worked, she'd lure him in and get him interested in her as a single mother. Once he got used to the idea that the woman he was attracted to had a thirteen-year-old son, she'd reveal herself—and Richard—and hope that Colt had fallen so in love with her he didn't turn tail and run.

She wondered if her response would grab his attention. Would he catch her reference to their one teenage tryst in the back seat of her mother's car, or would her note be buried in all the other replies to his ad? He was too damn handsome—he might be overrun with would-be wives.

Heather's hand hovered over the keyboard. She wasn't sure she was ready to post the e-mail. Colt would probably—

"Mom? Mom!"

Heather hit send, then slapped the laptop shut to hide Colt's ad just as Richard barged into her bedroom.

"Can I have the leftover pizza?" Richard skidded to a halt near her desk.

"As long as you have some fruit, too. Hurry up; we have to be at the airport by one-thirty." That was close— he'd nearly seen what she was doing. She took a deep breath to try to calm her racing heart.

Heather stood up and followed Richard into the kitchen. She grabbed an apple from the refrigerator and tossed it to him before sliding the leftover slices of pizza onto a baking sheet and putting them in the oven to warm up.

"When do you think Dad will come home?" Richard took a seat at the kitchen table. She glanced at him, wondering if he'd seen Colt's ad on her screen after all, then decided he couldn't have.

"I don't know, honey. Soon, I would think."

"I wish we knew where he was."

"I know."

Colt's work as an Air Force combat controller terrified her. She remembered when she'd looked it up on the Internet after talking to his brothers last summer. She'd barely breathed for days. A combat controller entered a region ahead of troops—by parachuting in or by other more dangerous methods—and then acted as an air traffic controller for everyone else. They worked under deadly conditions in hostile regions, paired with small groups of Navy SEALs or other Special Forces teams that had little chance of battling their way out again if they were discovered. Heather couldn't believe Colt would put himself in such danger, but the more she thought about it the more she understood why the Air Force would choose him for such a job.

Colt had always been capable. As the youngest he didn't always get the respect from the others that he deserved, but back when they were teenagers, back when she was still dating Austin, she'd noticed his father always chose Colt when the job was really difficult. He flourished in a tight spot and his sharp brain saw things the others didn't. His absolute confidence was one of the things that had attracted her to him back when they were teens.

"You don't think he's dead, do you?"

Heather snapped back to the present. "Of course not." It was her worst fear, but the man had just placed a wife-wanted ad. He had to be all right, didn't he? She wondered if he'd gotten in touch with his brothers yet. The last she'd heard, they were still waiting to hear from him, but once Regan told Mason she'd found his ad, Heather was sure Colt's brothers would track him down. She pulled open the oven to check on the pizza. She'd stayed up more nights than she cared to admit worrying about Colt and all the bad things that could happen to him. She was glad she knew as little as she did about military operations, and she refused to watch war movies. The action sequences hit too close to home.

"We don't know for sure, though."

Her heart ached for her son. He'd never even seen Colt in the flesh. She knew Richard worried that Colt wouldn't like him, or that maybe his father would think he didn't stack up. Richard had taken to emulating his uncles in everything—right down to training as hard as he could on the side-by-side obstacle course Colt's father had built for his sons on the ranch so long ago.

Already he'd developed new muscles in his arms and legs. He reminded her so much of the Hall men when they were young that sometimes tears came into her eyes when she looked at him. Those happy-go-lucky boys, always competing on that damn obstacle course, had turned overnight into men when their father died. She wondered what Richard would be like when he grew up. Would he join the military?

Her heart gave a little lurch.

"Mom? What's wrong?" Richard peered at her. "Did you hear something about Dad? Is he all right?"

Heather fetched a plate and napkin and placed them near him on the table. She grabbed herself a banana. "I'm sure he's fine. I was thinking about the past." And the future.

"About when you and Dad were dating?"

You could barely call what they'd done dating. "Yes.

I guess so."

"When he comes home, will you get married?"

His words cut right through her. She wished it was that simple. No relationship—not that she'd had many—had felt as right as being with Colt. "No one's talking about marriage."

"All my other uncles had to marry to get the ranch. Dad has to marry, too." He slid a look her way.

"Where did you hear that?"

Richard shrugged and Heather told herself she shouldn't be surprised. Little pitchers had big ears and all that. "I'm sure he will." She hoped Richard would drop the subject.

"Maybe he'll marry you."

"Honey, I think that ship sailed a long, long time ago."

"Maybe you should try harder."

Try harder? She was trying as hard as she could.

CHAPTER THREE

A COWBOY STOLE my heart once, but he walked out my door when I was only seventeen and I've missed his brand of loving ever since. Could you be the cowboy who will bring my heart back to me? I could use a man like that right now.

Colt stifled an oath. Just what he needed: a romantic. He'd just finished clearing out his inbox when this new message appeared. Thank God they weren't all like this one. He was pretty sure he'd already found his woman—one Melanie Monroe, who was plain spoken and matter-of-fact, just like he'd hoped for. Melanie planned to open a spa. The money she'd earn by pretending to be his wife would add up to the down payment she needed to get started. She was perfect and he hoped to sew up the deal before the day was done.

So far this Helena Warner woman wasn't even in the running.

I don't need diamonds or a fancy wedding, and I've always liked the back seat of an old Impala better than a soft bed in a four-star hotel.

The back seat of an Impala? Instantly his mind slipped into the past—to the one time he'd made love to

Heather. He had to agree with Helena on that one; he'd give anything to be sixteen again with Heather in his arms—

No. Colt shook his head grimly. He didn't want to go back, even to relive his one roll in the hay—or romp in the back seat—with Heather. If he'd never loved her, he wouldn't have raced past his father that day. He would have seen him crumple to the ground, called for help, and Aaron might still be alive. Knowing that his father's last thoughts about him were filled with disappointment had rubbed at him for years like a jagged pebble in his shoe.

He stared at Helena Warner's photo. She didn't just share Heather's initials, she even looked like Heather— albeit an airbrushed, polished model version of the girl he'd known. She was blond, like Heather was now, but she was thinner than Heather had ever been, so thin her collarbones protruded. Colt suspected her breasts had been augmented; no woman that skinny was so endowed in his experience. The real girl had a body like an old fashioned pinup. She was curvy and sexy and delicious— without any need for silicone.

I can be simple and temporary. I can be complicated and permanent, too. It's up to you.

The last thing he needed was complicated and permanent. He didn't have plans beyond securing the ranch and confessing his mistakes to his brothers. He didn't even know if he would stay in Chance Creek. That depended on the reception he received. He'd marry Melanie, not Helena, and certainly not Heather.

So why were his fingers typing a reply?

Helena,

I might be a cowboy, but I don't have your heart. I've got nothing you'd want to have.

I'm not looking for romance, or for anything resembling permanent, so I'll have to sign off here and wish you well.

Colt

That ought to scare her off. Colt deleted her message.

Just as quickly he hit *undo*.

He read her words again. As wrong as she was for him, he couldn't make himself delete her e-mail. Her reference to the backseat of an Impala stopped him each time he went to press delete. Those few stolen moments he'd had with Heather had been some of the happiest of his life. He hesitated, then archived the e-mail instead.

Time to answer Melanie's message. Might as well get down to brass tacks.

Melanie,

I can meet you at eight in the morning on January 7th at the Chance Creek Regional Airport with a money order for the first half of the payment I mentioned and a pre-nup for you to look over. Once you've signed the document before a notary, we will set up the wedding as soon as possible.

I expect all paperwork pertaining to my inheritance to be completed by mid-April. Until then you

and I will live at Crescent Hall, my family's ranch, as
husband and wife. At the end of our time together, I
will give you the second half of the payment and wish
you well.

Colt

Heather's phone chimed to announce an e-mail, and
she straightened in her chair in the waiting area of the
Chance Creek airport when she saw who it was from.

Colt.

Had he read her message, guessed who she was, and
raced to get in touch? She hurriedly clicked on the e-mail
but frowned when she read the first line. *Helena.* So he
hadn't guessed it was her. She scanned the rest of his
short note. He wasn't interested in her either. She'd
obviously blown it by going for the heartstrings rather
than answering his ad in the spirit in which it was
written. Colt had made it clear in his ad he wanted a fake
wife. Why had she made a play for something more?

"Mom, they called our plane," Richard said, tugging
at her impatiently.

"What? Oh." She came back to the present and gathered her things. They were flying to Colorado where her
grandparents had retired and her whole family planned
to gather for New Year's. She followed Richard, thinking
about her answer.

Because she would answer. Colt couldn't shake her
that easily.

PING.

Another e-mail. From Helena. Colt sat up on the motel room bed and pulled his laptop closer. This time he'd trash the message—right after he read it. He'd made his offer to Melanie and he hoped she would take it. Helena wasn't right for him at all.

Okay, you don't want forever and you don't want romance. How about a three-month-long adventure you'll never forget? I'm something special, in bed and out of it, and I promise you won't regret spending some time with me. Come on, Colt—if you're not going to marry for real, your fake marriage should be something special, right?

Give me a chance.

Her words intrigued him. He looked at Helena's photograph again and somehow knew it didn't do her justice. She would look sexier than the woman onscreen, just like Heather did. She'd be more real—rougher around the edges. Just like Heather. She'd laugh at his jokes, match him drink for drink, and take all his hard-earned money when they played poker. She'd throw her head back when he moved inside her and cry out his name when she—

Shit. Who was he kidding? Colt moved impatiently on the bed.

Still, he read the e-mail again, and couldn't help comparing it to Melanie's earlier note. Melanie was all facts and common sense, like he wanted his fake wife to be. Helena was a bundle of energy and excitement. Her references to sex were part of the attraction. He'd been alone a long time and his body ached for female company as much as he tried to deny he wanted it.

Before he knew what he was doing, he was typing a reply.

Helena,

I'm already well on my way to being engaged to a woman who would suit me fine; she wants nothing from me but my money. Next week I'll meet her at the airport and I suspect I'll be a married man before the month is out.

But I'm not engaged yet.

He hit send before he could stop himself, wondering all the while what game he thought he was playing. Melanie was everything he needed. There'd be no fuss from her when the deal was done and it was time to walk away.

Helena was a wild card whose next move he couldn't predict. Was that what attracted him to her—his affinity for trouble? She might remind him of Heather, but she was a total unknown.

Colt took a swig of beer, picked up the remote and clicked the TV on.

This time when the laptop pinged, it was Melanie writing back. He dropped the remote again.

Colt,

Sounds good. I've attached all the necessary information for you to purchase my plane tickets. See you on the 7th.

Melanie

Now that was a woman he could deal with, Colt thought. Why couldn't everyone be as sensible as she was? If Helena wrote again he wouldn't answer, he decided, and closed the laptop's lid with a snap. But as he picked up the remote and turned up the volume on the television he knew he was fooling himself.

He would read it. And he just might write back.

I'M NOT ENGAGED YET.

Heather's heart plummeted as she hid in the bathroom at her grandparents' condo and read through the latest e-mail from Colt. After she had answered his last message, she had put away her phone during her flight and hadn't allowed herself to look at it again until she was alone. She'd been so sure he wouldn't answer at all she'd thought she'd never want to look at it again. He'd answered, but that was little consolation. Not engaged yet but nearly there. That meant someone else had answered his wife-wanted ad. Someone more suitable.

Fear twisted her insides. She was losing him. Her references to the past hadn't snared his interest. Neither had her promise of future excitement. What else could she do, tell him who she really was?

No. Definitely not.

Tell him she'd take half the money to act as his wife?

No, Colt had never been thrifty.

Sext him?

Heather bit her lip, her face warming with the audacity of the idea. Could she do that? Colt sounded awfully matter-of-fact these days. Had his time in the military hardened him until he didn't even care about the physical side of life anymore?

She stifled a laugh. Colt? Turn his back on sex? She doubted it.

But how did one go about seducing a man over the Internet—a man she hadn't seen in years? She thought back to their one time together. Colt had loved every bit of their fumbling lovemaking. So had she—until guilt kicked in afterward. What she remembered most was the time he'd lavished on her breasts. Even in high school they'd been ample. They'd embarrassed her until Colt got his hands on them. He'd made her see how glorious they were—at least in his eyes.

She looked at her phone and then down at her cherry red holiday sweater.

She couldn't.

Could she?

Today she'd followed Camila's advice and ditched her bland work pants for a pair of jeans that hugged her curves. Her supple leather boots completed the outfit. She'd been relieved when she'd stood in front of the mirror this morning to see she hadn't lost her looks.

Now she shrugged at her reflection. Maybe she could do it. She tapped a finger on the counter. Might as well give it a try. What could it hurt, after all? Colt didn't know she was Helena, and as much attention as he'd lavished on them twelve years ago, there was no way he could identify her from her breasts.

Making up her mind, she yanked off her sweater and tank top then unstrapped her bra and shrugged it off.

Looking at herself frankly in the mirror, she was happy to see the years hadn't left their mark on her body yet. She tucked one arm under her chest to plump the girls out and held her phone in her other hand, aiming it at her reflection. She snapped a couple of shots.

"Heather? What are you doing in there?" A sharp rap at the door startled her and she almost dropped the phone when she heard her mother's voice.

"Shit!"

"Heather? What's going on?"

She rolled her eyes. Seriously—there were two other bathrooms. "I'm taking pictures of my breasts and sending them to a stranger!"

"Ha, ha. Hurry up—Grandma's got dinner on the table already."

"Be right there, Mom." Stifling the urge to giggle like a schoolgirl, Heather flicked through the photos, chose one, cropped it so that her face didn't show and sent it to Colt with the message, *Glad you aren't engaged yet—sending you this would be wrong if you were. Good-night.*

Maybe that would get his attention.

CHAPTER FOUR

H E'D OPENED HELENA'S e-mail.

He'd clicked on her attachment, too.

Now Colt gazed at a pair of breasts that begged to be touched, kissed, fondled—

Hell.

He shifted on the bed, surprised by the sudden rush of libido the image conjured up. Women's breasts had been the last thing on his mind these past few months. He was no saint. He'd seen his fair share of them and normally he had no issue maintaining control around a woman's body, but he hadn't been expecting these, not in an e-mail from sentimental Helena, and now he was half-hard and distinctly uncomfortable.

He pushed away the laptop, got up and paced the room. Coming back, he tugged the computer closer and took another look before pushing it away again.

He didn't plan to meet Helena, let alone fool around with her, but it had been a long time since he'd been with a woman, and the image filling his screen was definitely eye-catching. Why had he thought Helena had augmented her bust? These were obviously natural.

He looked again. Narrowed his eyes. Wait a minute. Colt's sharp gaze traveled upward to Helena's neck. In the photo she'd sent earlier, the ridges of her collar bone had been so sharp he'd noticed them before he'd been distracted by her similarity to Heather. In this photo, they weren't nearly so prominent. Intrigued, he toggled between the two and spotted something else: a small mole just below the hollow of her neck on Helena's newest photo that wasn't there on the original one.

He shut his eyes a moment, remembering another woman with a similar mole. Heather had squirmed when he kissed the small brown mark at the base of her neck all those years ago, and her movements had brought one nipple into his reach. Colt had bent to kiss that rosy target and they were off and running.

He found more differences between the photos but they were too subtle to confirm anything. Maybe Helena's first photo had been retouched while this newest one hadn't. Most men would have been so focused on her breasts they wouldn't have noticed anything else. Unfortunately for her, he'd been trained to look for details in every aspect of his job.

Gazing at the two photos again, Colt stiffened when he realized something he should have known from the start. Helena had snapped the photo of her reflection in a mirror she was standing quite close to. Behind her was a beige wall that was out of focus.

And if he wasn't mistaken those were photographs hanging on it. Curious, he got to work.

It took him some time to fiddle with software and

blow up the images so he could see them better. When he did, he sat back and swore, disbelief coursing through him.

The images were fuzzy at this resolution but he recognized one face even after all these years. Audrey Ward.

Heather's mother.

Which meant those breasts probably belonged to the woman he'd once loved.

And walked away from over a decade ago.

No wonder he couldn't get *Helena's* e-mails out of his mind. No wonder she had a mole right where Heather had one. Helena *was* Heather.

Which meant Heather wanted him. But why all the subterfuge? Why the fake photo, for God's sake? Unless she was afraid he wouldn't answer her e-mail if he knew it was her.

Which was fair. As far as Heather knew, he'd walked out of her life and never looked back. She probably thought he hadn't loved her and had used the excuse of his father's death to leave her behind. Maybe she thought he'd already gotten what he wanted: a quick lay in the back seat of her mother's car. Had she felt used all these years? Regret washed through him.

Now she was giving him another chance, and he admired the bravery it must have taken to reach out to him again. He couldn't believe she wasn't married already. Had she… waited for him?

He discarded that idea. She'd probably loved and lost several times over by now. Maybe she'd had an unhappy first marriage. Maybe she was married still, and simply curious about him. That could explain the fake name, too.

He sure as hell hoped he was wrong about that, though. Colt stopped himself. No matter the reason that she got in touch, he still couldn't be with her. It hadn't been right back then and it wouldn't be right now.

He closed the laptop. He simply wouldn't answer her message. Standing up, he paced the small room, but before he knew it he was back on the bed. He opened the laptop and pulled up her photo again. God, she had the most amazing breasts.

Little minx. She knew exactly what she was doing when she referenced the Impala and sent this photo, didn't she? She knew damn well he'd think back to the one time they'd made love. She was probably laughing at him right now—glorying in her ability to knock him off-kilter.

Two could play that game.

His resolutions forgotten, Colt had his pants down in a flash, his boxer-briefs, too. A couple of strokes had him standing to attention. It was awkward taking the photo, but after a couple of tries he got what he wanted.

He hesitated before he pressed send. He didn't intend to follow through with Heather. Shouldn't life have taught him to avoid trouble by now?

Hell, no. Apparently it hadn't, and as messed up as things were at the moment, why not throw caution to the wind and really start a fire? He quickly added a message.

Helena

I'm glad I'm not engaged, either, because if I was,

sending THIS would be really, really wrong. Enjoy.

Colt

He pressed send and laughed out loud for the first time in months. He pulled up Heather's photo again.

That was a fantastic pair of tits.

And if he remembered correctly, the woman behind them was pretty special, too.

HEATHER FELT HER phone vibrate in her pocket and tried to resist the urge to take a peek. Her grandmother was carving the roast beef she'd cooked for dinner. The rest of them passed around dishes of potatoes, beans, salad, rolls, and more. She fingered her pocket under the lacy tablecloth as Richard began to dig into his dinner. Her mother debated her grandfather over a program on World War II they'd been watching on television before the meal was served. No one was paying any attention to her.

She slid the phone out of her pocket, but kept it under the table so no one else could see. She tapped in her security code, called up her e-mail program, read Colt's message, and tapped on the image to take a look.

Her snort of laughter and shock made everyone turn her way. "Sorry," she said, holding back more giggles as tears sprung to her eyes. "Sorry. Swallowed something wrong."

"You haven't even started eating," her mother protested.

Heather pushed back abruptly and stood up. "Be

right back."

She made a dash for the bathroom, and exploded in laughter when she slammed the door shut behind her. What if someone had looked over her shoulder and seen that photo?

"Oh, Colt—"

She pulled up the image again and this time took a good, long look. Hell, he'd always been crazy. And hung like a horse to boot. The one time he'd pressed inside her she'd felt so good. So damn good.

She'd been with other men since then, but no one had grabbed onto her heart like Colt had way back then. None of them had matched his enthusiastic lovemaking either. Going back into her correspondence she pulled up his ad and looked at the photo he'd included in it.

So handsome after all these years. Where once he'd been a lean and rangy teenager, now Colt was all man. He was sharp in his dress uniform and his torso was trim. His eyes were wary, but his bearing was confident. He wasn't a man to toy with, so why was she toying with him?

Because she couldn't help it. Besides, he was toying with her too. She flipped back to the image of a certain attention-getting portion of his anatomy and a shiver of need whispered through her. It had been a long time. A really long time. When Richard was young she'd leave him with her mother from time to time and go out on a date, but as he grew older, she'd pulled back from trying to find a new relationship. She didn't want to confuse him. He was such a loving boy and she knew he'd get his feelings hurt if a man came into their lives and then left again.

She wished to God Colt knew about Richard and had helped her raise him. She wished they were the kind of family she'd always wanted to have.

She couldn't get all sappy now, though. What should she do?

Camila would know, she decided. Her friend was fearless. Heather texted her quickly.

I'm in touch with Colt, but he doesn't know it's me. I just flashed him my tits and he showed me his...well, you know. Now what do I do?

The answer came back more quickly than she expected.

Talk sexy to him!

Heather thought fast. What should she say? The seconds ticked by as she discarded line after line as too silly or too over-the-top. She was out of practice. Heck, she'd never been in practice. Finally, she began to type.

I thought I told you good-night, but you don't appear to be sleeping. Do you know how to use that thing or are you all flash and no fire?

She splashed a little cold water on her face after she sent the e-mail, and was preparing to leave the bathroom when her phone chimed again.

I know how to use it. Wish you were here so I could show you.

Heat rushed through her. Damn it, how was she supposed to get through a family dinner like this? She was hot and... wet and wishing he was here, too.

Hold that thought. Gotta go for a while. Be back in a few

hours.

She almost laughed out loud again when she pressed send. That ought to get a reaction.

Ping.

You're killing me. I'll be here.

CHAPTER FIVE

ONE HOUR STRETCHED into two and then three. Colt found himself flipping through the channels on the television over and over again, but he couldn't concentrate on any of the shows. Was Heather coming back at all or had she played him like a fine violin? When the time stretched out too long he found himself doing an Internet search. Heather Ward's name came up in a few links and when he switched to images there she was— not the teenager she'd been when they were together, but a mature, beautiful woman whose clear, direct gaze pulled him straight into the past.

She could have been his wife. She could have been the woman he grew old with, if only fate hadn't sent them into a tailspin.

When he couldn't bear to look at her any longer, he flipped to Melanie's e-mails and examined her image again. She was quite pretty with full lips, dramatic eyes, and dark hair pulled back into a long French braid that rested over one shoulder. She looked modern and capable, her stance upright and her smile friendly.

She was by far the more appropriate choice for a

fake wife, but he didn't feel like sending Melanie a dirty text.

His flirtation with Heather didn't mean he wouldn't go through with his business arrangement with Melanie, though. Heather couldn't blame him, either. He'd been up front about wanting a fake wife. He'd told her point blank he was practically engaged.

And then he'd exposed himself via e-mail. Classy.

A chime had him focusing on his laptop. Heather. Finally.

What are you wearing?

Heat spiked through him. They were going to do this, were they? He sat back down on the bed, his flash of interest cooling slightly as he faced the truth. He didn't intend to be with Heather, as much as he wanted to be. This was wrong.

Still, he typed, *Nothing. Didn't you see my photo?*

He waited for her response. In reality he was still in jeans, boxer-briefs and a shirt. He'd kicked his boots off, but wore socks—this was January in Montana after all.

By the way, he added. *Wouldn't it be easier to switch to chat? Better yet, video?*

Chat's okay—not video, she answered. Colt chuckled. Heather didn't want to expose herself. A few moments later, his laptop chimed with the information that *Helena* wanted to chat with him. *I don't buy that you're naked,* she wrote. *Take it all off. I want to have my way with you.*

He laughed and settled in. Heather was just as feisty as always and now their conversation could proceed at a quicker pace. *I thought that was my line.*

You thought wrong. Are you nekkid yet?

Colt wavered, knowing he shouldn't proceed with this game. He was playing with fire.

Playing with Heather's heart.

Still, online sex with the woman who'd featured in his dreams for years? What red-blooded man could resist? He reached out to answer and hesitated.

He should sign off. He should stop this before they went too far.

He didn't want to.

Colt gave in with a growl. What the hell—in for a penny, in for a pound. Why not have a little fun before he went home and faced the music? Maybe this was just what they both needed to get each other out of their systems.

He stripped down, strode to the heat register and turned it up, then climbed onto the bed, plumping the pillows behind him and bunching the covers around him to ward off the chill.

Yep. You?

Nope. I'm wearing a push-up bra, garters, silky stockings and mile-high cherry red heels.

I like it. He liked it a lot. Colt toggled the keys and pulled up both the image of Helena's breasts and the larger photo he'd found online of Heather fully dressed.

Another message chimed. *I'm letting you touch my breasts.*

Too late to stop this now. *I'm pulling the edge of your bra cups down and taking your luscious nipples into my mouth, tugging and teasing them until you moan,* he wrote back.

I'm sliding my hands all over your body, kissing your neck, your shoulders, your chest, she wrote.

He could almost feel her soft feathery kisses all over him. He leaned back, his pulse kicking up a notch, and took hold of himself, moving his hand in slow, languorous strokes.

I'm undoing the catch of your bra and sliding it off your shoulders, glorying in the way your breasts bounce free.

She wrote back quickly. *I can barely breathe for wanting you. I reach down and caress you, taking you into my hand.*

Hell. He wished Heather was here. Chat was all well and good, but it wasn't enough. *I slide my hand down your back, under your panties and between your legs.*

I'm wet, she messaged back. *So wet.*

Colt groaned, moving his hand faster. What would Heather be like to make love to now?

I want you inside of me, now, she wrote. *Please, Colt. Take me.*

He let go of himself to type quickly, *I toss you on your back, climb on top of you and push inside. I pound into you until you scream my name and come.* Not elegant, but true enough to the way he'd act if she were here.

He pushed the laptop aside, needing all his attention for the task at hand, pushing all conflict to the back of his mind. Wrapping his fingers around himself, he allowed his imagination to run free. There were so many things he wanted to do with Heather—so many positions, so many—

He came with a grunt and a shudder, working himself until he was drained. Leaning back, breathing hard, he turned his head to see the laptop's screen.

OMG, you are so big, Heather had written.

And then added a smiley face.

Colt snorted, then laughed out loud. The computer chimed again.

You fill me perfectly, she said. *You make me moan out loud. You make me—oh, Colt!*

A few seconds later another chime sounded. *Heaven.*

Heaven, indeed.

No reply came for a few minutes. Was Heather lying in her own bed and thinking the same things he was? He took the opportunity to clean up a little.

Finally she wrote again. *Colt, that was good, but it wasn't as good as having you here would be.*

Know what you mean, he wrote back, although his emotions were far too confused to make sense of.

I have to be real here for a minute, she said. *I loved showing you my breasts. This wouldn't have been nearly as fun if I hadn't—if I didn't think you were aroused by me—but I can't have that photo out in the world.*

He smiled again at those amazing breasts. It would be a shame to erase that photograph, but he'd honor her request. It was the least he could do, considering their situation. He hit delete.

Your photo is gone. I'll miss it and the girls. They made a mighty pretty picture, he wrote.

Your photo is gone, too.

He wondered why she thought she had to delete it. Was she married, after all? Pain lanced through him, and he forced himself to sit with it. After all, he wasn't going to marry Heather, was he? She was supposed to be off limits to him.

Memories of the last time they'd been together flooded back into his mind, and the guilt he'd carried all these years flared up. He'd betrayed Austin again. He'd betrayed Aaron's memory.

Colt? You still there?

After a long moment, he answered, *Yes.*

Tell me something about you. Something no one else knows. I want to feel close to you.

He stared at what she'd written, the mood between them spoiled by his memories. *I killed my father*, he wrote before he could stop himself. *Do you feel close to me now?*

ALONE IN THE bedroom her grandparents had allocated to her in their spacious condo, Heather clutched her phone until her fingers turned white.

I killed my father, she read again. This was worse than she'd thought. She knew their time together and his father's death were tangled in Colt's mind, but she'd never guessed he actually thought he'd caused Aaron's aneurysm. How could he have? That's not how aneurysms worked.

She worried at her lower lip with her teeth, caught herself and stopped. If Colt thought their being together had killed Aaron, did that mean Aaron knew about them? Was that it?

A sinking feeling in her gut told her she was right. If Aaron had known, had he forbidden Colt to be with her? If he had, and Colt had disobeyed...

Heather closed her eyes. No wonder he'd never spoken to her again. Things between them were even more impossible than she'd thought. It was bad enough they'd gone behind Austin's back to be together—she still cringed to think of how quickly she'd moved from Austin to Colt. If Colt thought he'd caused Aaron's death, there was no way he'd ever want to be with her again.

She wanted to ask Colt what he meant straight out but she couldn't without telling him who she was. She had to tread carefully.

If you really killed your father, you wouldn't say so outright. So you must mean you think you did something that inadvertently led to his death, and now that he's gone you feel guilty for that.

Am I right?

She waited for hours, but Colt didn't write her back. Camila did around midnight.

What's happening?

I blew it, Heather texted back.

CHAPTER SIX

HEATHER'S WORDS HAUNTED Colt all the next morning as he cooled his heels in the Billings motel room. Yes, she was right; he did feel guilty about what he'd done. His father hadn't wanted him to be with Heather. He'd obviously worried that Colt and Austin would fight when Austin found out. Colt wasn't sure how his father had discovered he was seeing Heather, but he figured that what had seemed clandestine to a sixteen year old had been patently obvious to a grown man. Austin had been mooning around the house for weeks over the way Heather had dumped him. That hadn't stopped him from planning his Army career, however. As far as Colt could tell, it was his decision to enlist that had broken him and Heather up in the first place. What had he thought Heather would do during all the years he planned to be away—wait for him?

Colt supposed that was exactly what Austin had hoped.

They were just kids, though—all of them. His father had to know they'd grow up and move on. What were the chances that any of them would marry his high school sweetheart?

The answer made him shove his feet into his boots, grab his coat and head out the door. His parents had been high school sweethearts, and if Heather had been a certain kind of patient woman, she and Austin might have married someday. Austin was loyal.

Heather hadn't been. Neither had he. Colt shoved his hands into his pockets against the chill Montana wind. None of this had any bearing on his present circumstances. Nothing he did now could bring his father back. Austin had moved on and married Ella, a former Hollywood actress who now had an interest in equine therapy and screenwriting. He should be able to get past his guilt and move on, too, but he knew it wasn't as simple as that. Not by a long shot.

His phone vibrated, startling him, and he pulled it from his pocket.

A message from Heather's fake account.

Are things looking any brighter by the light of day?

He looked around him and realized he ought to pay more attention to where he was walking. He was in a retail section of Billings, trudging down a snowy sidewalk as cars and trucks edged past carefully on the slick roads.

A little, he typed.

Glad to hear it.

He waited for her to ask him about what he'd said last night and was relieved when she didn't.

Got any clothes on? he wrote and pressed send. He immediately wished he could erase the words. He had to stop this before they both got hurt.

Unfortunately, yes. I have to go to a family gathering soon. I'm going to wear my most boring outfit.

He smiled. *You could wear your stilettos.*

I wish I could wear sweatpants.

Another fantasy goes up in flames, he typed quickly.

LOL. Maybe I'll slip into something less comfortable tonight for you.

If you do, I'll help you get up to all kinds of trouble, he said.

I bet trouble is your middle name.

Colt paused. Hadn't Heather said that to him once before? *Trouble is your middle name, Colt.* The memory overtook him—on their first date he'd told her about the time he and a few friends had taken a car for a joyride and nearly wrecked it. That was how she responded, with a light in her eye that told him his recklessness turned her on a little.

Yeah, you might say that.

My mother would say that about me, too. I got in a lot of trouble when I was young.

He wondered if Heather's mother had found out about their tryst in her car.

I bet you're the pinnacle of responsibility now.

Really? I flashed a stranger my breasts.

The stranger appreciated it a lot.

I'm not usually like this, she said. *Something about your ad captured my imagination.*

Your responses have captured my imagination, too. He knew he should cut this short, but he was hoping he and Heather could chat a while longer.

Heather? He typed a few minutes later when she

didn't respond, then deleted the name quickly. *Helena, you still there?*

He got no reply.

WHEN RICHARD FLUNG her bedroom door open again, Heather shrieked and tossed her phone across the room. "Richard! Knock first!"

"What're you doing? Why aren't you dressed yet?"

"I'm e-mailing friends. You scared the daylights out of me."

Richard went to fetch the phone, but Heather leaped from her bed and snatched it away from him. "No way, buster. That's mine!"

"You're acting weird."

"And you're supposed to knock."

"Sorry. I'm hungry."

"You're always hungry." She cringed. What kind of mother got angry because her son interrupted her flirting session?

The kind who had sex over the Internet, apparently. No wonder she was jumpy; she was taking a hell of a risk doing these things with Colt. It dawned on her that her conversations with him would never go away. They would be in Colt's e-mail records even if she deleted hers.

Worse, as far as Colt was concerned he was fooling around online with Helena—a total stranger. She was basically helping the man she cared for cheat on herself.

He hadn't sought her out the way she had looked for him. And judging by the eager way he'd fooled around with *Helena* last night, he wasn't exactly pining for her, either. Colt had moved on a long time ago. Any more conversations between them were just going to increase her pain when she watched him marry someone else. She got up, shooed Richard out the door, turned off her phone, plugged it into her charger, and swore she wouldn't talk to Colt again.

An hour later, sitting in the back seat of her grandfather's truck squashed between her mother and Richard, Heather felt a bit like a child herself. She wished it was true and she could start all over again—

She glanced at Richard and amended that thought. Not for the world would she give up her son, even if it meant she could have created a different life for herself. It was just that sometimes she thought that all the adventures in her life were over. It felt like everyone else had jumped on a fast-moving train and left her behind.

But that was silly. Richard was thirteen. In four and a half years he'd go to college. In eight years he'd head out on his own. By the time she was forty she'd have an empty nest. Heck, many women were just starting their families then—she wasn't washed up yet.

As the landscape passed by her window, she wondered about the other adults in the truck. Had they ever felt a sense of disappointment in their lives?

She turned her head and caught her mother watching her.

"What?" she asked.

To her surprise her mother took her hand and squeezed it. "It'll get easier, honey."

Heather checked to make sure Richard was chatting with her grandparents and asked Audrey in a low tone, "Did you ever feel restless when you were raising me alone? Like maybe you were missing out? I mean, I love Richard so much—"

"Of course you do. And yes, I felt restless. You do what you have to do when you're a parent. When you're a mother." Heather's father had left when she was very young and Audrey had never dated during her childhood. Heather wondered why she'd never married again, but her mother had always discouraged those kinds of conversations.

"Do you still feel restless?" Heather asked cautiously.

"Sometimes," Audrey admitted.

"There's nothing to hold *you* back. You could have an adventure," Heather said, surprised by the sadness in her mother's voice.

"I could," Audrey said. "Maybe I should. I don't seem to know how to start."

"Neither do I."

"New Year's is a time for resolutions." Her mother lifted their clasped hands. "Should we tempt fate?"

"And resolve to have adventures?" Heather thought about that. "Why not? That sounds like a terrific idea."

"Then I resolve to have an adventure in the coming year," Audrey said.

"I resolve to have an adventure in the coming year, too." Heather grinned at her. She couldn't remember the last time she felt on the same page as her mother. It felt good.

"I want an adventure," Richard piped up.

Heather's smile faltered. She'd forgotten for a minute that Colt was coming home. That might be adventure enough. "I have a feeling you will."

Don't suppose I could get you back in those high heels, Colt typed that evening. He'd expected Heather to contact him but so far she hadn't, so he decided she was waiting for him to take the next step.

You could try, but I'm slippery from the coconut oil I just spread all over myself. I'd probably get away.

He grinned at her quick answer, his body stirring with interest. *I could help you rub it in.*

I'd like that.

Where are you?

Warming myself by the fire. On a bearskin rug, of course.

He liked that visual. *Of course. If I was there I'd heat you up right quick.*

I bet you would.

I'd start by oiling myself up too.

That might be dangerous, she wrote back. *What if you slide right off me?*

Then I'd climb back on and rub myself all over your body, he went on. *When you were good and hot, I'd slide right in.*

Sounds good. I like the way you make love to me, Colt.

He hesitated. *I like the way you let me make love to you.* He wished Heather was here and he could explore her body in real life like he was in his fantasy.

Are we ever going to make this real, Colt?

He thought about that. *I don't know.*

HEATHER NEARLY GROWLED in frustration. She was hot and bothered and wanted Colt to take her right now, but he was hundreds of miles away and he didn't even know who she really was. The coconut oil she'd mentioned was imaginary, as was the fireplace. In reality, she was back in her sweatpants and T-shirt, sitting in her bed in her grandparents' guest room.

I'm Heather. The woman you left behind. The mother of your child, she typed, and then quickly erased the words again. She knew Colt; the direct method would never work. If she wanted to get him hooked on her she'd have to try something different.

Forget sex, she typed. And hit send.

Forget sex???? he wrote back.

Just for now. Let's get to know each other a little better. If we have to.

She laughed. Vintage Colt. *We have to. We each get three questions. I'll go first. If you could be anything, what would you be?*

There was a long pause before he wrote back. *I was going to say I wanted to be in the Air Force again, but that's not true. I want to be a rancher, like my father was.*

Heather sucked in a breath. That was huge for him to admit. *Now you ask me a question.*

What's your biggest regret?

That I let the love of my life get away from me. Would he know she meant him? Of course not. But she wished he did. *What's yours?*

Another pause. *I have two. Trouble is, they contradict each other. I regret I disappointed my father when I was young. He wanted me to stay away from a woman and I didn't listen to him.*

On the other hand, I regret I didn't hang onto that woman when my father died. What's the best sex you ever had?

Heather blinked back the sting of tears, even as she laughed at his sudden change of topic. She bet he wanted to lighten things up, but his answer to her previous question warmed her heart. He *had* loved her once.

Apart from yesterday? The best sex I ever had was in the back seat of my mother's car with a hot young cowboy who rocked my world. What's one place you'd like to have sex with me?

Right here in my motel room. What's your favorite position?

She pulled up Colt's photograph and imagined what it would be like to be with him. *However you want me. As often as you want me.*

She waited for him to answer. After a minute, her phone chimed. *No more questions?* he asked.

That was three. I'd better go. She didn't want to, but it was late and Richard would be up early. So would her grandparents. Tomorrow was New Year's Eve, which meant an endless day and night of cooking, eating, friends and parties.

I didn't even get to fondle your breasts yet.

I'll see you in your dreams.

I sure hope so.

Night.

Good-night.

CHAPTER SEVEN

*T*ALK TO ME, *Helena*, Colt typed on New Year's Eve. He'd never thought of himself as a drinking man, although he could hold his own, but the pile of empty beer bottles stacked up on his bedside table signified something else. Time was passing and soon he'd have to leave this sanctuary. He'd decided he would give his brothers one last day of peace tomorrow to sleep off any New Year's hangovers they might acquire. January second would find him home at Crescent Hall, ready to face his future.

His phone chimed almost instantly with an answer.

Thank God you got in touch. All my relatives are playing a trivia game and I'm dying of boredom.

You don't like trivia games?

I hate them. I've been sitting here in a crowd of people and I've never felt lonelier. Hold on, I'm going to move where I can have some privacy.

He gave her a minute, then typed, *That's too bad. Wish I could be there.* It was true. He wanted to be with Heather and not just because he was horny. He was also feeling sentimental. He thought he'd like to kick back and watch the countdown with her. They could share a beer and catch up on the years they'd been apart.

I feel like time is getting away from me, she wrote. *My life isn't turning out like I'd planned.*

What's missing?

She didn't answer right away. *I guess I thought I'd be married by now—for real.*

Do you want a family? He wasn't sure what made him ask, except every time he pictured him and Heather together, the scene came complete with a house and a dog and a kid or two.

Very much. I guess it's clear I don't really want to be a fake wife at all. I guess that's not really my style.

Maybe I don't actually want to be a fake husband, either. Maybe I want more than that. He pressed send before he could stop himself.

There was a long pause before she answered. *I thought you wanted something temporary.*

It took him a while to formulate his answer because that's exactly what he'd told himself he wanted—or needed, at least.

It was always my dream to be like my dad. I wanted to be a rancher just like him. I loved my home.

So why not go home and become that rancher?

I'm beginning to think that might be possible, but first I'll have to repair the damage I did when I was younger. You're right; what I did didn't kill my father, but it might as well have—it was the straw that broke the camel's back. I have to mend fences with my brothers and see if they even want me to stay. If not, I'll have to make another plan.

What about you? she wrote back. *Do you want a family?*

Yes, he typed, only realizing at that moment it was true. *I want that more than anything.*

When Helena didn't text back, Colt grew anxious. *What's going on over there?*

I'm here. I'm just surprised. You're a complicated man, Colt.

BACK IN THE guest room at her grandparents' condo, Heather could barely see the screen on her phone for the tears that filled her eyes. Colt wanted children. He wanted a family. She'd been terrified all these years of the day he discovered what she'd done, and now she knew how he really felt. She wouldn't fool herself; he might still be furious that she'd hidden Richard from him, but at least he'd embrace the boy as his own. As frightened as she'd been of his reaction to her, it was fear of his reaction to Richard that had kept her awake at night since Mason arrived in Chance Creek last spring to herald the Hall boys' homecoming.

She never wanted her son to be hurt. It had been bad enough when Austin got home and thought Richard was his. Both of them had been angry at her, and angry again when she told them the truth. She'd been so terrified that Colt would deny he was Richard's father and refuse to have a relationship with him.

She'd been wrong.

You have a child, she typed, then erased it just as fast. She couldn't possibly tell Colt that news like this. She needed to do it face to face.

Did you go home for the holidays or are you still deployed somewhere? she wrote instead.

I almost went home. Didn't quite make it.

Heather frowned. *Where are you?*

Billings. Where are you?

Heather breathed a sigh of relief that she could truthfully tell him she was in Colorado.

Colorado? Damn, Heather, I wish you were closer.

Heather stared at the words on her phone, so shocked she couldn't breathe. That was *her* name, not Helena's. Had Colt known who she was all this time?

I'm sorry, Helena. Wish I could blame auto-correct. You remind me of her sometimes. Heather was my first real girlfriend.

That's okay, she swiftly keyed in, disappointment crashing over her. She told herself it was a good sign he was thinking of the past, but it was a bitter pill to swallow to realize he'd simply made a mistake.

Gotta go. Talk soon, he wrote.

Bye.

Colt didn't answer. Heather turned off her phone, but she didn't get up and rejoin her family. She was still shaken by what he'd written and kept replaying their conversation in her mind. Something wasn't right here. Why had he called her Heather in the middle of a discussion about Colorado? Was he telling the truth? Had she just crossed his mind?

Or was Colt lying?

She turned her phone over and over again in her fingers. What if he actually did know who she was? Could he have figured it out somehow?

He was a member of an elite military team. So were

all his brothers. He probably had access to all kinds of methods to get at the truth. With the name she'd picked and the stock photo that looked a lot like her, she'd given him some pretty generous clues—why wouldn't he be able to track her down?

After all, it wasn't like she was some kind of computer genius—her fake e-mail was linked directly to her real one. Maybe that was easy to trace. Heather had no idea.

But if Colt knew she was pretending to be Helena, why hadn't he said something? Was he waiting to see how far she'd take the pretense?

Did he like baiting her?

She clutched at her bedspread. Maybe everything he'd said was a joke. Maybe he'd been making fun of her the whole time.

She turned her phone back on and sent a quick text to Camila. *Colt knows who I am, but he's pretending he doesn't! What do I do now?*

That rat-bastard! Camila swiftly replied. *You've got to get him back. Call his bluff!*

How? Heather typed.

She laughed when Camila told her the plan.

CHAPTER EIGHT

DAMN IT, HOW could he have screwed up so badly when the last thing he wanted Heather to know was that he knew her real identity? Colt dropped his head in his hands and wondered if she'd believed his explanation. She had to, or he was in trouble.

He looked back over their last few messages. Would she think he'd made an honest mistake and cut the conversation because he'd gotten embarrassed? Or would she see through his lie?

If she did see through his lie, what would she do next?

Colt groaned. One thing was for sure—staying cooped up in this motel room was driving him certifiably insane. He couldn't believe Heather had gotten him to admit he was thinking about life after the military— about settling down and having a family.

He didn't know what to do about Melanie, either. His heart told him to give her the heave-ho and see if things could work out with him and Heather. There were several problems with that, though. For one thing, he'd be taking a risk. His deal with Melanie was cut and dried:

she'd already committed to pretending to be his wife until he and his brothers got the deed to the ranch. If he tried for a relationship with Heather it would be far more complicated. Their wedding would be real, which meant that everything had to go right between them in the meantime. What if he got to Chance Creek, met Heather in person and found out they'd grown too different over the years to have a relationship that could go the distance? If Heloise knew they were dating but things didn't work out, she'd never believe it if he pretended to meet and fall in love with a new woman directly afterward—even if he could find a suitable fake wife at such a late date.

And what about his brothers? This wasn't just his own future he was playing with. If he screwed up and they lost the ranch, too many people would be hurt. Not to mention the awkwardness of having a relationship with Heather while living at the Hall with Austin. While common sense told Colt it wouldn't matter to Austin anymore if he and Heather paired up, he figured common sense had little to do with love. If he chose to be with Heather, wouldn't that widen the divide between him and his brothers?

He pulled up Melanie's e-mails, read them over again and decided it was too early for him to call things off with her; he didn't know how things would progress with Heather. Better to wait a day or two—until he returned to Chance Creek and saw the lay of the land. Plenty of time for him to make up his mind then.

His laptop chimed. He bent to look at it. Another e-mail from *Helena*.

He clicked on the message.

Pretend I'm Heather.

He blinked.

I'm serious, Heather typed. *Look. We're not going to be together long term. You already said you're practically engaged. It's been great to pretend that maybe we had a shot, but apparently we don't. So why don't we have some fun instead?*

Colt ran a hand over his short hair. What kind of game was she playing now? Was this some sort of brinksmanship to force him to admit he knew who she was? Or did she still think she was fooling him?

After another moment's thought he wrote, *What do you have in mind?*

She answered swiftly. *Let's meet in person. I'll come to your hotel in Billings for one night. You'll have all the lights off and the windows covered. You'll leave the door unlocked and I'll let myself in.*

Colt snorted. *Why? So you can murder me?*

Maybe that had been her goal all along.

Heather typed back. *No. So I can slide into your bed and make love to you. No strings attached. No heartfelt talks. Nothing but us—together.*

Colt's body thrummed with a need that took him off guard, but he didn't trust Heather's motivations. *What do you get out of this?*

It's been a long time since I've been with a man, she said. *I'd like to be held for just one night. Then I'll go back to patiently waiting for Mr. Right.*

The idea of her with another man made his fingers

clench. Maybe she did think she'd fooled him. Maybe she thought this was her last chance to be with him if he planned to marry someone else.

Did Heather have the kind of regrets he had? Did she wonder what would have happened if he'd stayed in Chance Creek? The idea that she might be alone somewhere, ready to go to extremes to share a single night with him, changed the whole equation of his thoughts.

Why the darkness? Two could play at brinksmanship.

There was a longer pause this time. *Because I've seen your photo, Colt. I'm pretty sure if I looked into your eyes while you made love to me, I wouldn't be able to walk out your door the next day.*

Colt swallowed hard in a suddenly dry throat. It hadn't occurred to him she'd been looking at his current photograph the way he'd been looking at hers. Maybe she'd traced the lines of his face and taken in all the differences in his body since she'd seen him last, just like he had when he looked at her photo.

I won't leave my door unlocked, he wrote back when he'd thought it through. *I'll open it for you and frisk you before I let you into my room.*

That ought to break the ice, Heather wrote.

Colt chuckled. She was right. *When can you get here?*

Tomorrow night around eleven o'clock. I looked at a map and the airline schedules and should be able to make it by then. I'll message you when I'm near. Tell me the name of your hotel and your room number.

Colt rolled his eyes. Heather hadn't had to look at any map to know where Billings was, but he wouldn't end their game now before he knew what she meant to do next. Tomorrow night. He wasn't sure he could wait that long. He swiftly keyed in the information she asked for.

Can't wait.
Me, either.

HEATHER'S HEART POUNDED when she pulled into a parking spot down the street from the Four Spruces motel in Billings the following evening. She, Richard and her mother had flown home from Colorado that afternoon and her mother had been happy to keep Richard overnight.

"Going to make a start on having that adventure?" she had asked and Heather was sure she'd blushed.

"Maybe. I could use a night alone," was all she said. Her store was closed for New Year's Day, but she'd have to get up early tomorrow morning to drive back to Chance Creek to work. She'd asked Susan to open the store just in case she got held up, but after being in Colorado these past few days she couldn't take any more time off.

It was Camila who'd come up with this outrageous idea. "Colt's a man," she'd said when Heather protested there was no way he would agree to it. "He'll definitely agree to it."

She'd been right. Colt apparently thought he'd covered his tracks when he apologized to *Helena*. Now that she knew he knew who she was, this whole enterprise had taken on another dimension. Colt didn't want to sleep with Helena; he wanted to sleep with *her*. He hadn't asked her to be his fake wife, though, which left her uneasy. He'd mentioned another woman when they'd first started to communicate and she wondered if he'd contracted her to play the part already or if he was biding his time.

Camila had suggested she get Colt naked, tie him to the bedposts and leave him there as payback for playing games. Heather told her that was far too predictable. Besides, she didn't want payback. She wanted Colt to fall in love with her. She planned to use this night to make him remember how good it was when they were together. She wouldn't let him go without a fight.

She was taking a big risk. If it turned out Colt only wanted a one-night stand to slake some kind of curiosity about her, she would have bared herself to the worst kind of rejection. It would be hard to continue to live in Chance Creek and watch Colt marry someone else after renewing their intimacy that way.

The alternative was even worse, though. She'd spend the rest of her life wondering if she could have had Colt if she'd just fought a little harder. She thought she knew why Colt was holding back. He felt guilty about being with her when Austin had still wanted her, and about his father's death, as well. She needed time to convince him neither of those things made it wrong for them to be together now.

Could she do that in just one night?

She hoped so.

Heather pulled up the hood of her wool winter coat

and tucked all her hair inside of it, refusing to dwell on the future. Since the coat's hemline fell well below her knees and it was big enough to wear over her bulkiest winter sweater, it made it seem like she was doing her best to hide her identity. She hoped that Colt would keep to his promise to cover his window and keep the lights off. At the end of their tryst, if he didn't want to marry her, she needed to be able to pretend that he didn't know who she was if they were going to live in the same town. Bad enough she'd have to watch him carry out his married life in front of her while Richard shuttled back and forth between them. She needed him to be full of guilt and longing for her each time they met, and she needed to be able to play the innocent, too—even if it was clear to both of them she wasn't.

Her throat was tight and her hands shaking by the time she found Colt's room and knocked on the door. She tugged her hood further forward and angled her back to the door when she heard someone turn the handle.

A man's voice sounded behind her, so familiar and yet so different. "Helena?"

She nodded. Good, he meant to keep to the pretense.

"Come on in. The lights are out, just like you wanted." He chuckled. "I improvised with duct tape and a sleeping bag. It's dark as hell in here."

"Thank you," she whispered and hurried past him, aware of the trace of perfume she left in her wake. That had been Camila's idea too. She'd told Heather to dab it on a little heavier than usual to be sure Colt noticed. Then when they met in Chance Creek, her scent would trigger the memory of their night of passionate lovemaking, even if they never discussed it again.

As soon as the door shut behind him she found he was right—it was inky black inside. The unzipped sleeping bag covering the motel room's single wide window was far more substantial than normal drapes.

"I took you at your word," he said behind her. "I figure if you're willing to come here to be with me, the least I can do is make you comfortable."

"Thanks," she muttered again. She turned to face him, unable to see more than his outline in the darkened room. She hadn't realized how easy it would be to recognize his voice—and that he'd be able to recognize hers just as easily. She jumped when he took her hand.

"The bed's over here. We can sit and talk or we can…"

She couldn't talk. If she did, it would take all of thirty seconds for this farce to become unsustainable. Heather moved forward, using her hands to find his shoulders and then his neck and then his jaw as she reached up on tiptoes to press a kiss to his mouth.

"Or we could do that," Colt said when she pulled away, his voice low and husky with interest.

She reached up and kissed him again, willing him to know that was all she had to offer him. She'd love nothing more than to sit and catch up and learn everything about him, but since that was out of the question she'd take what she could get. Would he go along with her plan? Or would he call her bluff right now?

After a moment, Colt returned her kiss, gently at first and then with a hunger she recognized. It must have been a long time for him, too. She moved her hands to his shoulders and braced herself against him as he deepened the kiss and let his need for her show. As he pulled her closer, raw desire bubbled through her veins. It had been so long since she'd done this with anyone and even longer—far longer—since she'd been with Colt.

"This was a good idea," Colt murmured against her mouth.

"I'm full of them," she said in a breathy voice, doing her best not to sound like herself.

"I'm glad to hear it."

Heather knew now Colt would play her game. They had all night together and she wanted to make it last, so she kissed him again and kept on kissing him, making out with Colt like they were teenagers. Colt followed her cues, kissing her back for a long time before he slid his hands up between them to undo the zipper of her coat. Heather opened her eyes to make sure he still couldn't see her and was satisfied when she was unable to discern more than the shape of his face even this close. She let him pull the jacket off her shoulders and toss it aside, then braced herself in anticipation of the feel of his hands on her body. He didn't disappoint her, sliding his hands down her back and sighing with what sounded like contentment.

"You feel great, Helena."

She rolled her eyes at his use of her fake name, but didn't say a word. She trailed a hand over his shoulder and down his muscled arm. Colt had always been in great shape, but his biceps today were big enough to make her weak in the knees. "Strong," she said, her voice husky.

"Credit the Air Force for that. It whipped me into shape."

"Sure did."

Heather leaned forward to press a kiss to his collarbone, tasting the saltiness of his skin. He pulled her closer and cupped her bottom. Her pulse spiked and she pressed herself against him, wanting to feel more. Colt skimmed his hands up again and palmed her breasts. Heather gasped.

"Too fast?" Colt stopped.

"No."

He chuckled at the desperation too clear in her voice. "That's how I feel. I want to strip you down, toss you on the bed and make love to you until the cows come home."

"Why don't you?"

He stilled. Reached up to cup her chin. "You giving me permission, *Helena*?"

She nodded, unable to speak.

He kissed her again, long and hard. A demanding kiss that left her breathless when he pulled away. He slipped his hands under the hem of the clingy black shirt she wore and tugged it up and over her head. Plunging his hands down her pants, he had them pooled around her ankles in a moment. He palmed her breasts again, skimming his hands all over her body, chafing her skin to warm her as he kissed her again. With a growl low in his throat, he undid the clasp of her bra, untangled her from it and tossed it away. He bent to take a nipple into his mouth and Heather clutched his shoulders, biting her lip to keep from crying out. She hadn't realized how much she'd missed being with a man until this moment. Her whole body responded to the feeling of his tongue on her skin and as he licked and laved and tugged at her sensitive nipple, the ache between her legs intensified.

He moved to lavish attention on her other breast until Heather was trembling with desire, then just when she thought she couldn't stand it anymore he reached down, tugged her panties down and slid a hand between her thighs.

A garbled sound escaped her and all she could do was cling to him as he teased her into a feverish peak. She shrieked when he picked her up suddenly and made good on his threat to toss her on the bed. Laughing when she hit the mattress and bounced up and down a couple of times, she yelped again when Colt leapt on top of her and pinned her to the mattress.

"I've got you now," he said in a mock growl.

"You do," she said. She let him lift her hands over her head and shifted beneath him as he settled between her thighs, his desire for her all too evident as he pressed against her. He began a slow exploration of her body, trailing kisses down her neck, to her breasts, to her belly and back up again.

He released her hands and shifted downward, kissing

a path down her belly again lower and lower until he found her core. Heather arched her back and twisted her fingers in the bedspread as he teased her with his tongue, his movements making her hum with desire. He slid his hands under her bottom and lifted her to give him deeper access. She wouldn't be able to hang on much longer.

"I have a condom. Should I put it on?" he rumbled against her.

"Please." She'd long since given up using the Pill.

He moved quickly to fetch it, sheath himself and nudge her thighs further apart with his knees. Taking up his position between them again, he pressed against her with the tip of his hardness.

"You're beautiful, *Helena*."

Heather closed her eyes at the sound of the false name on Colt's tongue. He was goading her to fess up about the truth. He was—

"Oh," she breathed as he pushed inside of her, filling her with one long stroke. Colt slid out of her and pushed in again, and Heather couldn't think coherently anymore. She didn't care what name Colt called her, and didn't care what would happen next. All she wanted was to be here—in Colt's arms and in his bed—with him inside of her.

As he thrust again and pulled back out, each stroke lifting her to a higher level of desire, she wrapped her arms around his broad back and held on tight, determined to let him control this ride. As his strokes picked up speed, she surrendered to the sensation of his lovemaking, unwilling to miss a moment of it.

Colt rode her hard, each stroke bringing her closer and closer to her release. When she came, calling out in incomprehensible syllables, Colt grunted and came with her, pounding into her, pushing her into a second orgasm that shuddered through her with earth-shattering strength.

By the time they were done, she was panting for breath, and so was Colt. He collapsed on top of her and she bore his weight gladly, clinging tightly to him so that he wouldn't pull out and move away.

"Don't think I'm done with you, sweetheart," he said, nuzzling her neck. "We're just getting started."

"Thank God," she breathed, laughing a little.

"Not satisfied yet?" he asked, running a hand down the length of her spine.

"Not by half."

"Damn, Helena. A man could get used to this."

As COLT MADE love to Heather again and then a third time he marveled at the ease with which they had come together, as if the years they'd been apart had never happened. He was able to anticipate her needs and she his until every stroke felt like a choreographed move in an intricate, loving ballet. He'd long since given up worrying about tomorrow. Tonight was all he cared about—being joined to Heather, loving her and being loved in return.

It was after two in the morning when they lay panting in each other's arms again. As Colt's heartbeat slowed, a warm glow took hold of him he hadn't known since before his father's death. Cradled by it, he floated in the sensation, his mind almost devoid of thought, but after some time passed he began to picture Crescent Hall the way it had looked when he'd gone home for a couple of days for Mason's wedding last June. By now his brothers would have completed all the repairs on the Hall and outbuildings and would be hunkered down for the winter with their wives.

A wave of nostalgia overtook him and visions of his childhood on the ranch paraded through his mind. Helping Aaron with the cattle, mucking out the horse stalls, running the obstacle course over and over again with his brothers.

It had been a damn good childhood for him.

It could be a damn good childhood for his own children. Was he making too much of his part in Aaron's death? Was it possible Austin was long over any jealousy he might have felt about Heather?

"What will you do next? After I leave." Heather still spoke in a husky whisper, as if that could disguise her voice.

"I guess I'll go home. For a bit." Curled up with her under the covers in the absolute darkness, speaking in whispers, he felt like a child at a sleepover. His sleepless nights were beginning to catch up to him and he stifled a yawn. "They're not going to be too happy to see me."

"Maybe it will go better than you think."

He frowned, glad she couldn't see him in the dark. "I doubt it; in my experience life's never that easy."

"There was a time when I thought everything would be simple," she said. "I thought I would meet a man, get married, be a wife and mother. I wonder why it all has to be so hard?"

"I don't know. Seems simple enough between you and me." He snuggled in closer to her, loving the feel of her body against his. His eyes drifted closed. He blinked and forced them open again.

Heather chuckled. "Really? Seems pretty complicated to me."

Was that regret he heard? "Tell me what you want out of life." His eyes drifted closed again, and he settled in to listen to her answer.

"I want a husband who loves me," she began after a moment, relaxing too. "A man who wants to be a father. A man who—"

Colt fell asleep.

THANKS TO SEVERAL years' practice when Richard had been a fussy baby who had to have her nearby to settle down at night, Heather was a pro at slipping away without waking someone. Richard used to fall asleep just like Colt had tonight, gripping her firmly as if to make sure she couldn't escape.

She lay beside him for several hours, cherishing this time with Colt, but she knew she had to leave before he woke up. As soon as the sun came up there would be no way to pretend he didn't know who she was, whether or not the sleeping bag covered the window. Even though she'd asked him what he planned to do next, Colt hadn't asked her to marry him. He wasn't planning for a lifetime with her. All she could do now was slip away and hope he came after her.

Her heart ached as she crept from the bed and dressed carefully, finding items of clothing, her purse, her coat, and her shoes by touch. She sent one last longing glance back toward the vicinity of the bed before she headed toward the door on tip-toes. She'd fooled herself into believing her trick would work and Colt would fall passionately back in love with her. She hadn't pictured herself sneaking out of his motel room the following morning.

She found the doorknob and was about to turn it when a light switched on.

"Heather, where the hell are you going?"

Heather froze. Footsteps behind her told her Colt had climbed out of bed. When he touched her shoulder and turned her around, she closed her eyes.

"Too late for that," he said, smoothing a thumb over her cheek.

She couldn't think of an answer and he chuckled. "Come on, you knew I knew who you were."

"But I didn't know if you knew that I knew." She opened her eyes and found him gazing at her with affection.

"Christ, woman, what were you trying to prove?" His hands fell to her waist and stayed there. His presence had overpowered her when she couldn't see him. Now that she could, his raw maleness set her heart beating.

"I wanted... I wanted you to remember me when

you married that other woman."

"Hell, I never stop thinking about you. How's a fake marriage going to change that?"

This time when she closed her eyes, it was from the pain. He meant to go through with the fake marriage after everything they'd done together. She reached blindly for the doorknob, but Colt stopped her. "Hey, I'm talking to you."

"I can't do this."

"What can't you do?"

"I can't watch you marry someone else."

His hands came up to cup her face. Before she could protest, he bent to kiss her thoroughly, sending her pulse racing and scattering her thoughts until he pulled away.

"Who says I'm going to marry someone else?"

"But—" She stared in shock as Colt lowered himself to one knee. Naked, he was more magnificent than a man in a tailored suit. He had no ring, but Heather didn't care.

"Heather Marie Ward, would you do me the honor of becoming my wife?"

It had to be a dream, but when Heather blinked he was still there, still on his knees, still looking at her like she was all he'd ever wanted. A tear spilled down her cheek. "I…"

"Say yes," he coached her.

"I…"

"Y…E…S," he said slowly. "You can do it, baby."

Heather laughed. "Yes!" A fleeting image of Richard flashed through her mind. She should say something.

She should tell Colt he was a father. But Colt surged to his feet, tossed her coat and purse aside, and pushed her up against the door as he bent to capture her mouth with his again. Helpless to withstand his passion, Heather forgot everything else as he kissed her senseless, the taste of his lips and tongue overriding all of her instincts. He tugged her shirt up and over her head and captured her wrists in one hand as he unhooked her bra. When he lowered his head to cover her nipple with his mouth, Heather was lost.

They didn't make it back to the bed. When she couldn't wait another second, Colt lifted her up, wrapped her legs around his waist and took her right there. His thrusts bumped her up against the door, but she didn't care what the neighbors thought. Possessed by him, brought to the brink of ecstasy, she gave herself up to his touch and when she went over the edge into her release, Colt cried out and bucked against her in the throes of his own.

LONG AFTER THEY returned to bed and Heather slipped into a light sleep, Colt realized he was shaking. At first he thought it was from his time outside of the covers naked in the cool room, but while his skin warmed the fine tremors that slipped through him didn't stop.

Was this...? Colt shied away from the word fear. He wasn't afraid of anything. Scratch that—he was afraid of losing Heather again now that he finally had her.

She'd said yes.

He couldn't describe the emotion that had filled him

when she'd agreed to be his bride. It was like time had reversed itself and he was sixteen again, whole and happy just to be alive.

That didn't mean all would be smooth sailing, though. He wanted to be with Heather and after touching her again there was no way he'd give her up, but he still had to face his brothers when he took her home. Even if Austin was married to someone else now, he might resent it if Colt was with Heather. And Austin and Mason might be angry about what he'd done the day Aaron had died, too.

If tensions ran too high between him and his brothers, he would need to convince Heather to move away from Chance Creek. He supposed she would agree to that once he had a chance to explain things to her. They didn't have to go far, after all. They could land in any of the towns between Billings and Bozeman, close enough to visit her mother and his family from time to time. He'd find work on a ranch. She could get whatever job pleased her. Still, even when she woke and they kissed again, he found himself reluctant to discuss that possibility.

"Now what do we do?" she asked, sitting up. The covers slipped down, giving him a view of her beautiful breasts. Colt sighed. He guessed they couldn't make love forever.

"I think it's time to go home."

She glanced at the clock on the bedside table and stiffened. "You're right. I've got to get to work." She scrambled to her feet and began to pick up her clothes.

"What do you do for work these days?"

"You'll never guess." She moved toward the bathroom and a moment later he heard the shower come on.

"Then tell me." He got up and followed her.

"I own Renfree's Home Décor now," she said when he joined her in the shower. He grabbed the soap, lathered up, but when he went to soap down her body, Heather wasn't having it. "I've got to hurry. My employee is opening for me, but at this rate I won't get there until after lunch," she said, but stood on tiptoes to kiss him.

Colt sighed. "An entrepreneur, huh? I always knew you'd do well for yourself."

"It's harder than I thought it would be. Sales are down from last year. I'm afraid the store won't be a success." She made quick work of washing her hair and scrubbing her body, then stepped back to give him a chance under the shower. Colt followed her lead and didn't linger.

"Is there anything I can do to help?"

"Just keep looking at me like that."

He knew what she meant. It was as if for the moment they shared a protective cocoon of love, and it was all the more precious because it was fleeting.

When he was done, Colt turned off the shower, then moved around the motel room packing while Heather got dressed. She used the blow drier that came with the room to dry her hair, then quickly pulled it up in to a ponytail.

"I like your hair that color. Blond suits you," Colt

said.

"You don't think it's too much?"

"I think it's perfect."

She smiled, gazed around the room and nodded. "I think that's everything. I guess I'll head out and see you soon, then." She shrugged on her winter coat and strode to the door.

"Wait. Hold up, there. I meant let's go back to Chance Creek together." He crossed the room to block the door. "What's your hurry?"

"I told you, I have to work." She didn't meet his gaze and for a second he wondered if she was having second thoughts.

"We need to go to Crescent Hall and tell everyone our news."

"Right now?"

"Why not?" Colt suddenly felt energized. Why wait a moment longer to face down the demons of his past? He'd carried his guilt with him for far too long. It was time to finally set that burden down. If his brothers were angry with him he'd find some other way to make things right. With Heather by his side he could do anything.

"But I have work."

"It won't take long."

"But—"

"But nothing. Let's go." He grabbed his bag and jacket and hustled her right out the door. A quick stop in the motel office let him pay his bill and he walked Heather to her truck, eager to get on their way. "Follow me, okay?"

"Of course." But she didn't seem happy. She raised a hand to tuck back an errant strand of hair and Colt realized why.

"First things first. You need a ring." How could he have forgotten that? He pulled out his phone and searched for the nearest jewelry store.

"Colt, I—"

"You don't have to say anything. I know; I'm a complete idiot for forgetting."

"That's not—"

"Just follow me. We'll get the prettiest ring they have." He kissed her cheek and jogged to his own rental car, knowing Heather would feel better as soon as he'd put a ring on her finger. He had to remember this was as strange for her as it was for him. He wasn't going to give her enough time to think of all the reasons it couldn't work.

Fifteen minutes later, both of them pulled into the parking lot outside of the store. Taking her hand when they met up, Colt hurried her through the door and tugged her to the jewelry cases that featured a selection of rings. The store was empty of customers so early in the morning, but Colt figured that worked to their advantage.

"I mean it; we have to talk." Heather dung in her heels and stopped him.

Colt turned her to face the rings. Hell, no. He didn't want to hear why they should slow things down, or put the wedding off. He'd asked her to marry him and she'd said yes. If they talked about it, they'd be buried under all the reasons they shouldn't do it. He could count them on his fingers right now. They hadn't dated in years. They'd barely dated at all. They'd betrayed Austin. Aaron had died alone. Just thinking about all of it made his chest tighten. The way he saw it, their one chance at happiness lay in not thinking or talking until they were married. If they stuck to making love everything would be fine.

"Later. Pick a ring."

"But—"

"How about that one?" He pointed to a beautifully cut diamond on a platinum band. Fairly traditional, but special all the same, just like Heather. Colt gestured to a clerk who came to open the case.

The clerk handed the ring to Colt and he slid it on her finger. "What do you think?"

She softened. "It's wonderful. Colt—are you sure?" He knew she was asking about more than the ring.

"I'm sure. You and I are meant to be together. That's all that matters, okay?"

She hesitated.

"Try on some more," he said, picking another one out. He did his best to ignore the worry he saw in her eyes. He'd set his course and he meant to keep it, no matter what.

Heather did try on a few more rings, but in the end she returned to the one he'd chosen.

"I like this one best."

"We'll take it," he said to the clerk.

They picked a wedding band to match and one for Colt as well, although the store didn't have one in his size. He got the next larger one, knowing he could get it resized at the jewelry store in Chance Creek. The clerk put the bands in small velvet boxes, but Heather kept the engagement ring on her finger. Colt settled the bill and they emerged back into the crisp daylight.

"I feel… official," Heather said.

Colt lifted her hand. "You are official. Officially about to become my wife. We'll schedule the wedding soon. I don't want to wait."

An expression he couldn't decipher flitted over her face, and she opened her mouth to speak. Colt sensed trouble again, so he leaned down and kissed her. "Come on. Let's go surprise the hell out of my brothers."

There it was again—that look of… Colt couldn't pinpoint her expression. Worry? Fear? He led her to her truck. Too bad if Austin was angry. Too bad if everyone else thought it was wrong. He'd never let Heather go now.

"But, Colt—"

He opened the door for her and helped her in. "See you at the Hall."

"Colt!"

He closed the truck door firmly and strode to his car. There might be a hundred reasons why they shouldn't get married.

He didn't care about any of them.

"YOU'RE WHAT?" CAMILA squeaked over the phone when Heather called her. Heather put her on speaker phone, fired up her engine and backed out of her parking spot.

"Engaged—to Colt." Heather was so excited she could barely speak, and at the same time she was terrified. She wanted to tell Camila everything, but she knew her friend would die if she found out Heather still hadn't told Colt about Richard. She'd tried, but every time she opened her mouth, he cut her off. He was excited, too, and that thrilled her to the core. Still, she didn't know what to do.

"That's amazing! See, I told you my plan would work!"

"I thought your plan was for me to leave Colt tied up."

"My plan was for the two of you to be in the same place at the same time—with at least one of you naked. Where are you now?"

"Leaving Billings. I can't talk long." She wished she could. She needed Camila's advice more than ever.

"Are you coming back to Chance Creek?"

"We're on our way to Crescent Hall. Colt wants to announce our engagement to the rest of his family. He bought me a ring."

"Take a picture and send it to me."

Heather stopped the truck in the middle of the lot, quickly took a photo with her phone and sent it. Glancing up, she saw Colt looking at her through his rear-view mirror. He lifted up his hands in a *what's going on* gesture. She waved at him.

"Just sent it, I've really got to go."

"I'm so excited for you! So Colt was okay when he

found out about Richard?"

Heather winced as she put down the phone again and began to drive. She followed Colt to the lot's exit. "Listen, I can't talk. I'm about to get on the highway. See you soon!"

She hung up before Camila could say another word, pulled out into the traffic, and trailed Colt down the road, but as she drove, her worry grew. Why wouldn't Colt let her tell him about Richard? It was as if he knew she had something to share he didn't want to hear, and now they were headed for disaster. She had to tell him before they reached Crescent Hall, but she could barely keep up with him, let alone pass him and try to get him to pull over. She couldn't message him and drive at the same time, either. She'd have to intercept him before he went into the Hall.

When they got to Chance Creek, however, Heather got caught at a light and she was a half-mile behind Colt when he turned into the ranch's driveway. By the time she pulled up and parked, he had walked up the steps to the porch and was opening up the front door.

Heather leaped from the truck. "Colt—wait a minute!"

She was too late. The door swung open and Mason appeared. Slightly taller than Colt, he had the upright bearing and muscled body of a long time Navy SEAL.

"Colt!" he boomed. "What are you doing here?"

Heather rushed up the stairs, but her chance to speak to Colt alone was gone. Austin, Zane and Regan crowded into the entryway, followed by Austin's wife, Ella, who was tall, blond, and as glamorous as the movie star she used to be, even if her belly was nearly as rounded as Regan's was.

"Colt!" Zane said, tugging a third woman forward. "Meet my wife, Storm!" She was blond, too, but her hair fell like a waterfall of light to her waist, and even in the dead of winter her California tan hadn't yet faded.

"And this is Dan, a friend of mine who's come to stay," Mason said gesturing to a man Colt didn't recognize. "He used to be a Navy SEAL, too. He'll have to tell you all about the extreme training camp he's opening here—his fiancée, Sarah, will join us in the spring."

Colt leaned forward to shake hands. "Glad to meet you. Glad to see you all! I've got some news, too. Heather and I are engaged." He turned back to Heather and pulled her forward, lifting her left hand to show them the new ring that graced it. She wished she could disappear in a puff of smoke, but all she could do was hold out her hand and let everyone exclaim over her ring.

"You're engaged?" Regan flung herself at Heather and hugged her. "I'm so glad you two worked everything out!"

"How come you didn't tell us your mission was done, Colt?" Mason said.

"I didn't think you were rotating stateside so soon," Zane echoed, coming to clap Colt on the shoulder.

Heather noticed Austin hung back and Ella wasn't smiling. Any minute someone was going to spill the beans about Richard.

"How long do you have before you go back?" Mason said.

"Here's the thing," Colt began. "I'm not going back."

CHAPTER NINE

COLT'S STOMACH TIGHTENED as his brothers' expectant gazes turned to shock and confusion. Crowded into the entryway as they were, he and Heather had barely made it into the house. He'd thought about holding off until later to spill his news, but had decided it was best to get it all out at once. Now that he'd announced their engagement, nothing could stop his wedding to Heather from moving forward. He was ready to sort things out with his brothers and get on to the good part of moving home.

"I separated from the Air Force earlier this month," he said.

The small room went quiet. "Does that mean you're home for good?" Mason said.

"Maybe." That depended on their reaction to what he had to tell them.

"Don't you want to stay?" Zane asked, frowning.

"Of course I do. But—"

"Where else would you go?"

"I don't know. We haven't decided—"

"What about Richard?" Austin sounded angry.

Colt broke off, confused. "Richard?"

"Colt, we really need to talk. Now," Heather said urgently.

"Uncle Mason!"

A boy careened down the hallway and came to a stumbling halt when he took in all the adults grouped in the entryway. He was nearly as tall as Colt and his brothers, and had the Hall blue eyes and frank features.

"Richard! What are you doing here?" Heather looked as shocked as Colt felt about this sudden interruption.

Richard turned to her. "Uncle Mason said I could come over for the day. But, Mom—what's going on? Is that—?" The youth's voice cracked uncertainly and he stared at Colt as if he'd seen a ghost.

A chill traced down Colt's spine. *Mom?* Heather had a son? Who was his father?

He stared back at the boy. Was he Austin's? Or...

Suddenly dizzy, Colt reached out and steadied himself with a hand on the wall. He turned to Heather. "That's your boy?" Why hadn't she said anything?

She nodded. He could tell she was struggling to speak. "Yours, too," she said finally. "I tried to tell you."

He looked the boy over again, too stunned to comprehend. "Mine?" He had a son? "How old?" he managed to rasp out.

"Thirteen. His birthday was in November."

Thirteen years. All that time ago he'd made love to Heather, and nine months later she'd given birth to his son.

And she'd never told him.

He scanned the room. No one else seemed the slightest bit surprised by this revelation. The floor seemed to tilt beneath his feet.

"We found out last summer," Austin explained. "You were already overseas."

"We didn't want to tell you until we could speak to you face to face." That was Zane. "I don't understand, though. You two are engaged. Didn't you know?"

Come home now. He remembered Zane's messages and the truth of it hit Colt like a thunderclap. All these years he'd been throwing himself in harm's way, taking the most dangerous assignments, almost daring fate to end his life. Trying to hide from the pain of his father's death.

And all this time he'd had a son?

The boy stared back at him, waiting for his reaction, so anxious Colt could tell he was trembling. He wanted to go to him, to pull him into a hug, to tell him... something.

But what? That he was happy to find out he'd missed his first thirteen years? That he didn't care Heather had hidden their baby away—kept him all to herself because she thought him unworthy to even know he existed?

Anguish tore through him and he felt more alone than he ever had in his worst assignments overseas. As he looked around at everyone looking back at him he couldn't stand it anymore. They'd all known about his son, and no one had told him. It wasn't enough that the woman he loved had kept him from Richard; his brothers had helped her. Why had they done that... unless they thought he didn't deserve to know? Colt staggered back, reached blindly for the door and yanked it open when his hand finally closed around the knob. He lurched outside and slammed it behind him hard enough to rattle the Hall's windows. Sick to his stomach, he stumbled down the stairs. Was that true? Was what he'd done so bad he didn't deserve to know about his own son?

When he reached the bottom of the porch steps, the door swung open again and Mason hurtled after him.

"What are you doing?"

"Leaving."

"That won't solve anything!"

"It's what you want. What all of you want! Isn't it?"

Mason caught him before he could open the driver's side door. "That boy has waited months to meet you. No, not months—years. He tracked down Austin last summer because he thought Austin was his father. It broke his heart to find out he was wrong. Since then he's waited for you."

"She never told me. Heather never said a word."

"Because she was trying to protect you. To protect all of us. She thought if she told you it would split up our family."

"That's bullshit." Colt slammed his palm against the hood of the truck. She'd secretly despised him all this time. She had to, or she'd never have done this.

"No, it's not. We'd just gone to Florida when she found out. Dad was dead. The rest of us were in shock. We were hurt, furious, spoiling for a fight. She knew if she spilled the beans that the two of you had been together, Austin would have lost his mind. She did what she thought was right."

"Does she love him?" Colt turned on him and searched Mason's face for an answer. "Tell me! Does she still love Austin?"

"No. She loves you. She just did what she thought she had to do."

So had he. He'd joined the Air Force. Taken every mission offered to him. Exiled himself from Chance Creek.

While his son grew up without him. He held his hands wide in defeat. "I can't do this. I just... can't."

"Well, guess what? You have to."

"Really? Why the hell are you in such a damn hurry to get me back in there? You've all done just fine without me, haven't you? Austin's the saint. I'm the loser who can't even be told about his son. So let him take over."

"Colt—you're being ridiculous!"

"Am I?" He was so overwhelmed he couldn't think straight. "Or maybe this isn't about me at all. Maybe this is about the ranch. You're afraid you'll lose it if I don't marry her."

Mason's expression hardened. "Why wouldn't you marry her? You loved her enough to steal her from Austin in the first place. She's the mother of your son. You put a ring on her finger. You belong together."

Colt remembered Heather in the motel room, throwing her arms around him. Making love to him over and over again with the abandon of a teenager. Had it all been a setup? Had his brothers used Heather to lure him home? A raw pain ripped through his heart to think that all of it was a lie.

"For God's sake, Colt—you're the one who left her behind and never got in touch again. If anyone should be angry, it's Heather!"

Colt stiffened. "Did she say that? She's angry at me because I left?"

"Of course she was angry. But now you're back and the two of you are getting married. She's forgiven you. Why can't you forgive her?"

Colt could only stare at him. Had Heather forgiven him? How could she when he'd made her pregnant, then walked away without saying good-bye? The more he thought about it, the more it didn't make sense.

Maybe she hadn't forgiven him. Maybe she just needed to marry him to get the ranch. The ranch her son would one day own a part of. He saw now how neat and tidy it all was. That's why she'd answered his ad under a fake name: to lure him in and make him fall in love with her before she revealed her plan.

He felt like a bear caught in a trap he would have entered willingly. He loved Heather and now that he had a son he would love him, too. All he'd ever wanted was to find a way back home to this ranch. Why couldn't they see that? He looked past Mason, took in the Hall and the pastures surrounding him and came to a decision. It didn't matter now how he'd come to be here. Fate had given him a chance and he meant to take it. He'd make his last stand right here. He'd try to be worthy to be Richard's father. To be worthy to be Heather's husband. To be worthy to be his father's son. Then, and only then, Heather would forgive him. They would start again and find the love they'd lost so many years ago.

"Okay," he said but his voice was rough with pain.

"You'll stay?" Mason watched him worriedly.

"I'll stay."

WHEN COLT WALKED back into the Hall, followed closely by Mason, Heather's heart started to pound all over again. She'd thought Richard would make a break for it out the back door as soon as Colt had raced out the front—the stricken look on his face nearly broke her heart—but Austin had leaped to stop him, gripped the boy's shoulders and talked to him in a low, earnest voice. Storm had come to touch Heather's arm and ask if she was okay. Heather hadn't been able to answer.

She stepped back as Colt re-entered the house. He looked defeated and her heart throbbed to know she was the cause of all his pain. If only she'd acted differently when she'd found out she was pregnant with Richard. She hadn't wanted to break up Colt's family, but that wasn't the only reason she hadn't called Colt. She'd been too afraid he'd reject her again. When he left Chance Creek she'd been able to tell herself grief had made him leave her behind, but if she'd told him about the baby and he'd refused to return, she'd have to admit to herself he'd been using her from the start. Now she knew what her pride had cost all of them.

"Richard," Colt said from his place in the doorway. "I'm glad to meet you."

Richard nodded warily as Heather held her breath.

"Everyone else, I'm sorry for the disturbance. I didn't mean to cause a fuss the moment I came home. I was just… surprised. Maybe you all can understand." He moved to Heather's side and to her surprise he gripped her hand. "I wish I'd known about you a lot sooner, Richard, but that's neither here nor there now. I'm looking forward to the release party in a few days time. I'm home and I'm going to marry your mother. I'm going to make sure we get our ranch. We'll be a family."

Richard nodded. Heather felt a ray of hope. Did he mean it?

"Congratulations," Regan said suddenly, breaking into a smile. "I know you'll be very happy together!"

"Congratulations, to both of you… and Richard," Zane chimed in.

The others murmured their congratulations, too— even Austin, although he stumbled over his words.

"I could use a minute alone with Heather," Colt said to the group when the conversation died down again. Heather swallowed as everyone nodded and drifted away. Austin put an arm around Richard and led him toward the kitchen.

"Colt, I'm sorry I didn't tell you about Richard," she said as soon as they were alone. "I wanted to, but—"

"What's done is done. It's in the past. It's time for us to build our future."

AS HEATHER STARED up at him, Colt wondered if there was any way to repair the damage they'd done to each other. One thing was clear. They both needed time to process what had just happened. If they tried to push forward now, they were likely to make things worse. And then there was Richard. Colt thought about the anxious way his son had watched him.

"I'm going to ask you to do something you're not going to like," he said.

"What?"

"Leave—for now."

"O-okay." A tear streaked down her cheek. Colt reached out and wiped it away.

"Just for a few days."

"I understand. I'll go get Richard."

"I'd like Richard to stay if that's all right with you."

Heather stilled. "Without me?"

Colt nodded. "I'd like a chance to get to know him."

"Of course." But her eyes were filled with pain.

"I'm not trying to take him away," Colt assured her. "I want to answer his questions. I want him to know I... care."

"I never meant to hurt you. You must know that. I—"

"Heather, I never got to see him as a baby, or teach him to walk, or buy him his first bike. I missed... everything." The catch in his voice surprised him as much as it did her.

Her eyes filled. "I'm sorry."

"Then give me a chance with him."

She nodded slowly. "Okay. Just promise me…" She broke off. "Richard's ready to love you. Let him."

Before he could answer, Richard came up the hall. "Mom? What's going on?"

She took a deep breath. "You're going to stay here with your Dad so the two of you can get to know each other."

"What about you?"

"I need to work. It'll just be the guys for a couple of days."

Richard hesitated. "Cool," he said finally.

Heather shut her eyes as if he'd stabbed her in the heart.

Colt hurried to intervene. "Go tell your Aunt Regan you'll be staying here. I'll be there in a minute."

"Okay." Richard turned to go.

"I love you," Heather called after him.

"I know."

When he was gone, Heather said, "I'll bring by some clothes for him later." Her voice was husky with unshed tears.

"Okay." Colt eased her toward the door. If she stayed much longer, he'd lose his resolve. Her pain was palpable and he understood it all too well, but he needed time to get his thoughts together.

"He goes to sleep at nine-thirty usually, but I let him stay up late on vacation. School starts up on a few days—"

"Heather." Colt waited until she stopped talking. He opened the front door. She walked through it and stood on the porch, her eyes shining with tears. "I got this."

She nodded. "I know."

HEATHER HAD NO idea how she ended up at her mother's house. She needed to get to the store, needed to focus on her business, but she couldn't face any of that. When Audrey opened the door, took one look at her and pulled her inside, she was grateful for her familiar embrace. She sobbed as she recounted Colt's return.

"I don't know what I'm going to do. Colt hates me, and he's taken Richard away. What if Richard starts hating me too?"

"Take a deep breath, sweetheart," her mother said, leading her into the living room and sitting her down on the green plush couch. "First of all, Richard won't hate you. You're the one who raised him from birth and he knows how much you adore him. Colt won't be able to poison him against you in a couple of days."

"Colt is so hurt. So angry." Heather scrubbed her arm across her face, trying to dry her tears on her sleeve.

"Of course he is. You must have anticipated that."

"I did, but that doesn't make it any easier."

"Did he say anything about custody? Is he going to take you to court?"

"Not exactly." Heather wasn't sure how to tell her mother what had happened so she blurted it out. "He's going to marry me."

Audrey stared at her. "He's... what?"

"Going to marry me. At least, he was before he saw Richard."

"I don't understand." Audrey reached for a box of tissues on the end table and handed it to Heather. Heather plucked one out gratefully and dabbed at her face.

"I stayed with him last night and he proposed this morning. I thought he loved me and I said yes, but when we got to the Hall and he saw Richard he turned white as a ghost. The way he looked at me—it was like I'd stabbed him in the heart. And now he has Richard. What if he won't give him back?"

"He can't keep him and you both know it. He doesn't have custody. It sounds like he just needs time to calm down." Audrey patted her hand. "Mason's there, right? And so is Regan and the rest of them. Nothing's going to happen to Richard. It might be a good opportunity for them to get to know each other without your interference."

"My interference?" Heather's voice rose. "I'm his mother!"

"And Colt's his father. As soon as he simmers down a little and gets used to the idea everything will be fine. In no time he'll send for you, too."

"No. Not now. If he decides to still marry me, it'll only be to get the ranch. I told you about Heloise and her requirements."

Her mother eyed her shrewdly. "Colt Hall never did anything he didn't want to. If he marries you it'll be because he wants to."

"He wants to get back at me, you mean."

"There are plenty of easier ways to get back at you

without involving God and the state of Montana," Audrey countered.

"Mom—"

"Don't Mom me. I know what I'm talking about." Audrey smiled suddenly. "Well, all's well that ends well."

"All's well that ends well? Are you crazy?" Heather stood up and paced around the room. "How can you even say that? Don't you see what's going on?"

"You're going to marry the man who fathered your child. A man who owns a quarter share of a ranch that should do exceedingly well for itself for years to come. A man who calls Chance Creek home just like I do, which means I can keep seeing my grandson on a regular basis. What's the problem?"

"He hates me for what I've done to him!"

Audrey patted the couch beside her. "Like I said before, Colt doesn't do anything he doesn't want to do. If he's marrying you, it's because he loves you. Soon you'll be one big happy family."

Heather sighed at her mother's naïveté and plopped back down on the sofa. They'd be a family, but she didn't think happy would have anything to do with it.

CHAPTER TEN

COLT GLANCED BACK over his shoulder at Richard. The boy was riding Sable, the black gelding he'd said was his favorite, with an ease that told Colt he wasn't new to the activity.

Colt had chosen a gray stallion called Star for the white patch on its forehead, and was leading the way. With Heather gone, he'd thought he'd have the chance to be alone with his son, but he'd forgotten that Crescent Hall was filled with his brothers and their wives, so he'd suggested the ride. The sun was out, sparkling on the icy crust of the hard-packed snow, and the fresh air was cleaning the cobwebs out of his brain. Out here under a wide Montana sky, anything seemed possible. Maybe he could salvage the mess he'd made, after all.

"No need to lag behind me—there's plenty of room for us to ride side by side," he said.

Richard was slow to catch up to him, and Colt knew he had to repair some of the damage between them— fast.

"You know it's not my fault I wasn't around all these years, right? I would have been here if I'd known about you."

Richard didn't answer, but his expression became downright mutinous.

Colt scowled. That wasn't what he expected. "I'm not lying," he said. "Your mother didn't tell me."

"Maybe because she didn't like you."

The bald statement hit him like a slap and Colt reared back in surprise. "She liked me well enough," he said. "I think you're evidence of that."

Without another word Richard wheeled his horse around and urged it into a gallop. Colt swore, sawed at the reins of his own horse, and tried to follow him. What a stupid thing to say. He was blowing it with Richard before he even got started.

He managed to turn the gray around and went after Richard. "Hold up, now. Come on—let's give each other a chance before we start scrapping." He kept pace with his son, resisting the urge to lean over and grab Sable's reins. "I just want you to understand I didn't turn my back on you intentionally."

"You turned your back on my mom, though, didn't you?" Richard shot back over his shoulder, not slowing down. "You walked out of here without looking back."

"I can't have this conversation while we're riding; I can barely hear you. Slow down or forget it."

Richard reined Sable in, making soothing sounds to his horse when Sable danced to a halt. "Mom said you never once wrote or called. So you obviously weren't in love with her."

"Yes, I was." It surprised Colt how much conviction

rang in his words. It was true—he had loved Heather desperately back then. He loved her desperately now. It stung to know Richard blamed him for what he'd done.

"Then why didn't you call?" Richard sounded like the teenager he was—uncertain, plaintive.

"Did your mom tell you what happened?" Despite what he'd said, he was glad they were on horseback. It was much easier to have this difficult conversation man to man over their horses' twitching ears than it would have been in any other arrangement.

"A little."

"I was sixteen. Just three years older than you are now." He let that sink in. "Your mom was dating your Uncle Austin and, man, that riled me up. She never seemed to notice me, no matter how well I rode my horse or ran the obstacle course or drove my dad's car. She was Austin's girl through and through—until one day she wasn't. She and Austin broke up and it turned out she had been falling out of love with him for a while. Still, we knew it wasn't exactly right for us to be together."

"Because you shouldn't date your brother's girlfriend?"

Colt grinned at Richard. "Not if you're following the rules."

"But you didn't follow the rules."

"Nope. Not that time. I couldn't get her out of my mind. She was all I thought about night and day. I finally asked her out and she said yes. We went out a few times—sneaking around behind everyone's backs. I didn't like how that felt, but at the same time it made it more exciting too." He shook his head over the memory. "I was stoked about dating her. I couldn't believe it."

"So what happened?"

Colt looked at Richard, who hunched over Sable's neck and listened to every word intently.

"The last time I went to see your mother, my dad caught me sneaking out and he knew what I was up to. He told me I needed to stop—that it was wrong and it would cause trouble. I went and saw your mother anyway. You were conceived that day. When I got home…" He broke off. Could he really tell this to Richard? What would Heather want him to do? He didn't know, but he figured Richard deserved the explanation. "… my dad was dead."

Richard pulled back. "Grandpa died the day I was…"

"The day you were conceived. That's right. Uncle Zeke—my dad's brother—kicked the rest of us out of the Hall two weeks later. My mom couldn't stand to stay here once she lost her husband and her home. That's why we went to Florida."

"But why didn't Mom call you?"

"Did you ever ask her that?"

Richard nodded.

"What did she say?" Colt was curious about the answer.

"She said she didn't want you and Uncle Austin to fight."

"That's what she told me, too." He couldn't keep

some of the bitterness out of his voice, though. He'd lost thirteen years of time with Richard and he'd never get that back.

When he looked up, Richard's gaze had narrowed. "You don't believe her."

"I don't know what to believe." Colt worked to control Star when the horse side-stepped anxiously. "I just found out I have a thirteen-year-old son... who wouldn't be confused?"

"If you're so confused, why are you marrying her?"

Smart kid, Colt thought, surprised at the question. "Because..." What was he supposed to say? Because last night he hadn't been able to get enough of her? Because even now he couldn't bear to be apart from her?

He took in Richard's watchful expression. "Because families are meant to be together. Now come on—let's get back inside out of the cold."

"THE WAY TO Colt's heart is through his—"

"Camila!" Heather glared at her friend across the cozy booth they shared at Fila's two days later. It was the middle of a weekday afternoon, a slow time at the restaurant, and Camila had taken a break to help Heather brainstorm her next move. A large plate of nachos draped with cheese and butter chicken sauce sat between them. Heather held a chip in her hand but had yet to bite into it.

"I'm serious! Give him a wedding night he'll never forget and everything will be fine."

"I doubt it. I don't even know if we're going to have

a wedding now." She was calmer now. She'd brought a suitcase full of clothing to the Hall for Richard the first night he'd stayed there, but Regan had been the only one home: Colt had taken Richard ice skating. She'd texted Richard and he'd answered hours later, his short notes making it all too clear he was having fun hanging out with his dad. That was exactly what she had wanted to happen, but she couldn't help feel left out.

"Heather—"

"I mean it. You should have seen him, Camila. People keep telling me it will all be okay, but he was so hurt and angry at me. I'm not sure he can forgive me for what I did."

"And now he's got Richard to himself for a few days."

Heather shrugged. "Or maybe more. Maybe Colt won't give him back, or maybe Richard won't want to come home after he spends time with his dad."

"Okay, first of all? Breathe," Camila said. "Let's look at this logically. The worst is already over. Colt came home. He proposed. And now he knows the truth about Richard. One night with you was enough to convince him to marry you, right? A few more romps in the hay and the two of you will be good as gold."

"I wish someone would take this seriously."

"I am taking it seriously, and I think the next step is for you to spend more time with him. Time in close quarters."

Heather sighed. "Close quarters, huh? How do I do that?"

"You could ask Mason or Regan if you could move into the Hall."

Heather thought about it. "That's not a bad idea. Do you think they'd let me? Ella might not like it. She's friendly, but she always keeps her distance, you know?"

"I think that's mostly in your head. She's busy, that's all. She's trying to start a business, too, you know."

Heather nodded. "Equine therapy. Regan told me about it."

"She wants to work with children, but without a degree she can only teach them to ride horses, she can't qualify as a therapist herself—she'd have to go back to school for too many years. I heard she's been trying to find someone who would sign on to work with her, but the therapist she had lined up backed out at the last minute. That has to be frustrating."

"I guess I heard that too." She hadn't taken that into consideration. Maybe Ella was simply too stressed out to be friendly. Heather knew how that felt.

"Anyway, I heard she's found someone new now, so give her another chance." Camila shrugged. "Might be better to know what you're up against now rather than later, too."

"You're right." Heather pulled out her phone. "I'll call Regan and ask her what she thinks."

"GOOD-NIGHT," COLT said when Richard leaned into his bedroom to say he was heading to bed. They'd established a basic routine over the last couple of days and Richard had relaxed around him somewhat. It helped he already knew Mason, Austin and Zane so well, although sometimes Colt resented that they'd gotten to spend so much more time with his son than he had.

Each morning he woke Richard up when it was time for chores. He'd expected his son to grumble about that but Richard was used to it from previous visits to the ranch, and he seemed to enjoy being treated like one of the men. He wolfed down as much breakfast as Colt did when they returned to the house and spent the rest of the time following Colt like a shadow. At first it had unnerved Colt the way his son watched his every move. He'd wondered if Richard was looking for things to criticize, but then he'd realized that wasn't it at all. Heather might not think him fit to be a father, but Richard couldn't get enough of him. In just a few days his son had started to walk like him, talk like him and even dress like him as much as he could. The boy had obviously longed for a father. How could Heather have kept them apart?

In quiet moments he was forced to consider his own part in the matter. He tried to put himself in Heather's shoes as she waited for word as his family had packed to leave. In this small town, she would have heard about the rift between Zeke and his mother. Had she kept close to the phone, wondering why he didn't call? And what had it felt like when she'd heard he was gone and knew he'd never come back?

He couldn't imagine how it had been to be seventeen and read the positive pregnancy test several weeks later. Audrey must have been furious. Some of her friends would have stuck by Heather, but others would have ditched her. There'd have been gossip and cruel remarks. If she'd felt like he'd abandoned her because he didn't care, she must have felt truly alone.

Would everything have been different if he'd only said good-bye before he left town? If so, he wished he could turn back time.

"I'm going home tomorrow, right?"

"That's right." Colt tried not to bristle at the question. It was only normal for Richard to miss his mom, but he couldn't bear the thought of how empty the Hall would feel without Richard.

"See you in the morning."

"Come here."

Richard made a face and crossed the room, but when Colt gave him an awkward hug, Richard hugged him back. "Night." He slipped back out the door. Colt heard his footsteps pace down the hall and climb to the third floor room he used when he stayed at the ranch overnight.

Alone again, Colt sat on his bed and pulled out his laptop. Running a cursory glance over his new e-mail messages he spotted one of Melanie's lower on the list. He'd only thought about her in passing over the last couple of days and he knew he needed to get in touch with her right away. He pulled up their thread of messages and read over it again, hit reply and began to type.

Melanie,

There's been a change of plans and I'll need to cancel our agreement. I realize this is last minute and I will

*compensate you for any inconvenience. Just tell me
where to send the money.*

Colt.

A soft knock sounded at his door, startling him. He looked at the clock. That wouldn't be Richard up again; the boy pounded when he wanted entry anywhere. Colt shut his laptop, stood up and crossed the room. It must be Mason or Zane or…

"Heather?"

She carried a suitcase in each hand and a pillow under one arm.

"Hi. I'm moving in."

For a swift moment, Colt wondered if he'd fallen asleep and was dreaming this scenario, but when Heather brushed past him into his bedroom he realized it was real. "What do you mean you're moving in?" God, she looked good. She must have changed after work because she wore poured-on jeans and a soft, silky top that had no shape of its own but somehow managed to accentuate her every curve.

"Do you want me here with you or should I take a room upstairs next to Richard?" The look in her eye dared him to send her packing, but he saw vulnerability, too.

"You didn't even ask—"

"The others took a vote and it was unanimous. They want me here." Heather stood her ground.

"Maybe I'm not ready to have you here." He was, of course. Already his body was responding to her presence here in his bedroom, and lascivious thoughts insinuated themselves into his brain. His bed was only a couple of feet away…

"Then it's seven against one. I'll find a room upstairs." She turned to go.

"Heather."

"What?"

"Get over here," he growled. Leaning forward, he pulled the suitcases from her hands. Her pillow dropped to the floor and he kicked it away.

Her protests cut off when he covered her mouth with his. Heather was far too tempting to let escape. No matter what had happened, if she was going to sleep in Crescent Hall then she was going to sleep with him.

He buried his hands in her hair and kissed her until she stopped fighting him. When he finally pulled back she said, "What was that for?"

"Because you're here. Because I can't help myself."

"Does that mean you've forgiven me?"

"It means you're driving me insane."

"I'm driving *you* insane?" She untangled herself. "Maybe I'd better sleep upstairs after all."

He caught her hand. "You can't expect me to figure all this out in a couple of days."

She searched his gaze a long time before looking away and he had the feeling that what she'd seen didn't satisfy her. "I guess so."

He tugged her closer more slowly, giving her time to put up a fight. She let him pull her in and this time when he bent to kiss her, she wrapped her arms around his neck.

"Just tell me the truth," he murmured into her hair. "Did you think I wasn't fit to be Richard's father?"

She stiffened and tilted her head back. "I didn't think you wanted me."

It was his turn to pull back. "Of course I wanted you."

"You left."

His arms tightened around her. "I was scared."

"So was I." He felt the dampness of her tears against his neck. "I was afraid you and Austin would fight. I thought your family would fall apart if they knew. I wasn't sure... what you'd say if I told you. I couldn't bear to be rejected again."

Every word she spoke was a blow to his heart.

"I shouldn't have left you. This is all my fault."

"No—it was—"

He kissed the rest of her words away. He'd had no idea how good it would feel to finally man up and shoulder the blame. Now he could cross the gulf between them. They'd been so young. So unprepared for what life could throw at them. They'd both done their best but it hadn't been good enough. Now they could give each other another chance. He bent to kiss her, and she met him eagerly. Heather's kisses inflamed him just as much as they always had. He couldn't get enough, and soon his need to be with her—to be inside her—outweighed everything else. When he led her to the bed, she needed no more persuasion to join him there.

She unzipped her jacket and laid it on the easy chair

tucked in one corner of the room. Then she began to undress, piece by piece, until Colt couldn't stand it anymore and moved to help her. Heather batted his hands away. "Just sit down and watch the show."

He did what he was told, but it soon became a kind of sensual torture to watch her without joining in. He unbuttoned his own shirt and shrugged out of it, then shucked off his jeans, socks and boxer-briefs, too. Heather wasn't the only one who could get naked, although she exhibited a certain style about it that he didn't seem capable of. She unhooked her bra and laid it on top of the other items of clothing she'd already discarded and when she bent to slip down her barely-there panties, her breasts hung heavy and all-too-tempting in front of his face.

Colt couldn't restrain himself anymore. When she was naked, he set his hands on her slim waist and lifted her onto his lap before palming her breasts and covering one nipple with his mouth. Heather moaned, and shifted herself closer, wrapping her legs around his waist. When he moved from one breast to the other and back again, she closed her eyes and tilted her head back, giving him easier access.

Sliding a hand down her back and over her bottom, he didn't know why she felt so good—so much better than any other woman he'd known. Was it something about her body that made her just right for him, or was it their souls that matched up? Whatever it was made her irresistible, no matter what had happened in the past.

Maybe this feeling told him everything he needed to

know about her actions, too. Maybe she had done her best to make a good decision.

Maybe there hadn't been any good decision to make.

All he knew was that pressed against her like this, she was all he could think about—all he wanted. He longed to be inside of her. As if she'd heard his thoughts, Heather wrapped her arms around his neck, lifted herself up and lowered herself down. Colt moaned as her hot, slick folds slid around him. Working solely on instinct, he began to move and she clung to him, murmuring phrases of encouragement into his ear as his pace increased. It turned him on to know she still wanted to give herself to him so freely, and the fact that she'd given him control over their lovemaking—and was so obviously blissed out by every move he made—set him on fire even more.

As she leaned back to fully enjoy the ride, her breasts lifted and Colt was swept away by the view. Heather was beautiful, sensuous, made for him, and he couldn't help but love her no matter what she did.

He gave himself fully to the experience, thrusting into her until she came with a cry that he hoped wouldn't wake the rest of the house. He came, too, a wave of love for the woman in his arms washing over him as he spilled into her. Heather belonged with him. Belonged to him. He wasn't going to let her go again.

Spent, exhausted and energized all at the same time, Colt fell back, drawing Heather down on top of him. He kissed her, and only then noticed that Heather had suddenly gone rigid in his arms.

"What's wrong?" Fear made him gruff. If she said this was a mistake he didn't know what he'd do.

"Condom. We forgot the condom. Colt, I'm not on the Pill."

SHE HAD NEVER, ever made this kind of mistake since the first time she and Colt had unprotected sex in the back seat of her mother's Impala. In fact, she had prided herself on being a modern, capable woman who regularly stocked her bathroom cupboard with a fresh box of condoms even when months went by without a single date, let alone a passionate liaison. On the few occasions when her infrequent relationships had made it that far, she'd spoken up loud and clear about the need to use protection. Why had she forgotten all of that now with Colt, for God's sake? She tried to sit up and untangle herself from him but he caught her up in his arms.

"Wait."

"Wait for what? I can't believe we didn't—"

"It's all right." He leaned back and began to laugh.

"What's so funny?"

"Us! Don't you see? Here we are in the same position we were back when we were teenagers. Driving each other wild. Making love without protection. Guilty as shit about being together. Worried about what everyone else is going to say."

Heather buried her face against his chest. "What are they going to say?"

"They're going to say we love each other." He sat up, moving her with him. "They're going to say we should have saved everyone a lot of heartache and married each other back then. We were obviously meant to be together."

"I can't be with you if you think I ever wanted to hurt you, Colt."

"I know you didn't. I guess I wanted to be angry at you so I didn't have to be angry at myself." He lifted her hand and pressed a kiss into her palm. "I was stupid to leave without saying good-bye. Every time I think about it I want to say, 'But I was only a teenager.' Trouble is, if I use that as my excuse, I have to admit it's your excuse, too. We were so young."

"We really were. We don't have that excuse now, though."

"Who cares? We're in love, we're going to get married. We're allowed to have more children if we want."

"Shouldn't we at least make it through twenty-four hours without an argument first?"

"Do you have any more deep, dark secrets to reveal?"

"No. How about you?"

"Not a single one. So how about this: we'll start over. We'll rewind to the night we made love in your mother's car and pretend the rest of it never happened. Come here." He rolled her over onto the bed and began another thorough exploration of her body with his mouth. At first she held back, feeling like there was more to say, but soon his kisses inflamed her senses again and before she knew it, he was pushing into her.

"Colt." She looked up at him, wishing she could read

his mind. Was he forgetting again? "Protection?"

"Do you want to use it?"

"Are you saying you want... a baby?"

He leaned down to kiss her. "That's exactly what I'm saying. Come on, Heather, let's forget our past mistakes. Let's make this real. Let's make a family with our eyes open."

"Are you sure?" She couldn't stand it if he changed his mind again.

"I'm sure. Are you?"

Was she? Reason told her they were rushing this, but looking into the oh-so-handsome face of the man she'd loved since she was seventeen, Heather knew reason didn't come into it at all. She wanted to take this leap with Colt and believe in their future together like he did. If he could see past the fact she'd hid Richard from him, and glimpse a future in which they'd be one big happy family, who was she to say no?

Heather didn't answer in words. She slid her hands down his back and urged him inside of her. He obliged with a strong stroke that made her moan aloud. The thought of Colt making her pregnant because he wanted to—because he was in love with her—turned her on more than she could say. She closed her eyes and feathered kisses along the edge of his jaw. He laced his fingers in hers, lifted her arms over her head and moved purposefully within her.

With each stroke her fears dissipated and her heart filled with a blissful knowledge that Colt was right; they did belong together. With his hands braced against the mattress, every muscle in his arms was defined. He was so strong, so handsome and every bit as reckless as she was. He was the man she'd always loved and that would never change. As he increased his pace, she let go of everything else and let him carry her up and over the edge of ecstasy. He muffled her cries with kisses and when they were done, she found that her cheeks were wet.

"Why are you crying?" He wiped his cheek across hers to dry her tears.

"Because I want you so bad."

"You've got me."

"I'm afraid I'll lose you again."

"You won't. I swear to God, Heather. Nothing's going to break us apart again."

Wrapped in his arms, pinned by his weight, Heather let go of the last of her fears. Colt had come back to her, and together they would add another baby to their family.

Colt pushed up on his elbows and looked down at her belly. "I'm not sure you're pregnant yet."

She laughed and scrubbed the rest of her tears away with her hand. "You're right; we might need to try again."

"I thought you'd never ask." Colt rolled over and pulled her up on top. "Your turn to do the hard work." He closed his eyes and flopped his arms out to the sides, but straddling him, she felt the truth of the matter; he was ready to go again.

She dipped down to brush her nipples across his chest as she pressed a kiss to his mouth.

She was ready, too.

CHAPTER ELEVEN

"TWO WEEKS IS nowhere near enough time to plan a wedding," Zane said at breakfast the next morning when Colt announced the date to his brothers. He and Heather had already broken the news to Richard together. Richard played it cool but he'd had a hard time hiding his happiness. It warmed Colt's heart to know how important he already was to his son. Especially since Richard already meant the world to him.

It was a cold, windy day, which meant morning chores hadn't been pleasant, but Colt couldn't remember feeling the nip of the stiff breeze when he'd been outside. Richard had worked alongside him as diligently as if he'd ranched all his life, and Colt was still buzzing with the after effects of making love to Heather the night before—and the idea that even now Heather could be pregnant again. Every time he thought about it, he grew half-hard. He was sure before the day was out they'd find a few more opportunities to try again. Good thing it was a school day. His brothers would respect a locked door, but Colt wasn't sure Richard would, and their bedroom door would definitely be locked.

The first thing he'd done this morning was find the draft of the e-mail he'd written to cancel his deal with Melanie and send it. With that chore out of the way, he could dedicate himself wholeheartedly to his future with Heather and Richard.

"I don't see why not. What's there to do? I'll talk to the minister today." Colt dug into the big breakfast the women had prepared. He'd missed food like this and he was making up for lost time.

"There's a lot more to it than that," Regan said.

"You have to hire a caterer, get music together, decorate the Hall. You can't do it half-assed, either; this is a once-in-a-lifetime kind of thing," Zane said.

"Don't forget the wedding dress and the brides-maids' dresses. Even if they buy off the rack, they have to be tailored to fit. It's intricate work and it takes time," Mason said.

"Then there's the flowers for the church and reception hall, and Heather will need a bouquet," Austin added.

Colt looked from one to the next of them and shook his head. "Are you sure you're my brothers? They used to have at least one cock between them."

Dan guffawed and the women chuckled. His brothers didn't find it funny.

"Three weddings." Mason held up a corresponding number of fingers. "We've pulled off three weddings in the last nine months. We know what we're talking about."

"They really do," Ella said.

Storm nodded. "You'll be impressed."

"That'd be a first. Hey!" Colt scowled when Zane flicked water on him from his glass, but his heart lifted when he saw Zane's smile and he knew the attack had been good-natured. He'd missed this kind of camaraderie with his brothers. "I still intend to marry Heather two weeks from Sunday."

"Then you'll have to work fast. Start with the minister and we'll go from there." The satisfaction on Mason's face told Colt his brother couldn't wait to have ownership of the ranch sewn up. He couldn't blame him. Mason had spearheaded the whole campaign of winning back Crescent Hall and he loved the ranch as much as Colt did. The knowledge that marrying Heather fast would settle things for everyone satisfied him, too. Everyone was much more relaxed this morning and Colt knew that was because it was obvious he and Heather had made up. He couldn't hide his happiness today and neither could she.

"What about you, Heather? Are you okay with such a short time frame?" Ella asked.

"I am, except... I still want all the traditional wedding things, you know? I want my dress to be beautiful."

"Of course," Regan said. "And you need to pick a theme and flowers and invitations."

"You'll have to send those invitations really quickly!" Storm broke in. "Don't forget the bachelorette party. I'll take care of that if you like!"

"We'll do the rehearsal dinner," Zane said. He looked at the other men. "We can handle making a reservation at a restaurant, right?"

"I can call Mia Matheson right after breakfast if you want to hire her to plan the wedding," Regan said. "She has all kinds of contacts that can speed things up."

"That sounds great," Heather said.

"We'll all pitch in and do what it takes to get it done," Zane said.

Everyone nodded, even Austin, who for the most part had kept his distance since Colt had come home. Sooner or later, Colt knew he and Austin would have to mend fences.

"Who's going to be the best man?" Dan asked.

Colt smiled. He'd already figured that one out. "Richard."

"THERE SHE IS," Susan proclaimed when Heather walked into Renfree's later that morning. "You're just the woman I need to talk to. You told me last month you would show me how to install laminate flooring. Could we set a time for that soon? I want to get my living room done before spring."

"Of course," Heather said, feeling a pang of guilt. She'd been putting Susan off for far too long. "Maybe we can do it tomorrow. Let me put my things away and we'll look at the calendar." Heather hurried toward the back of the store. She felt calmer now that she was at work, where she called the shots and knew how to handle problems. Her upcoming wedding thrilled her and worried her in equal measure. She knew they could pull off the ceremony and reception, but everything felt so rushed. She'd just adjusted to Colt being back in her life and now she might be pregnant. Laminate flooring was a welcome relief.

A woman popped out from behind a display of window screens, startling Heather. It was Donna Richmond, a retired teacher. "Laminate flooring? I want to learn how to install that. I've been asking my son to come and put some in my pantry for months. He says he doesn't have time. Could you show me, too?"

"Of course, Donna. I'll call you when I've set up a time."

"Excuse me." A woman Heather didn't recognize came around the corner. "I didn't mean to listen in, but did you say laminate flooring? I want to put some in my basement to make a sewing room for myself, but my husband's back won't let him do the work. Could I really do it myself?"

"Sure," Heather said. "I tell you what; give Susan up front your name and number and I'll call when I've picked a time. I'll hang up a flyer on the door, too. Then anyone can join us."

"Terrific!"

Heather left the pair of excited women and continued toward the back room. She wondered if anyone else would want to join in. Probably, she decided. She'd print up that flyer and post it in the store for everyone to see. Her mind shifted to practical considerations. She wondered what time was best to hold such a demonstration. Maybe early in the evening so that people who worked could come?

When she returned to the front of the store, she found her employees talking excitedly.

"I think your demonstration is going to be a hit. I'll bake some brownies and bring them in for it," Susan said.

"You don't need to do that."

"Yes, I do. My mother always said give the people food and drink and they'll follow you anywhere. You'd better stock up on some juice, too. The good stuff, not the cheap kind."

"Yes, ma'am."

Susan scowled at her. "Don't give me any lip. You'll see."

"I could make the flyer for you," Allison said.

"Really? You know how to do that?"

"Sure!" Allison looked excited for the first time in weeks. Too often the young woman radiated boredom. She was a recent hire and Heather was afraid she wouldn't work out.

"Okay, have a go at it," Heather said after a moment. "You can use my laptop in the office. I'll get you set up."

Ten minutes later, Allison was typing happily and Heather returned to the front of the store.

"That was a good idea," Susan said, leaning against her checkout counter. "She needed a project."

"I'm not sure how she'll do," Heather said. "She hasn't been too enthusiastic so far."

"I think she'll be enthusiastic now."

Susan was right. An hour later, Allison poked her nose out of the office. "Heather, can you come here for a minute?"

"Sure."

"Here you go." Allison gestured to the laptop when Heather joined her. "I set up the flyer and I set up a newsletter, too, that you can send out each time you plan a demonstration."

"Each time? I don't know if I'll ever do another one."

"You should have a newsletter anyway. You can tell people about upcoming promotions and things like that. I updated your website with a form for people to sign up for your mailing list. You can also take people's names at the tills and I'll add them to the list every now and then, if you like."

"How on earth did you do all that so fast?" Heather peered at the laptop and then looked back at the nine-teen-year-old. "I can't believe how professional this looks."

"It's easy. I can show you how I did it." Allison bit her lip. "I hope you'll let me keep doing them, though. It's more interesting than running a till."

"Of course you can keep making the newsletters." Heather had no desire to learn a new program when she had so much on her plate already.

"I was thinking," Allison said. "Maybe you should start sending out printable coupons in the newsletters, too. You could tie them in to something you want to highlight. Also, did you know you're not on any of the social media sites? And your website is really lame, even with the newsletter signup. Sorry," she added, "but it is."

"I know it is." Heather thought fast. She didn't feel like she could pay someone to do that kind of work, but could she really afford not to? She wasn't very tech savvy herself, but she still used the Internet all the time—for everything. So did everyone else. If she didn't invest in an online presence she'd get left behind. "How would you like to take that on, as well?"

"I'd love it! We should look into online advertising, too."

"One thing at a time!" Heather laughed. "I like your enthusiasm, though."

"This is what I really want to do," Allison confided. "I mean, I'm glad you gave me the job; I need to make money if I'm ever going to move out from my parents' house, but I want to do online marketing."

"Well, I'll be your guinea pig, then. I'll still need you on the floor most of the time, but we'll squeeze in the online work whenever possible."

"I'll drum up so many sales you'll need me full time!"

"I hope so." Heather smiled, and for the first time in weeks she felt like things were looking up for her home décor business.

"Can I make another suggestion?" Allison asked.

"Sure." Heather braced herself. She didn't think she could keep up with her newest hire.

"Change the store's name. You aren't Renfree. You're Heather. You have to let people know that." Allison waved a hand. "While you're at it, change the décor, as well. Update the place."

"You might be right," Heather said, wondering why

she hadn't thought of changing the name. Maybe she hadn't given herself permission to actually own the store yet. Maybe she'd been so afraid she'd lose it again she hadn't been ready to invest her soul into it when she'd invested her money.

She was ready now.

THE MINUTE COLT walked into the Chance Creek Reformed Church, its plain white walls and peaceful atmosphere transported him back to childhood Sundays when his parents would herd their four children through the crowd down to their pew. Back then church had seemed designed to keep him from what he really wanted to do—head to the fishing hole in summers, or out to build forts in the snow in wintertime. For the first time in his life he appreciated the building's clean lines and promise of solid answers to the soul's difficult questions. He hadn't thought much about his faith in years, but as he sat down on a hard wooden bench he remembered the clear, shadowy night in Afghanistan when his father had whispered into his ear it was time to go home.

Was his father's spirit in some heavenly realm? If Aaron was looking down on him now, what did he think of the path Colt had chosen? It sure involved a lot of twists and turns.

"Colt! I'd heard you were back in town. Good to see you home safe and sound!"

"Reverend." Colt stood up and met Halpern halfway down the aisle. The Reverend was a hearty man in his sixties with grey in his hair and a friendly smile.

"What brings you to church today? I've enjoyed see-ing more of your family on Sundays recently."

Colt found that interesting. His brothers had become regular church goers? His mom would be pleased. "I hope you'll help me get hitched the week after next. Sunday afternoon. After your service is done, of course."

"Of course." Halpern's smile told him he knew Colt hadn't even thought about the services when he'd planned his wedding. "I think you're in luck, but let's check just to be sure. You Halls don't believe in long engagements, do you?"

"No, sir." He left it at that. He didn't know how much Halpern knew about Heloise's conditions for them to inherit Crescent Hall, and he didn't want to get into that with the reverend. Halpern led the way to his small office, sat down at his desk and checked a calendar.

"If you can make it for about four o'clock, I can of-ficiate."

"That'll work just fine."

"And the young lady in question is?"

"Heather Ward."

Reverend Halpern closed his eyes. "Hallelujah." He opened them again. "That's a prayer answered. I'm happier than I can say that you two found your way back to each other."

Colt reminded himself this was a small town. He shouldn't be surprised that Halpern knew all about him and Heather. "I'm happy, too."

"Here are some forms to fill out. You can take them

home and discuss them with Heather. Bring them back as soon as possible so we can make sure to set everything up the way you want it."

"Sounds good." He took the folder Halpern handed him. "Reverend, do you believe—" He cut off, unsure if he really wanted to talk about what had happened in Afghanistan.

Halpern waited for him to finish.

"Do you believe in messages from… the beyond?" Colt finished lamely, wishing he'd never started the conversation.

The reverend sat back in his chair. "What was the message?" He gave Colt his full attention and to his relief, Colt didn't feel judged. Instead he thought Halpern was genuinely interested.

"To come home." He shifted uncomfortably. Halpern was taking him seriously but he still felt foolish even bringing it up.

"Sounds like it was a helpful message for you to get. Do you mind if I ask who gave it to you?"

"My dad."

"Ah." Halpern smiled. "Aaron Hall always did have a powerful spirit. I have a feeling if anyone would stick around to see his boys settled and happy, it would be him."

"Yeah, well…" Hell, he was making a fool of himself.

"I believe that all kinds of things are possible, Colt. That's why I chose this career." Halpern stood up and clapped him on the shoulder. "Come on, I'll walk you out."

SUSAN WAS RIGHT; the following night the break room at Renfree's was crowded with women eager for a demonstration of how to correctly lay laminate flooring. Heather couldn't believe how many had come on such short notice. After a busy day that included a preliminary meeting with Mia to plan the wedding, Heather and Susan had emptied the room of everything but chairs, but it was still hard to find enough space to demonstrate the techniques she was trying to show her audience. The juice and brownies soothed the crowd's rough edges, though, and the women acted as if they were at a party rather than a flooring lesson.

It didn't surprise Heather that the participants were all female, like the majority of her customers these days. She'd noticed as soon as she took over Renfree's that Chance Creek's male contractors stopped coming to the store. It steamed her that they wouldn't at least give her a chance. She still stocked quality inventory and provided great service, just like Renfree always had.

She forgot her worries as she spoke to the gathered crowd, however. Heather went through all the steps several times and passed around examples of the materials and tools required. She let everyone who wished take a turn fitting the pieces together and using a mallet to bang them into place. By the end of the session the women seemed confident they knew what to do.

"Heather, could you demonstrate how to lay the type of vinyl flooring that looks like wood?" Carly Russell asked.

"I want to learn how to tile my bathroom walls," another woman said.

"Heather, I saw in a magazine how someone had built a bookcase headboard for their bed and I want to do that. Could you show me how?"

"I want to learn to build a bookcase, too."

As the women clamored around her, Heather felt overwhelmed. She didn't know how she was going to keep her store open, let alone plan a bunch of extra demonstrations.

"Here." Susan waved a piece of paper. "Anyone with a demonstration request, write it down here and include your name and e-mail. Heather is going to put together a calendar. If you want to sign up for a monthly newsletter that will list all the upcoming classes, jot down your e-mail addresses here." She slapped a second piece of paper down on the counter near the sink.

The women crowded around the pieces of paper, leaving Heather free for the moment.

"Why don't you go freshen up," Susan told her. "I'll start herding everyone out front. It's time to close up."

Heather agreed gratefully, but when she emerged from the washroom five minutes later she found the store still full of women. Sidling up to Susan's till at the front she whispered, "I thought you were going to shoo them out."

"Look around you," Susan hissed back. "They're *shopping*."

Susan was right. The women pushed carts around

the store and were loading up on supplies. A group of them were clustered around the laminate flooring display debating over the different styles.

"Better grab some coffee," Susan advised. "I think we'll be here a while."

"Do you have any brownies left?" Allison asked. Her wide grin told Heather she was enjoying all the activity.

"I've got a whole other plate." Susan beamed. "I knew they'd be a hit. I'll put them up front."

"I've got an idea," Allison said. "Take my till, Heather." Heather opened her mouth to answer this surprising request, but the young woman dashed away into the small front office. A moment later, a catchy song spilled out of the loudspeakers. Heather recognized it from the constant airplay it was receiving on all the country music stations. A few of the shoppers cheered, and Carly yelled, "Now it's a party!"

Heather laughed. "It's working," she whispered to Susan as the other woman passed by.

"Of course it's working."

The front door opened and a man stuck his head in. "You open for business tonight?"

"Yes, we are, Tom—come on in!" She'd known Tom for years and was thrilled to see him in her store.

"Looks like you're celebrating."

"We're just having fun," she told him. "Can I help you with something?"

"You sure can. I've got a new project…"

When Heather finally shut the door on the last customer over an hour later, she was exhausted but triumphant. She gathered her small staff together and gave them both a big hug. "You are geniuses. I couldn't have done it tonight without you. Susan, your brownies and Allison, your music made it so much better!"

"We have to do it again," Allison said.

"Definitely. You're right, Susan, I will make a calendar. We have to do this on a regular basis. I hope Tom Hennessey tells all his friends about the good deal he got out of me tonight. He's a contractor, you know."

"I'm sure he will. You did good tonight, boss." Susan patted her arm. "Now, let's get out of here. I'm dog tired."

"Me, too."

CHAPTER TWELVE

"RICHARD, LET'S GO!" Colt called up the stairs the following morning, and realized how normal it felt to do so. It still amazed him he was a father, but it was beginning to feel comfortable, too.

Richard clattered down the stairs. "Gotta grab my lunch." He kept going through the dining room into the kitchen, where Colt heard him talking with Regan. Heather followed close behind him, looking beautiful but harried. Colt had kept her up late last night and in bed far too long this morning. He couldn't help it. He felt insatiable around her and apparently she felt the same way. She lifted up on tip-toes to press a kiss to his cheek as she passed him, then hurried to pull her coat on. "I'll see you tonight. I might be late—I'm supposed to talk to Mia again. Planning a wedding this fast turns out to be a stretch. The poor woman is beside herself."

Colt tugged her closer. "I'd like you beside me," he began, but Zane walked through the entryway on his way to the stairs and interrupted them.

"Looks like someone's coming." He gestured out the window.

"Who's that?" Colt didn't recognize the car he saw bouncing its way up the snowy driveway. It pulled to a halt in front of the Hall.

"It's a woman, but I don't recognize her," Zane said. "Heather, is that one of your friends?"

"I've never seen her before in my life."

Colt's heart, which a moment ago had hummed with contentment, sank to the pit of his stomach as a tall, beautiful brunette exited the vehicle. He recognized her pretty face and the French braid tucked over one shoulder.

Melanie.

He stepped closer to the window.

Why was she here? He'd told her the deal was off.

She hadn't written back, though, Colt realized suddenly. Hadn't she gotten the message?

"Colt, do you know her?" Zane asked.

Colt pushed down the panic beginning to churn in his gut. "It's Melanie," he said, his voice tight. He turned to Heather. "The woman I hired to be my fake wife."

Heather's mouth dropped open. "You didn't cancel…?"

"Oh, shit," Zane said. "Colt—that's Heloise pulling in behind her."

Colt looked out the window again. Zane was right. Another truck had entered the driveway and he could see his aunt sitting in the passenger seat. Allen James, an old family friend, was driving. Colt watched in horror as Allen parked the vehicle and Heloise got out with an alacrity that belied her age. She leaned on her cane heavily when she walked, but she caught up to Melanie and the two women climbed the stairs together.

"What do we do?" Heather hissed. "Why didn't you tell her not to come?"

"I did tell her. She didn't listen!"

"We don't have time for this." Zane gripped the handle when one of the women outside knocked.

"But—"

"Just play along," Colt told her, but he knew her panic must be reflected in his eyes. He nodded at his brother and Zane opened the door.

"Hi, Heloise, come on in. You're up early on a cold winter's morning."

"I'm no lie-abed if that's what you mean." She pushed her way past him into the crowded entryway. "Having a party, are we? I see I wasn't invited to this one, either. Come along, whoever you are," she said to Melanie. "Don't dawdle on the doorstep like an encyclopedia salesman."

"Isn't James coming in? Here, let me take your coat." Zane held out a hand for it, but she waved him off.

"I won't stay long enough for that. James will wait for me in the truck. I just came to find out why I haven't been invited to my nephew's wedding! I had to hear about it in town. What do you have to say for yourself?" She poked Colt in the arm.

Colt didn't think things could get any worse. His only hope was that Melanie would keep quiet. He couldn't meet Heather's eye. "I haven't sent out any invitations, Heloise."

"Haven't sent them out? Two weeks before the wedding?"

Melanie looked from Heloise to Colt, and suddenly exclaimed, "It's all rather last minute, isn't it?" She flashed Heloise a thousand-watt smile, took Colt's arm and leaned her cheek against it, as if she'd decided she'd better step straight into her role in order to save the day. "I told Colt here we should wait at least three weeks, but you know him. Always so slap-dash and devil-may-care!" Heather made a kind of sputtering noise. Colt only just stopped himself from shaking Melanie off. Slap-dash and devil-may-care? He had to stop her before she ruined everything.

"Who is this?" Heloise gave Melanie a look-over that could have stripped paint off the side of a house.

"I'm Melanie. Colt's fiancée! I can't believe I'm finally here, darling! Can you believe it?" She stood on tiptoe and planted a big kiss on Colt's mouth before he could answer. Colt stifled a groan. How the hell was he going to fix this now?

Heloise's expression hardened. "I wasn't told about any Melanie." Her gaze scoured the small room. "Heather, isn't that a ring I see on *your* finger?" When Heather didn't respond, she turned back to Melanie. "Where's yours?"

Melanie looked to Colt. "You said we'd get it as soon as I arrived, didn't you, honey?"

Colt could only stare at her. Zane signaled to him from behind Heloise's back to say something, but what could he say? He'd always prided himself on his quick thinking, but nothing in his life had prepared him for this.

"Uh… yeah, I guess so."

"I thought Heather was your fiancée. Well?" Heloise demanded when he didn't answer. "Which one are you marrying?"

"Uh… It's…"

"I thought I made it clear I wouldn't be toyed with again," Heloise snapped. "Obviously, none of you took me seriously. Two brides. That's ridiculous even for you, Colt." She turned to go.

Colt thought fast to come up with an answer, but he was trapped. How could he deny that Melanie was his fiancée when she was leaning all over him? But if Heloise had already heard Heather was his fiancée, he couldn't acknowledge Melanie even if he'd wanted to. Which he didn't.

"Heloise, you've made a mistake," Heather blurted just as the old woman's hand grasped the doorknob. "If someone told you I'm marrying Colt, they're wrong. He's engaged to… Melanie."

Colt heard running footsteps behind him, turned his head in time to see Richard bolt back down the hall. When he turned back Heather's face was white, but she stood her ground. He wanted to chase Richard down and tell him it was all a mistake, but Zane's presence reminded him why he had to stand right here. The fate of all of them rested on what happened next.

"Then who are *you* marrying?" Heloise demanded of Heather.

Heather paused only a second. "George Buckley from Silver Falls," she said in a rush. Colt didn't know whether to be grateful or horrified that Heather had intervened to save his skin. Every second this farce went on, they were digging themselves deeper into a trap they wouldn't be able to get out of.

"I'm not familiar with the name." Heloise didn't sound convinced, but she turned her focus to Melanie. "What's your story?"

"I'm Melanie Munroe." She held out her hand and shook with Heloise. "I'm not surprised you haven't heard of me. Colt and I have had a difficult road. We fell in love with each other back when he first went to basic training, but I knew I couldn't be a military wife and Colt couldn't bear to leave the Air Force. We tried to forget each other but it didn't work. Each time we met again it was as if we'd never been apart. Finally, Colt made the ultimate sacrifice and gave up his career for me."

Colt wanted to throw up his hands. Could Melanie be more theatrical?

Heloise snorted. "If he'd made the ultimate sacrifice, he'd have come home in a casket."

Tears filled Melanie's eyes. Colt blinked, somewhat impressed. "Don't even say that! Your nephew put his life in danger countless times while he served his country. If he'd been killed, it would have killed me too. But he didn't die. He came home to me and now we'll spend the rest of our lives together." She gestured to Colt. "I love everything about this man."

"What about Colt's son? Do you love him, too?"

He had to credit Melanie; she barely blinked before saying, "Of course I do. I intend to raise him like my own."

Heather made a strangled noise and Colt couldn't even look at her. She must be livid. How had everything gone off the rails so quickly? He knew Heather meant to help him when she'd blurted out her explanation, but now he'd been backed into a corner he couldn't get out of. He didn't want to marry Melanie, but he couldn't tell the truth, either. All he could do was follow Heather and Melanie's lead.

"It was like this, Heloise," Colt began. "When I got home and found out about Heather and Richard, I thought I should marry Heather instead and be a father to Richard, but after a while, I..." He didn't know what to say. "I guess I...I guess I realized that wasn't going to work. Melanie's the one for me." It killed him to say it, but he pressed on. "Anyway, we'll be married in a couple of weeks."

"Well, this is a fine kettle of fish." Heloise tapped her finger on her cane. "But I guess if that's the way it is, then that's the way it is. Heather, congratulations on your upcoming wedding. Colt, well... I hope like hell you know what you're doing."

With that, she headed for the door, but she stopped with a hand on the knob. "But if I think for a minute that you three are lying to me, there'll be hell to pay."

"We know, Heloise," Colt said wearily. "You'll give the ranch to Darren." He didn't know what satisfaction she'd get from it. His cousin had once been their biggest rival for the property, but several months ago, Darren had confided to Colt's brothers he didn't even want it.

Colt brightened a little. Maybe Heloise should give it to Darren and then he could pass it on to them.

As if she'd read his mind, Heloise said, "To hell with Darren; he point blank told me he's done with ranching. I'll sell it to those nice men from Chicago who approached me last month about developing the property."

"Developing it? For what?" Zane demanded. He'd been quiet since Heloise came in, but now his alarm was all too clear.

"A housing tract, they said. Claimed Chance Creek was due to expand soon. Something about minerals up north. Showed me plans and everything. Over a hundred houses to be built in three stages."

"You can't build houses on the ranch!"

"She wouldn't do that. She's just trying to scare us," Colt told his brother.

"Go ahead and believe that if it makes you sleep better," Heloise said. She tapped the door with her cane and Zane opened it. "I'll choose a housing development over lies any day. Besides, I'd like to be rich. They say it's nice in Hawaii this time of year." They watched her go.

"Careful on those stairs, Heloise," Zane called after her.

"I know how to walk; I'm not senile yet!"

Zane shut the door behind her. "Well, that's that. We're going to lose the ranch."

"We're not going to lose the ranch." Colt turned on Melanie. "What the hell are you doing here?"

"I came to marry you—just like I said I would. What's going on? And who's she?" Melanie pointed to Heather.

"My fiancée—the one I told you about. I e-mailed you and called everything off. Why did you still come?"

Color flushed her cheeks and Melanie closed her eyes. "Shit!" Opening them again she confessed, "I broke my phone this weekend while I was visiting my grandma. I figured I could get a new one here. Oh my God, Colt. Did I just ruin everything?"

"Yeah, you did."

"It's not her fault. It's yours," Heather said. "What were you thinking, having her come here?"

"I was making sure my family inherits this ranch. Like I said, I called it off."

Zane shook his head. "I'm going to go get the others." He strode away down the hall.

"Richard just heard everything, by the way," Heather said. "I'd better go talk to him. You straighten this out."

"I can't straighten it out. Not now."

"Well, you can't marry Melanie!"

When the silence stretched out between them, Melanie dropped her hands and stared at them. "I'll leave. I'll leave right now."

"It's too late! That was my aunt Heloise who barged in," Colt said, as much to remind Heather as to explain it to Melanie. "She's the whole reason I placed that ad in the first place. She owns this ranch and she won't hand it over until I marry. All three of my brothers have done their part to inherit the ranch. I can't let everyone else down. We'll have to go through with it." He turned to Heather. "It's only temporary—just for a few months. You know I wouldn't do this if there was any other way."

"You've got to be kidding." When he didn't answer she made a noise of disbelief. "You're really going to marry her?"

"What else can I do?"

"I don't know. There has to be another way!"

"Tell me what it is, and I'll do it!" Colt waited, hoping like hell Heather could come up with a plan. He couldn't see his way clear to one. All he knew was that he couldn't be the one to lose the ranch for everyone else. He already had too much on his conscience.

Melanie shook her head. "I'm not going to go through with this. I won't break up your relationship with your fiancée or hurt your son."

"You don't have a choice. None of us do." Colt blew out a breath. "Come on, we'd better go find Richard and let everyone know what's going on. Maybe someone else will have an idea. Heather." He took her hand. "Look, I love you. I promise it's all going to be all right."

She only shook her head at him in disbelief.

He knew exactly how she felt. He led the way down the hall feeling like he was walking to his execution. A half-hour ago he thought he was about to step into the life he'd always wanted. Now everything was a mess. When they reached the living room, Richard stood alone in one corner, his arms folded and his face flushed with anger. Everyone else had gathered on the sofas and chairs, waiting for him.

Colt took one look at them and knew this wasn't going to go well.

"YOU DON'T UNDERSTAND everything that's happened," Heather said to Richard. She tried to keep her voice low and steady as she talked to him, but tears stung her eyes and she had to keep blinking them back. She hadn't had time to process what had happened herself. All she knew was that she'd acted on instinct. Colt and his brothers were about to lose the ranch they'd fought so hard to win, and she couldn't be the reason for that loss, even if it meant giving up her own chance at happiness.

Her decision to proclaim Melanie as Colt's wife had been made in an instant and she'd regretted it just as fast, but there wasn't anything else she could have done. Not with the ranch on the line.

"You're supposed to marry Dad."

"I know. It's... complicated. Richard, you know that your dad and all his brothers have to marry in order to get Crescent Hall, right?"

He nodded once, but his expression didn't change. He was fighting tears of his own and thirteen-year-old boys didn't appreciate that kind of emotion.

"Before your Dad and I talked it out and decided to marry, he didn't think he'd be able to find a wife, so he put up an ad and met Melanie. I think they came to an agreement to marry temporarily." She heard herself speak as if from a distance and was amazed by how calm she sounded. Inside she was anything but calm.

"Temporarily?" Richard put a teenager's scorn into the word.

"That's right." Heather did her best to make it sound reasonable. "Just long enough to get the ranch."

"So he was going to lie to Aunt Heloise?"

"He was going to… Yes, he was going to lie to her." There was no way to soften the truth. A fresh rush of sorrow nearly overwhelmed her, but she forced down all thoughts of the future. She had to concentrate on the now, which meant she needed to forget she'd have to postpone her own wedding to Colt.

"You always get mad when I lie!"

"I know." There was nothing else she could say.

"What if she won't go afterward?"

"You mean Melanie?" She'd never considered that possibility, but Richard was right; conceivably Melanie could refuse to divorce Colt. She could drag things out in court, or ask for more money than he'd offered in the meantime.

What if she angled for a piece of the ranch?

"I don't know. I don't know any more than you do right now, okay? We're all going to have to figure this out together."

"I've already figured it out." Richard pulled away from her. "And it sucks!"

"Richard!"

He stormed across the room, but Colt collared him. "Have a seat."

"No." Richard tried to push past him, but Colt wouldn't let go.

"I said, sit down! Heather, are you ready?"

She nodded and came to sit on one of the sofas. After another brief struggle, Richard tore away from Colt and took a seat on the edge of one of the easy chairs, looking poised for flight. Colt straightened. "I'm glad everyone's here. I'm sure you've all figured out what's going on. This is Melanie." He quickly explained the situation. "Now Heloise thinks she's my fiancée," he concluded.

"You have to tell her the truth," Regan said firmly.

"If he does that, we could all lose out," Austin countered.

"Austin's right," Colt said. "She's not talking about giving the ranch to Darren anymore; she says there's a developer interested in buying Crescent Hall. They'll carve up the ranch and build houses here."

"She's got to be lying," Mason said.

"Are we willing to take that risk?" Austin asked. "Heather, you know what's going on here. You can wait for Colt, can't you? This ranch is going to be your and Richard's home, too."

"It's too much to ask for her to wait," Storm said.

"But it's only temporary," Mason countered. "We'd all do what we can to make it bearable."

"I don't think we should put that on Heather," Ella said.

"I think we have to let Heather decide." Zane sat forward. "Heather?"

This was exactly the moment Heather had dreaded. Everyone waited for her answer. Colt stood with his arms crossed, his expression betraying nothing, while Melanie watched her with a concern that was all too evident.

Richard watched her, too, his face like thunder, but she knew underneath his anger lay disappointment. He loved his father and he loved Crescent Hall. She couldn't take either of them from him.

Most of all she was afraid of what would happen if she said no.

If Colt threw off Melanie and married her, everyone else would lose the home they'd worked so hard to get. She didn't think she could stand that. And if Colt didn't back down—if he went ahead and married Melanie—she'd have lost him forever because of her pride.

"Of course," she made herself say. She didn't know how she could watch him pledge his love to another woman, though. Even if everyone but Heloise knew it was a lie, he'd have to act like he loved Melanie and she'd have to stand by and watch.

Richard jumped to his feet and rushed down the hallway. A minute later the front door slammed shut.

Heather stood up. "I have to get Richard to school."

"Wait a minute. We have to get our stories straight," Austin said.

"Maybe you all do, but I don't," she countered. "I'm late." She hated the tone that had crept into her voice and if she didn't leave soon, she'd lose her cool.

"I'll walk you out," Colt said.

"Heather, please know I am so, so sorry for how I've messed things up," Melanie said as she passed. "I had no idea—"

"I know. I don't blame *you*."

Colt tensed as her barb hit home, but she didn't care. He had to know how badly this turn of events hurt her. When they reached the front hall and he took her arm it was all she could do not to pull away from him. She didn't want him to touch her.

She wanted to be alone.

"I never meant for this to happen. You have to know that," he said when they reached the entryway.

She pulled on her coat and boots. "Did you even actually send that e-mail canceling your deal with Melanie?"

"Of course I did."

"When? In the last couple of days?" That hurt the most; knowing he must have wanted to keep his options open.

"I only started talking to you a few days ago!"

"She obviously didn't answer you," she went on, ignoring him. "Didn't that raise some alarms?"

"I was too busy thinking about you." He stopped her when she reached for the door. "Damn it, Heather. I love you. I. Love. You." He cupped her face in both hands and leaned down to kiss her. Heather struggled at first, but this was Colt. She didn't know how to resist him, even now, but her acquiescence only lasted a moment. "No." She ripped herself away from him. "Not until she's gone." She opened the door before he could recover and ran down the front steps. When she got into her truck, Richard was already belted in.

"I hate him."

She started the engine, blinking hard against tears. "It's not his fault."

"Then whose is it?"

"Heloise's. All of ours."

"Then I hate Heloise."

She knew she should lecture him about forgiveness and tolerance, but she found she couldn't form the words. "I think right now I hate her, too."

CHAPTER THIRTEEN

WHEN COLT RETURNED to the living room, Melanie sat on the sofa and Regan sat next to her, a consoling hand on her arm. "This isn't your fault," she was saying.

"That's right; it's my fault. I should have followed up to make sure you got my message." Colt couldn't sit. Instead he paced across the room, then turned to cross it again.

"I still wouldn't have gotten your e-mail," Melanie said. "Not with a broken phone. It's my fault for not finding a computer and checking in one last time before I came."

"What's done is done," Zane said. "Now we have to make the best of it. Colt, is Heather on board?"

"For now. She's not happy, though. And Richard hates my guts."

"He doesn't hate you," Ella said.

"Of course he hates me. I just ditched his mom!" He scanned the worried faces looking back at him. "I shouldn't have let them leave like that, either. Whatever happens, they need to keep living here so I can keep close to Richard. I don't want to lose him over this."

"Of course not," Storm said.

"They should definitely keep living here," Regan echoed. "It's not like Melanie is trying to break you two up, right? We'll do everything we can to make this as easy as possible. We'll keep Richard busy and entertain Melanie and make sure she has fun while she's here. It will be like a vacation for you, Melanie."

"A really awkward vacation." Melanie twisted her fingers together in her lap. "Heather must despise me."

"No," Colt said. "I don't think so. If anything she's pissed at me."

"Are you sure I should stay? Because I think you should tell your aunt the truth about us—"

"No!" Several voices rang out together.

"You don't know Heloise," Zane said. "Although if there's any issue between you and Heather, Colt, then you have to do what's right for the two of you. None of us want to win the ranch if it's going to break you up."

There was an uncomfortable silence that stretched out just a bit too long before Colt said, "It's not going to break us up. Not if I can have time alone with Heather and Richard along the way."

"We'll all help with that," Storm said. The others nodded.

"I hate to bring it up, but we've got to be practical. You and Melanie better go buy a ring," Mason said. "Zane says Heloise thought it was weird you hadn't done that already."

Colt rubbed his neck. He'd already bought a ring for

the woman he loved, but Mason was right; Melanie would need one, too. "We'll do that later today," he said. "All right, Melanie?"

Melanie looked like she would object, but she took in the concerned faces surrounding her and her shoulders slumped. "Okay."

"YOU CAN'T LET Colt marry someone else!" Camila sat across from Heather at Linda's Diner later that afternoon. Heather kept an eye on the time. She wanted be there to pick Richard up from school as soon as the bell rang. He'd refused to talk to her when they drove into town this morning, and she knew that his anger masked a world of hurt. This situation required delicate handling.

She'd gone to work and done the best she could to keep up with her to-do list, but when Camila texted to say she was taking her afternoon break, Heather had jumped at the chance to meet her for coffee.

"What else can I do? If he doesn't marry her now, they'll lose the ranch."

"So let them lose the ranch! This is getting out of control."

Heather had to agree, but there was nothing for it. "What's done is done. We just have to get through the next few months and everything will be fine." Maybe if she told herself that enough times it would come true.

"Somebody needs to sort Heloise out. She's messed up."

"I agree."

"She—"

"Oh no." Heather fought the urge to drop her head in her hands when she saw who had just walked through the door.

"What?" Camila turned around. "Is that the fake fiancée?"

"Yep."

Colt paused in the doorway with Melanie, spotted them and led Melanie their way. Heather couldn't believe it; surely he didn't mean to join them.

Apparently he did. He gestured for Melanie to sit next to Heather and moved to sit by Camila. Camila glared at him for a long minute before she finally rolled her eyes and moved over.

"I'm glad we found you." Colt reached for Heather's hand, then pulled back at the last second. "Look, I know how awkward this is but I want you and Richard to keep staying at the Hall."

"I don't think that's a good idea. Besides, it's impractical. I can't leave my house empty for long and it's too hard to live out of a suitcase."

"You didn't mind that before."

"Things were different before."

"Then come and go, but if you move home now, Richard's going to feel like I've abandoned him." Colt's handsome face was tight with worry. Despite herself, Heather's anger decreased. She could see how much he had grown to love Richard and how it was killing him to let his son down.

"I've explained everything to him."

"That doesn't fix it, though, does it? He and I were

just starting to be comfortable. I don't want to lose him again."

"What will Heloise say?"

"She'll think it's crazy, but she won't be able to prove we're lying about my marriage to Melanie."

She could feel Camila willing her to say no, but Colt was right; Richard would pull back from him if they weren't in contact. "Won't it be hard for Melanie to have us around?"

Melanie shook her head vigorously. "Of course not! I want to do anything I can to help. Colt told me everything that's happened and I feel like such a fool for messing it all up. You three should live together. Richard needs to get to know his father and I'll explain the whole situation to him again if you think it will help."

A quick glance across the table told her Melanie's eagerness to please had undermined even Camila's ability to stay angry at her.

"Okay," Heather said reluctantly. She expected Colt to be relieved, but instead he frowned. He took her hand and lifted it up.

"Where is it?"

"Where's what?" But Heather already knew what he meant. She tugged her hand away. She'd taken off her engagement ring before she came in to work, unwilling to wear it if they weren't actually going to marry.

"Your ring? Where's your ring?"

"You're marrying Melanie. Maybe… maybe she should have it."

"Like hell!" Colt glanced at Melanie and lowered his

voice. "I mean—we're going to go get her one to wear for show, but it won't be real and we sure as hell won't use yours. You're acting like—ow!"

Heather kicked Colt when she spotted Heloise.

"Well, isn't this cozy!" Heloise made her way down the aisle toward them. Thank goodness Heather had seen her early enough, or who knew what Heloise might have overheard.

Colt turned and surveyed her grimly. "Isn't this a surprise."

"Maybe for you it is. I come for a slice of pie every week." Heloise scanned the occupants of the booth and her eyes narrowed when she focused on Heather's hand. "Heather Ward, where's your ring? Have you lost that fiancé of yours already? You're not very good at holding onto your men."

Despite herself, Heather felt her cheeks warm and it took all her will not to hide her hand. "I haven't lost anyone, Heloise. My ring is… at the jewelers. I'm going to pick it up when I'm done here."

"I notice you still don't have a ring, either," Heloise said to Melanie.

"That's our next stop," Colt said with forced cheer.

"It's your lucky day. I'm on my way to the jewelers, too. I feel the need for a new brooch. I'll back you up, young lady. Make sure that cowboy of yours doesn't act like a cheapskate when you pick out your ring."

"Oh, I don't want anything fancy," Melanie said.

Heloise chuckled. "That's what they all say until they get to the jewelry counter, eh, Colt? Let's get a move on.

You too, Heather."

Heather exchanged a helpless glance with Colt. "What about your pie, Heloise?"

"That can wait. First things first. Or maybe you don't want to go. Maybe you don't have a fiancé. Maybe everything the three of you have told me is a lie, and those developers are going to get Crescent Hall for a song."

Colt's gaze met hers and Heather knew the old woman had won again.

"Okay, let's go," she said and got up. Melanie stood as well. With a sigh, Colt got to his feet. "I'm not sure this is a group activity, Heloise." Camila kept to her seat, but shook her head slowly. Heather knew what she meant. They were all stark raving mad.

"It is now," Heloise said.

As COLT HELD open the door to Thayer's Jewelers, he wondered how best to survive this little field trip. Heather walked into the store first, shoulders stiff and head held high. Melanie hung back as if she wanted to hide. Heloise had a thin-lipped smile that spelled more trouble ahead. The jewelry store had changed since he was young. Back then Thayer ran it in a far more traditional manner, but a year or so ago, Rose Johnson had teamed up with Mia Matheson to purchase the place and run their businesses together. Rose ran the jewelry store and used one large wall as a gallery to display the landscapes she painted. Mia ran her wedding planning business from a small office off to the side.

Colt had no idea how this encounter would play out. Rose would certainly know about his engagement to Heather. Could he somehow signal to her that things had changed? He'd heard Rose had a special kind of intuition, but he doubted that meant she'd be able to read his mind. According to Mason, when she touched a couple's engagement ring, she got a hunch about their future prospects. It had pleased his brother when she pronounced that he and Regan would go the distance, but that wasn't any help to Colt now.

Rose came to meet them before he could think of a better method to fill her in on what was happening. "Hello, Heloise. Colt, Heather—congratulations, Mia told me your news!" She looked expectantly at Melanie.

Colt knew he had to work fast. He touched Melanie's arm and spoke clearly, hoping to make Rose understand how important it was to go along with what he said. "Hi Rose, I'd like to introduce you to Melanie Munroe—my fiancée."

Rose's brows furrowed. "Your... but... isn't..?" She looked from Heather back to Colt and worked to get herself under control. "Of course. Are... you two looking for a ring today?"

He admired her professionalism and the way she caught on so fast. "That's right. The prettiest ring you've got," he improvised.

"Why don't you start looking through the cases over there?" Rose pointed across the room. "So... ah... Heather. What can I do for you today?"

As Colt steered Melanie over toward the rings, he

listened for Heather's answer.

"I'm here to pick up my ring. You know, the one you were resizing for me?" She too over-enunciated her words.

Rose opened her mouth, shut it again. Cocked her head and said, "Of course. The ring. Could you remind me again what it looks like? I swear I've done a passel of them this week."

Colt didn't think he'd ever heard Rose sound so countrified, but then this situation would scour the varnish off anyone. He was happy she'd had the presence of mind to go along with their charade without tripping any of them up so far.

"Sure." Heather drifted toward the cases that held the rings, scanned them quickly and said, "Just like that one!"

Rose nodded. "Okay. I know exactly where it is. Heloise, is there anything I can do for you?"

"I have it in mind to buy me a new brooch. An expensive one. I have a feeling I'm going to come into some money soon."

"Of course! Take a look around. I'll come help you in a minute, after I fetch Heather's ring. Colt and Melanie, are you two doing all right?"

"Just fine," Colt hurried to say. Rose disappeared into the back room and he said a silent prayer of thanks that so far things had gone this well.

"About this fiancé of yours," Heloise said to Heather, "does he realize how intimate you plan to be with Colt?"

Heather's eyebrows shot up. "I... don't know what you mean."

"Colt's the father of your child," Heloise elaborated. "I assume you'll see him frequently—when he spends time with Richard."

"Oh... of course!"

"Heather and Richard are living at the Hall for now," Colt said. "I want to see my son every day."

It was Heloise's turn to blink. "Very enlightened of you," she said. She turned to Melanie. "And you're all right with this, young lady? Living with your stepson's mother?"

Melanie nodded quickly. "Of course. A child should be with both his parents."

"Well, when I said you'd be intimate before, I had no idea, did I?" Heloise turned back to Heather. "And your fiancé? He'll move into the Hall, too?"

"Um..." Heather looked to Colt.

"Sure. Why not?" he said.

"I'd better meet this paragon," Heloise said. "In my day the two of you'd be more likely to kill each other than live together under one roof. But they don't make men like they used to, that's for sure."

"I'm sure my fiancé would be very happy to meet you." But when Heloise turned away, Heather sent Colt an imploring look.

"He's a very busy man, though," Colt said.

"I'll see him tomorrow night for dinner," Heloise proclaimed, bending to look at a case full of necklaces. "At the Hall. Tell Regan to make those potatoes that I like."

"I don't think—" Heather began.

"Tomorrow," Heloise reiterated. "The man has to eat, doesn't he? No matter how busy he is."

To Colt's relief, Rose reappeared. "Here's your ring, Heather."

Heather took it from her and slid it on her finger. From what Colt could see, it was a passable double for the one he'd bought her in Billings. He hoped it would fool Heloise. He was still scrambling to think of what to say to deflect his aunt from her dinner plan. "I doubt George will be able to make it on such short notice."

"And I doubt George exists," Heloise said promptly. "So we'll eat dinner and when George doesn't show, you'll admit you all are lying and I'll sell the ranch to the highest bidder."

"What do you think of this brooch, Heloise," Rose blurted, pulling a large one out of the nearest case. "It's pretty expensive."

"I'm sure George will do what he can to make dinner if it's so important to you, Heloise," Heather said suddenly. "Tomorrow, it is."

"I'll see you tomorrow then." She examined the piece of jewelry in Rose's hand and sniffed. "I'll be going now. You youngsters have tired me out with your newfangled notions. And that brooch is dreadful." Heloise left without another word.

"Is someone going to tell me what the hell is going on?" Rose said.

THE DOOR OPENED again before anyone could speak, and Mason walked into the jewelry store. He navigated his way around the glass cases. "I saw your vehicles outside," he said, "and I saw Heloise leaving. Just wanted to make sure everything is okay."

"It won't be okay until someone tells me what's happening." Rose looked from Heather to Colt. "Weren't you two engaged?"

"It's a long story," Heather said. "It involves Heloise. That should pretty much sum it up."

"I have to marry Melanie first before I can marry Heather," Colt said. "That's why we need a ring."

"First? Polygamy wasn't legal in Montana the last time I checked."

"It's not like that," Heather said. "It's because of the ranch. I'll explain it later, Rose, but right now I'd better go." She handed the ring back to her. "As long as I don't see Heloise between here and home I won't need this."

"You can bring it back tomorrow if you want it overnight," Rose said. "But I still don't under—wait a minute." She pointed to the large front display window. "Isn't that Richard outside? Shouldn't he be in school?"

Heather turned to look and sucked in a breath. Rose was right; Richard was walking past, and it wasn't nearly time for him to leave school. She hurried out of the store and intercepted her son just as he was about to cross the street. "Richard?" She'd never seen the girl who walked beside him, a tall brunette whose spiky hair seemed liable to poke out Richard's eye if he came too close. The girl wore more makeup than Heather liked to see on someone so young, but it was Richard's presence that shocked her the most. "What are you doing here? Why aren't you in school?"

Guilt and a little fear flashed across his face, but then he glanced at the girl and straightened. "It's just gym class. I'll be back in time for math."

"You're... skipping class?" She couldn't believe it. Richard had never done such a thing. He'd never even said he wanted to. While he preferred the outdoors and ranch chores to class time, he had a lot of friends in school and had never made a fuss about going.

The girl rolled her eyes. "Everyone does it. It's not a big deal."

"Everyone doesn't do it, or the school would shut down. Richard, I want to speak to you inside."

The girl held up a hand. "I'm out of here. You know where to find me," she said to Richard and walked away. Richard took a half step like he was going to join her and Heather grabbed his arm.

"Oh, no you don't. You're going back to school and you're going to apologize to your gym teacher and tell him you'll never do this again."

Richard yanked his arm away. "Like hell I will."

Heather's mouth dropped open. Her son had nev-er—*never*—spoken to her like that before. "What did you just say to me?"

Remorse flashed across his face before he pulled himself together. Heather almost pitied him for how hard it obviously was to fake this bravado. *Almost*. She was too angry to pull it off.

"Catch you later," he said. He tugged his arm free and backed away.

Colt, who had followed Heather outside, strode past her and caught him. "Your mother's talking to you." He tugged Richard back to the sidewalk where Mason joined them.

"What's going on here?"

"Nothing." Richard glared back at them defiantly. "So I missed gym class. Big deal!"

"It is a big deal," Heather said. "Why would you skip school? You've never done anything like that before!"

"I bet Dad skipped school all the time."

They all swung around to look at Colt, who scowled. "I didn't skip school. Much," he added when Mason snorted. "And it didn't matter because I joined the Air Force and they were happy to take me."

"Maybe that's what I'll do. Maybe I'll drop out right now and join up." Richard's voice cracked and his face reddened.

"Not much call for thirteen-year-olds in the armed forces," Mason intervened. "And regardless of what Colt says, they have standards. You drop out now and you'll never get in."

"He's never getting in, anyway," Heather exclaimed. "I refuse to watch my son—"

"I'll sign up if I damn well want to!"

"What did you just say?" Colt turned on him, but Mason stepped in his way. "I'll take Richard back to school. You finish up your business here, Colt. Melanie is inside waiting for you. Heather, I imagine you need to get back to work?" Mason didn't wait for either of them to answer. He collared Richard and marched him to his truck. "See you at the ranch in an hour," he called back. A moment later, the truck pulled away.

CHAPTER FOURTEEN

"**O**F ALL THE nerve," Heather said.

Colt understood what she meant, but he couldn't help thinking Mason had done the right thing. He'd been too angry to deal with Richard properly. He needed to learn some parenting skills, fast. When Richard swore at Heather, he'd seen red. No son of his was going to talk to his mother like that—

"He's never acted like this before," Heather said.

"He's pissed off."

"Well, so am I."

"That makes three of us." Colt unzipped his coat, suddenly over-warm even though they still stood outside.

Heather made a face. "This day has been too crazy. I'm going back to the store."

"Heather, wait. I'll pick Richard up after school and have a little talk with him."

"Okay." She turned away.

"Heather," he called again.

She stopped at her truck. "What?"

"Boys will be boys. Don't take this too much to heart."

She nodded, but as she climbed in and started the engine, she didn't look happy.

Back inside the store, Colt found Rose and Melanie deep in conversation. They were bent over the display case of rings, so intent on the selection their heads almost touched. Melanie looked up when he approached.

"Is everything all right?" she asked.

Colt stopped himself from answering in the negative. Nothing was all right, but none of it was her fault. "Find a ring?"

"How about this one?" She was subdued as she raised her hand to show him the one on her finger, a plain diamond in a simple setting.

"It looks nice."

"It's cheap."

"I'll ring that up for you," Rose said quietly and took it from her. She winced and dropped it on the counter, then rushed to pick it up again and pop it into a velvet-covered box.

"Why don't you wait for me in the truck?" Colt said to Melanie. "I'll finish up in here."

She nodded and took the keys from him. When she was gone, Colt faced Rose. "Go on. Say whatever you've got to say."

Rose shook her head. "Melanie explained everything. I get why you're doing what you're doing. But Colt, when I held that ring just now—I've never seen such a bleak future. There's got to be another way."

He could easily believe she'd drawn a big blank when she'd held the ring. He and Melanie had no future.

"Believe me, if there was, I'd take it."

"Can't you explain to Heloise...?" She trailed off. "Of course you can't. I feel utterly irresponsible selling you this ring, though."

"Whatever happens, the responsibility is mine," Colt said, but as he paid for the ring and pocketed the box he had a feeling she was right; things were going to get worse before they got better.

The drive home from Thayer's was quiet and when they reached the Hall, Melanie claimed a headache and said she wanted to lie down. Colt accompanied her inside where they met Regan, who said she'd take Melanie up to the room she'd prepared for her. "Unless you plan to share Colt's room."

"No," both of them said at once. Regan led Melanie away without another word.

Colt knew he should join his brothers and Dan to help with the chores until it was time to get Richard, but he couldn't stop thinking about Heather and how she must be feeling. Secure in the knowledge that Regan would do all she could to make Melanie comfortable, he went back outside, got in his truck, and headed back to town. When he reached Renfree's, it struck him that he hadn't been inside the place since Heather took over. It looked much the same as always, except that without Renfree, it had a distinctly female vibe.

"Colt? Is something wrong?" Heather hurried to meet him.

"Everything's fine. I just wanted a chance to talk to you alone. I already dropped Melanie off at the ranch."

"Oh, okay. Susan, can you manage on your own for a while?"

"I've got it, boss," Susan called out good-naturedly. "I'll call Allison if I need help. She's working on that newsletter." Heather led the way through the store to a room in back that must have been the employees' lounge. She shut the door after he'd entered.

"What do you want to talk about?"

"What do you think?"

"I don't think it's a good idea to go into everything again." She moved to the counter and began to stack coffee cups from the dish rack.

He took the cups from her hands and turned her to face him. "I'm proud of you for what you're doing here. You're a great role model for Richard. Owning your own store; that's a big step."

"I'm kind of making a mess of it." Heather tried to tug her hands away but he didn't let her. He needed a physical connection to her since the world seemed so set on dragging them apart.

"Your sales are still down?"

"They've improved since I hosted the flooring demonstration. And one of my employees is working on advertising, but they're not where I need them to be yet."

"If you need any help, you let me know. Anything at all. You can boss me around and I'll do exactly what you say."

"That sounds fun." She rolled her eyes. "Listen to me. You're off limits."

"I'm only off limits when Heloise is watching." He

drew her closer.

"Colt." She tried to twist away when he bent to kiss her. "Not until after all of this is over. It's not right, me kissing you when you have a fiancée."

"You are my fiancée."

"Don't let Heloise hear that."

"Heloise isn't here." He backed Heather up until she bumped against the counter. Letting go of her hands, he lifted her up to sit on it. "No one's here except for you and me." He cupped her chin. Gently tugging her close, he managed to kiss her this time. He'd ached to kiss Heather all day. He wanted to let her know in the most direct way possible that no matter what happened next, she was the only woman he wanted. Heather kissed him back, but when he slid a hand down to her breast, she pulled away.

"No. I'm sorry, but I can't."

Colt heaved a sigh. Bracing his palms against the counter on either side of her, he said, "So now what do we do?"

"Now we find me a fiancé," she said. "You heard Heloise—she expects to meet him tomorrow night."

Colt couldn't believe he'd forgotten that in all the drama surrounding Richard's decision to cut class. He thought a moment. "I might know a guy."

"Seriously? You know a guy who would pretend to be my fiancé?"

"I served with him for a while and he lives not too far away. He used to have a knack for this kind of thing. I'll give him a call and let you know what he says later."

He leaned in for another kiss, but Heather cut this one short.

"I have to get back to work."

He didn't let her go. "Tell me we're going to make it through this."

"Colt—"

"Tell me. Or I'll call everything off right now. We'll go tell Heloise the truth."

"No. I don't want to do that. Despite everything—despite what Richard says now—one day he'll appreciate the chance to live on the ranch, so we have to play this out to the end." She looked away. "We'll make it through this."

The shine of tears in her eyes cut him to the quick. He hated that they'd been put in this position.

"I want to make love to you."

"We can't." She pushed him away and jumped down off of the counter. When he pursued her, she put up her hands to block him. "Not now, Colt."

When a tear spilled down her cheek, Colt wrapped his arms around her and crushed her against his chest. "I love you and only you. No matter what happens, you have to believe that."

She nodded, but when she pushed him away again, he let her go.

TWO HOURS LATER, Heather parked her truck in front of the Hall and wiped her eyes again. She'd been a wreck since Colt had left Renfree's and she'd been relieved when the day ended and she could close up the store.

She'd barely reached the front steps when the door swung open and Regan appeared.

"Oh good; you're home. I have to run into town to pick up a prescription refill. Storm and Ella are working on dinner. With everything that happened I forgot about tonight."

"What's tonight?"

"It's Cheyenne's birthday. She, Henry and the girls are coming for dinner. So are Darren and Belinda—and the Turners."

Storm had mentioned the plan earlier in the week, and Heather had picked up a gift, but she had forgotten it was today. The last thing she needed was an avalanche of guests, but there was nothing for it but to paste a smile on her face and keep going. "That's a houseful. Can I help?" Cheyenne was Storm's mother, who'd followed Storm to Montana from California. She'd married Henry Montlake recently and moved in with him on his large ranch. Zoe, Daisy and Violet were Storm's much younger sisters. They'd taken to Chance Creek like fish to water.

Darren had been the other possible heir to Crescent Hall, but these days he and wife, Belinda, were frequent visitors here. Belinda worked with Storm at Willow's. The Turners were another young ranching family who owned the Flying W, where Camila lived. Eli, Noah, Maya and Stella Turner were siblings. When their father retired from ranching, their cousins Brody, Liam and Alex joined them. Heather enjoyed the boisterous Turner clan and normally she'd be happy they were coming for dinner.

"I'm sure you can; we're all scrambling. Ask Storm!" Regan hurried off to her truck and Heather let herself into the Hall. She evidently wasn't going to get a minute of quiet. Maybe it was better that way.

Storm set her to work making meatballs. Ella was setting the dining room table. "How are you doing?" Storm asked quietly as she stirred the sauce.

"As well as can be expected, I guess. How about you? The store doing okay?" She didn't feel like talking about herself.

"It's doing really well, actually. I did great over the holidays."

"I'm glad to hear it. What about your mom and sisters?"

"Cheyenne loves it here. With her house in California sold and all her debts paid off she's a new woman. Of course, now that she's married to Henry she can be the stay-at-home mom she always wanted to be. I think Zoe, Violet and Daisy adore having her full attention."

Was that wistfulness Heather heard in her voice? She knew Storm hadn't had it easy growing up. Once her father had died, she'd filled his shoes and helped Cheyenne support her sisters. Heather could relate, although she hadn't had any siblings to care for, like Storm had.

"I'm glad they're so close. Otherwise you'd want to fly off to California all the time."

"I'm glad they're close, too. I would have missed them too much otherwise."

Ella entered the kitchen and opened the silverware

drawer. "Hi, Heather. Are you all right?"

"I'm fine." Heather deflected the question again. "How about you? Did I hear you'd found a therapist who was interested in working with you?"

"You heard right." Ella brightened. "Dr. Diane Wells from Bozeman. She loves the idea of equine therapy. We're working out the details."

"Tell Heather about your screenplay," Storm pointed her wooden spoon at Ella. "This one's been busy."

"Screenplay? What's it about?" Heather was happy things were working out for Ella, despite the awkward-ness between them. She knew it must have been hard for her to leave Hollywood behind for Chance Creek, but Ella never complained about small town life.

Ella blushed. "It's about four sisters who inherit a bed and breakfast."

"And don't forget the crazy aunt and her conditions for the inheritance," Storm sang out.

"She's a crazy *cousin*, but yes, she's modeled on someone we all know."

A smile crossed Heather's face for the first time that day. "That's perfect." Maybe Ella had hidden depths she'd overlooked before. Heather had to admit she'd always been so afraid Ella wouldn't like her she hadn't given her much chance to prove otherwise.

"I thought so, too," Storm said.

"I couldn't help but get a little revenge."

Heather enjoyed the banter, but she knew she'd nev-er truly feel like she belonged at the Hall until she sorted things out with Ella once and for all. Maybe now was the time to do that. "Will it bother you if I ever marry Colt and move in for good?"

Ella's eyes widened. "Of course not! I admit when you first showed up I worried for a minute you might still have feelings for Austin—or he might have feelings for you. As soon as I saw you with Colt, that fear went right out the window. I've never seen two people more in love." She lifted her hands helplessly. "I'm sorry it hasn't worked out the way it should have."

"We've got company," Storm cautioned them.

Heather turned to see Richard and Colt walk in. Colt came over and kissed her on the cheek. Richard hung back in the doorway.

"I'm sorry, Mom," he mumbled, leaning against the doorjamb.

"And?" Colt's deep voice prompted.

"I won't skip class again. And I won't swear... in front of you."

"Richard!"

"Okay, I won't swear at all. Much."

Storm coughed and hid a chuckle behind her hand.

Heather heard Colt's long-suffering sigh and suddenly saw the humor in the situation, as black as it was. She saw the saving grace, too: she wasn't alone in this. No matter how crazy things got, Richard had a lot of people pulling for him.

"Okay."

Richard's eyes widened when he finally looked up and caught sight of her face. "Mom?"

"It's okay," she assured him, realizing he must have

spotted the traces of her tears. "I'm just sad."

"Because of what I did?" Suddenly he was a boy again, stricken by the consequences of his actions.

"It's been a hard day."

Richard looked miserable. "Dad says I better do some chores."

Dad. Heather's heart contracted. Glancing at Colt, she saw how much it meant to him to be called that name by his son. "I agree with your father. You can start upstairs in the third-floor bathroom. Clean the tub and sink. Do the counters, too. Use the right cleaning products. They're in the pantry."

"Okay." Richard went to rummage in the pantry glumly and a few moments later she heard him trudging up the stairs.

"Thank you for talking to him," she said to Colt, who leaned against the kitchen island, watching her every move with a hunger she couldn't mistake.

"He's acting this way because of my mistake, right?" Colt straightened. "I'd better get back to my chores, too."

"See you at dinner." She went back to her work, stiffening when Colt came up behind her and dropped a kiss on the top of her head. She turned a questioning look his way. He shrugged and left out the back door, but the desire in his eyes lingered with her long after he was gone, making it even harder to accept the way things had turned out.

CHAPTER FIFTEEN

STORM AND REGAN must have made some phone calls because neither Darren nor Belinda batted an eye at the extra fiancée at the table, and Cheyenne, Henry, and her girls greeted Melanie as if they'd known her for years. The Turners were cheerfully oblivious to the undercurrents swirling around the large dining room table and helped diffuse the tension that otherwise might have overwhelmed the rest of them. Violet and Daisy immediately piled onto Richard and managed to coax a grudging smile out of him with their silliness. Zoe, who was twelve, chatted with him over their heads and soon Colt was convinced that Richard would be able to relax for the evening, at least.

"How are you feeling?" Cheyenne asked Storm across the table. "You're not showing much."

"I'm showing enough for both of us," Regan said, placing a hand on the rounded curve of her belly.

"You look terrific. So does Ella," Maya assured her. "Isn't that right, Eli?" Colt had met the Turners at Mason's wedding last spring and he enjoyed the whole boisterous family. Maya's teasing of her brother reminded him of the way he and his brothers used to interact. He hoped that someday they'd be able to relax and enjoy each other's company again.

Eli, looking embarrassed, mumbled, "Sure is."

"You look beautiful, too, Storm," Noah chimed in gallantly, raising a glass and toasting her.

"I may not be showing, but all my clothes are getting tight," Storm said. "It's lucky I own a clothing store."

"Do you still enjoy working at the store, Belinda?" Henry asked.

Belinda, who'd just taken a bite of spaghetti, nodded vigorously. When she'd managed to swallow, she added, "It's getting busy, though. Melanie's going to help us out for a while."

"Just for a while? Do you have something else planned, Melanie?" Cheyenne asked.

"I want to open a spa," Melanie said. "Someday." She toyed with her noodles and Colt wondered if she was thinking that enduring the next few months wouldn't be worth the payoff.

"Chance Creek desperately needs a spa," Stella said from down at the other end of the table.

"Oh, I don't think I'll open one in Chance Creek." Melanie shut her mouth with a snap and blushed when the Turners focused on her with interest.

Zoe had been following the conversation, too. "Where, then?"

Melanie bit her lip, as if unsure how to answer the dangerous question. Colt wondered how much Storm's younger sisters knew about the situation. "I haven't worked that out yet. Cheyenne, did you find it easy to move from California to Chance Creek?"

Colt relaxed as the conversation turned. He felt like he'd been negotiating a field full of landmines all day and it would only be worse tomorrow night when Heloise came for dinner. He'd spoken to his old Air Force buddy, Eric Rutherfield, who lived in Missoula, and Eric had agreed to play Heather's fiancé in exchange for a case of beer. "Nah, sounds like fun," he'd said when Colt offered him cash. "My life is way too boring these days. I guess I should have dodged that bullet." Colt knew he meant the one that had torn through his shoulder and messed up the rotation of his right arm just enough he had to leave the military. Eric worked for his family's sporting goods store now, and Colt understood why the man would be eager for a change of pace.

He and Heather were to meet Eric at Camila's place the following afternoon so they could synchronize their stories and practice acting like an engaged couple. He figured Heloise might barge in at the Hall, but she'd never think to look for them here. He trusted Eric to do the job right, but he was afraid Heather's patience had already been stretched to the breaking point. He hoped she could hold it together long enough to pull this off. Eric would stay for a couple of days and said he could come back if that become necessary, but Colt hoped that meeting George once would be enough for Heloise.

After Cheyenne opened her presents and they all ate cake, Richard and the girls left the table and raced upstairs to the third floor. The Turners excused them-

192 | CORA SETON

selves, too. "Sorry to eat and run," Eli said. "Got a heifer that isn't doing so well. We need to keep an eye on her."

"No problem," Mason said. "We know exactly how that goes."

"Come back soon," Regan said. "We don't see enough of you these days."

"I know." Stella gave her a hug. "We'll host next time."

Everyone chimed in with their good-byes, and Mason showed them out. Once the coast was clear and the rest of them were settled in the living room with coffee and tea, Darren spoke up. "So Heloise has you all in a bind again I hear."

"That's about the size of it," Colt said.

"You're really going to marry Melanie?" Belinda asked. "When Storm told me you were back with Heather I was so happy for you two. No offense," she added to Melanie.

"None taken," Melanie said. "If I could go back and change things, I would. I never meant to cause all these problems."

"Heloise saw Melanie when she first got here. What else could we do?" Colt shrugged. "She said if it turns out we're playing tricks on her, she'd sell the ranch to bunch of developers."

"Well, that's a new one." Darren leaned back on the couch.

"She'd do anything to get her way."

"Isn't that the truth?" Belinda sighed. "That woman would try a saint."

"You haven't heard the worst of it," Storm said. "Heloise cornered these three and made them invite her for dinner tomorrow."

"There was no inviting," Colt broke in.

"And not only that. She's forcing Heather to bring her fiancé!"

"Hold up," Cheyenne said. "You have a fiancé?"

"I do now." Heather tucked her feet under her on the sofa. "Colt found him for me. I get to meet him tomorrow. Maybe it'll be love at first sight!" Her quip pierced straight through Colt and an uncomfortable silence settled around the room. "I'm joking," she said, her exasperation clear. "For God's sake, if we lose our sense of humor, we're not going to make it through this."

"I'm with Heather. To a sense of humor." Melanie raised her cup.

"To a sense of humor," the rest of them intoned. Colt drained the rest of his beer.

They were going to need it.

"CAN I ASK you a personal question?" Melanie said later that night when she and Heather met in the third-floor hallway. Heather had said good-night to Colt downstairs and had just closed the door to Richard's bedroom. The boy was in a better humor after a few hours with all the other kids, but he'd been gruff when she tried to kiss him good-night.

"Sure. Why not?" Heather said. "We're just about sister-wives, after all."

Melanie chuckled. "You're taking this well."

"Not much else I can do." Inside she still ached at the injustice of it all and she knew she'd probably cry herself to sleep tonight. All she could do until then was cling to the remnants of her self-esteem.

"Anyway, my question is, why are you sleeping up here?" She indicated the room Regan had set up when Heather asked her to.

"Because Colt has a new fiancée." Heather leaned against the wall.

"A new fake fiancée, and everyone knows it except Heloise. You were obviously sharing a room with him before I came. I don't see why you'd change that now."

"You know, you're being awfully good about this, too. You stepped into a hornet's nest. Not to mention Colt's pretty handsome," Heather added. "I'm glad you haven't fallen for him."

"He made it really clear in his ad he only wanted a temporary wife. The last thing I needed was to set myself up for more heartbreak. Besides, he's not my type."

Heather considered her. "Has anyone even asked you why you answered the ad in the first place?"

"Sure they have. I'll tell you what I told them. For the money. I want to start a spa."

"What's the real story?"

Melanie made a face. "I needed somewhere to go. For a long time I'd gotten stuck in a rut that was just comfortable enough to keep me there. I worked at someone else's spa, my boyfriend paid me just enough attention to keep me happy and I saw my friends often enough that I thought they cared about me. Then in one week my boss folded the business without telling anyone and I discovered my boyfriend was cheating with one of my friends. It woke me right up. I realized I'd been living on auto-pilot. I needed a big change—and some money to start fresh. I don't know if I'll be able to open a spa with what I earn from doing this, but it will be a step in the right direction. And I've gotten out of Oklahoma. That's a plus."

"I guess it is."

"Anyway, enough about me. Go sleep with the man you love." Melanie waved her along and disappeared into her own room.

Heather hesitated, wondering if Melanie was right and she was being silly for not spending the night with Colt.

Then an image flashed through her mind of him standing in front of Reverend Halpern and pledging his love to Melanie. Fake or not, she wasn't in the mood to sleep with anyone tonight.

"GEORGE BUCKLEY, HUH? Not much of a ring to it," Eric said when Colt and Melanie met up with him outside Camila's cabin the following afternoon. The Flying W was a ranch similar to Colt's family's spread, with a sprawling old house and numerous outbuildings, including Camila's small home. He wished he was here on a social call; not on a mission to fool Heloise. Heather was due to arrive any minute, but she'd texted that she'd gotten hung up at work. Melanie had come along because Heloise would assume she'd met *George* before with Heather living at the Hall.

"You're lucky it isn't worse. Heather thought it up on the fly." Colt nodded at Camila when she opened the door and invited them in. He was well aware Heather's friend didn't think much of him right now. However, she exchanged a smile with Melanie, which relieved him a little.

"Think you can pull this off?" she asked Eric when they were settled in the living room. A woodstove in one corner kept the room cozy, and it was obvious to Colt someone had updated the cabin to make it airtight and comfortable.

"Absolutely. I managed to infiltrate a terrorist organization once. I doubt Aunt Heloise will pose that much of a challenge."

Colt chuckled. "You don't know Heloise. Don't underestimate the enemy."

"She's crafty," Camila agreed.

"Nice place you got here," Eric said to her. "Quite a spread." He indicated the view out of the large window.

"None of it's mine—I only rent this cabin. The Turners own the Flying W." She looked wistful and Colt wondered if country life was growing on Camila. From what he'd heard she'd only been in town about a year. He'd have thought the Montana winter would scare away a southern transplant, but Camila rarely mentioned Texas and bitterness was evident in her voice when she did.

"I love these ranches," Melanie said. "Where I come from everything is flat. Your scenery is lovely."

"This is Melanie Munroe, by the way," Colt told Eric. "She's my fake fiancée."

"You always were a trouble magnet, but you've outdone yourself this time, Colt. Of course your trouble is as pretty as ever." He smiled at Melanie and she smiled back.

"Here comes Heather." Colt gestured toward the truck trundling up the lane, and his spirits lifted as they always did when he caught sight of her. As Heather parked the truck, Colt went to open the door for her.

"Hi, sorry I'm late." She entered the cabin and shrugged off her coat. Dressed in her work clothes, she wasn't quite the carefree young woman he used to know, but she was still beautiful enough to take his breath away. Today she wore a form fitting tunic with leggings that showed off her shapely legs. Her boots were practical given the snow outside, but they were stylish, too. He felt a surge of pride that this complicated, sexy woman was the mother of his child. One day soon she'd be his wife, too—no matter how hard Heloise tried to keep them apart.

"No problem," Colt said. He led her to the living room. "This is Eric. Otherwise known as George Buckley."

Eric stuck out his hand and shook Heather's vigorously. "Good to meet you."

"Nice to meet you, too." Heather looked him up and down, taking the measure of her new fiancé, but Colt noticed that Eric's gaze had slid back to Melanie.

"We'd better get started," Colt said.

"I'll leave you to it," Camila said. "I have to get back to the restaurant. Lock up when you leave."

It took the better part of an hour to establish back stories for each of them and to take turns quizzing each other until they knew all the details of those stories.

Colt glanced at his watch. "I'm due back at the ranch soon. Heather, you and Eric better take some more time to get to know each other."

Heather nodded.

"Can you drive me to Willow's, Colt?" Melanie asked. "I told Storm I'd come in and help her today."

"You're leaving?" Eric seemed disappointed.

"I'm sure we'll meet up again soon." A becoming blush spread over her cheeks and a dimple Colt hadn't noticed before flashed in her smile.

"Come on, Melanie." Colt shot his friend a disgusted look over his shoulder as he led Melanie away. "Try to focus, you two."

"We will," Heather called after them.

"As for you," Colt said as he and Melanie got back into his truck. "No flirting with my fiancee's fiancé."

She laughed. "I'll do my best."

HEATHER FOUND ERIC to be a charming companion and partner in crime as they swapped backgrounds and concocted a storyline for their fake romance. He was nothing but friendly toward her. Still, she cringed when he brought up the question of public displays of affection.

"I'll hold your hand whenever I can," he said, doing

just that. Heather felt none of the thrill she got when Colt touched her. Eric's palms were dry and there was nothing objectionable about him, but there wasn't anything exciting about him either. She supposed that was a good thing overall.

"What about kissing?"

He smiled. "This is pretty awkward, huh? I didn't have to kiss any terrorists." He leaned in and brushed his lips over her cheek. It was nice enough, but again, no fireworks went off. Nuzzling her neck, he kissed her softly behind the ear and this time she shivered, but more from being ticklish than from any attraction to him.

"I think we can fool the old girl," he said. "You'll have to stop undressing Colt with your eyes, though."

"I don't do that."

He swooped in for a quick kiss on the mouth.

"What was that for?" Heather asked, wiping her lips with the back of her hand.

"To get it over with, just in case the situation calls for it. Next time try not to rub me off so quickly." He nodded toward her hand and Heather covered it with her other one.

"Sorry."

"That's okay. So, what's the story with Melanie? What will she do when this is over?"

"When Colt divorces her?" She hated to think about either the marriage or the divorce. "I don't know. I guess she'll go back to Oklahoma."

"She has someone waiting for her there?" He did a

good job feigning nonchalance, but Heather thought he had more than a passing interest in the answer. She didn't blame him; Melanie was beautiful. In fact, it had pleased her a little to see the way Melanie looked at Eric. She'd never looked at Colt like that.

"I don't think so. She mentioned that her boyfriend cheated on her and she wanted to get away."

"Ah, I see."

"Let's go over everything one more time." She made herself touch Eric's wrist lightly—to get it over with, like he said. She leaned in and swiped a quick kiss on his cheek. She could do this.

She hoped.

CHAPTER SIXTEEN

"WHERE'S MOM?" RICHARD asked as he reluctantly got into Colt's truck later that afternoon.

"She's meeting with a friend of ours. I wanted to talk to you a bit." Colt took his place behind the wheel and pulled out cautiously from the parking lot of Chance Creek Junior High.

"What if I don't want to talk to you?"

"Too bad. You're stuck with me." He turned the truck toward Crescent Hall and was struck again by how strange it was that he was the father now and Richard his son. He could remember many a ride like this in Aaron's truck. During some of them he'd been as sullen as Richard was now. "You know we're in a tricky situation with Heloise."

"I know you're lying to Aunt Heloise. Is that what you mean?"

"Yeah, that's exactly what I mean." Colt worked to control his temper. Richard had every right to be mad at him. "Heloise thinks your mom is engaged to a man named George Buckley."

"That's a stupid name."

"Well, anyhow, a friend of mine has come to town to act the part. He'll stick around at the Hall for a day or two and then cut out again. I expect you to be civil to him and if anyone outside the family asks, I expect you to go along with the story."

"You want me to say my mom's engaged to George Buckley?"

"Yes, I do."

"This sucks."

"Yeah, it does."

Richard shifted in his seat to get a better look at him. "You know what? I have a better idea. Maybe you should just go back."

Colt's fingers tightened on the steering wheel. "Back where?" As if he didn't know.

"To Afghanistan."

"Richard—"

"You just cause trouble. You're no good to anyone here."

Stung, Colt shot a glance his way. "That's not true."

"Sure it is. You keep hurting Mom. You've screwed everything up."

"Look, it's complicated—"

"How hard is it? You either want her or you don't. You either want me, or—" Richard broke off when his voice cracked. Colt took a hard right turn into the long driveway that led to the Hall.

"Is that what this is about? You think I don't want you?" He waited until he'd pulled to a halt in front of the house and shut off the engine to continue. "I want you.

You got that? I want your mom, too. No matter what happens."

"Well, I don't want you. Not like this." Richard opened the door and scrambled out.

Colt's temper flared. "All right, let's settle this once and for all." He pushed his own door open and climbed out, too. He slammed it shut behind him and strode around the truck. "Let's go."

"Where?" Richard crossed his arms and didn't budge.

"To the obstacle course."

At first he thought Richard might refuse, but with a shake of his head, the youth stalked right on by him toward the woods. "I'm going to kick your ass."

Big words, Colt thought, but he knew Richard's bravado was the only thing keeping him together right now. He was angry, and more than that, he was hurt. He needed to challenge Colt's authority, but ultimately he needed Colt to win to prove to him that he was loved.

"Here's the deal," he said as they approached the start of the obstacle course. "If you beat me, I'll go back to Afghanistan. If I win, you'll stick out the next few crazy months while I marry Melanie and get us this ranch. You'll wait until Heloise signs over the deed and Melanie leaves again, and then you'll be my best man when I marry your mother."

"I'm not going to be your best man." But already Richard was moving toward the starting line.

"If I win you will be, and you won't complain about it, either. We're making a deal and a man doesn't go back on his word. Got it?"

"Got it. You want me to watch you marry someone else, wait around for you to divorce her, then be your stupid best man." Richard glared at him.

"That's exactly what I want." He stuck his hand out. "Shake on it."

After a moment Richard placed his gloved hand in Colt's. It was nearly as big as his own, and his grip was firm, but his fingers were thin and childlike. Colt needed to remember that his son was just thirteen. When he beat Richard—and he would beat Richard—he would have to give his son room to vent his anger at the outcome.

"You call the start," Colt told him.

"On your mark, get set, go!" Richard rattled off the words and lunged off the starting line toward the monkey bars with a confidence that told Colt his son had been practicing—a lot.

Colt jumped too with the ease of long practice. He crossed the monkey bars quickly, jumped down and tackled the climbing wall next, feeling a rush of pride when Richard hoisted himself up and over the wall almost as fast as he did. He kept his objective foremost in his mind, however, and put on a burst of speed as he dashed to the next obstacle. A minute or two later he was well in the lead.

With one part of his awareness on Richard's progress, he found this race through the course harder than any other he'd run before. He'd never cared about the progress of his opponent the way he cared about Richard's and this split in his concentration caught up with him when he nearly tripped in the tire course.

Refocusing, he sped up again, but Richard had gained ground in the meantime. Colt increased his pace and put some distance between them. As he approached the high balance beam made out of large, rough-hewn logs, Colt knew he couldn't be distracted again no matter what Richard did. Thankfully the beam was free of snow and ice and he was able to run right up the inclined log that led to it. He was five feet along the obstacle when he heard Richard scramble up onto the other balance beam. Colt frowned. How had Richard caught up all of a sudden? Had he skipped an obstacle or two? Maybe he'd underestimated how much his son wanted him gone.

Colt sped up again and practically ran across the beam, something he did easily in lighter footgear in the summer. It was far more difficult in his heavy winter boots. He let his momentum carry him forward, trusting his balance to keep him atop the beam, but when a loud *crack* sounded above him, he nearly slipped, and flailed his arms to stay on the log.

Richard cried out, "Dad!" Before Colt could react, a heavy branch crashed down onto the beam in front of him. Running too fast to stop, he jumped up and over it to land skidding and wheeling on the other side. He slipped and slid along the remaining few feet of balance beam, tipped over the edge and crashed to the ground, somersaulting through the snow to land on his back.

"Dad!" Richard reached him a few seconds later and dropped to his knees by Colt's side. "Are you okay?"

"Yeah. Yeah, I think so." Colt sat up slowly, taking

stock of the aches and pains throughout his body. It occurred to him Richard could take this opportunity to race ahead and actually win. Richard looked over his shoulder at the course, then back again and Colt knew his son was weighing his options.

"Can you stand up?" Richard said. He climbed to his feet and held out a hand.

Colt took it, hoping the boy couldn't see how much the offer pleased him. He stood up, knowing he'd pay for that fall later.

"That branch could have crushed you."

"Nah." It was true, though. The branch was big and would have packed a lethal punch. He'd felt its impact throughout the length of the beam.

"Yeah, it would. You'd be toast!"

"Don't sound so happy about it."

"I don't sound happy." Richard was indignant. "Bet I could beat you now, though."

"Bet you could." Colt peered up at the trees that ringed them, wondering if more branches were ready to fall. He and his brothers would have to walk the course and look for deadfalls that might pose a danger.

He realized Richard hadn't moved. "Well, why aren't you running?"

"Doesn't seem fair." The boy shoved his hands in his pockets.

"That's honorable of you."

Richard squirmed under his scrutiny. "Plus, I still can't do the salmon ladder very well."

Colt stifled a grin. "Yeah, that one's a bear. You're

allowed to do chin-ups instead, though." He wondered what Richard's strategy would have been if the race had continued. Would he have done the requisite chin-ups, which took much longer, or would he have hung back until Colt was out of sight and skipped the obstacle altogether, like he had probably skipped one or two others?

"How old were you when you did the ladder the first time?" Richard asked casually.

"A little older than you, I think. Give it a year or so; you'll get it."

"Yeah."

"Maybe we better call it a day. What do you say we go see what Regan's got cooking in the kitchen?"

Richard brightened. "Sounds good! Race you there!"

He took off like a shot. Colt followed more slowly. He'd be sore tomorrow, but it was worth it to make a connection with Richard.

Inside, Regan was stirring a pot on the stove. She smiled at him and nodded toward the kitchen table where Richard sat, a plate full of cookies in front of him.

"Are you going to eat all of those?" Colt asked him and braced himself for a scornful answer, but Richard pushed the plate his way.

"Not all of them."

"I DON'T THINK I know any Buckleys," Heloise said sourly as Zane helped her to a seat at the long dining room table that night. She'd sailed into the Hall like a queen five minutes before but when Heather presented

Eric as *George*, she'd lost some of her momentum.

Regan and Ella had outdone themselves, Heather thought. The food they were bringing to the table smelled heavenly, but she wasn't sure she'd be able to eat a bite of it. Eric, sitting beside her, patted her knee comfortingly and left his hand resting there. Colt, sitting across from them beside Melanie, narrowed his eyes.

"My folks are from Idaho originally," Eric said smoothly, sticking to the story they'd agreed upon. "I'm still something of a newcomer to Montana."

"What's your line of business?"

"Outdoor gear."

Heather was glad they'd been so thorough in concocting their back story, because she could tell Heloise was taking mental notes and meant to check up on them later. As Heloise continued to grill Eric, Heather scanned the rest of the group, thankful that Richard had gotten a last-minute invitation and was spending the evening at a friend's house. Colt had filled her in on their competition on the obstacle course, and the conclusion. She hoped that Richard would be able to hang in there long enough for this insanity to pass. The others listened attentively, tense with the need to keep from making any mistakes.

"About that wedding," Heloise said to Melanie. "You're taking a lackadaisical attitude toward it, seems to me. Where are your folks?"

"Both have passed away, I'm afraid. I'm on my own."

Heloise pursed her lips and Heather had a feeling she was about to challenge Melanie. She spoke up to cut her off. "Melanie fits in really well here, though. We're her family now."

Heloise raised an eyebrow. Heather hoped she hadn't overdone it.

"What about you?" Heloise asked. "When are you two tying the knot?"

Eric took Heather's hand and pressed a kiss into her palm. "As much as I can't wait to marry Heather, we'll have to put it off until I'm back from Georgia. I leave soon for a two month training program."

"How soon?"

Heather squeezed his hand, sensing a trap. He needed to answer this carefully.

"In a couple of weeks."

Heather closed her eyes. *Shit.* He'd left them wide open.

"So you'll be here for Colt's wedding."

"Um…" He looked to Heather.

What could she say? "Of course. We wouldn't miss it for the world."

"I should say not, the way you all are so close." Heloise drummed her arthritic fingers on the table. "If you're going to be gone for two whole months, it seems to me you'd want to marry before your trip. You never know what you'll come home to if you don't."

Damn it. Just as Heather thought, Heloise was laying another trap. "He doesn't have to worry. I'll wait for him," Heather assured her. Eric smiled at her and bent to kiss her cheek. Colt frowned.

"Nonsense!" Heloise exclaimed. "None of us are

getting any younger. You all are such good friends now—family, even, didn't you say? Why not throw a double wedding?" Her eyes gleamed with diabolical satisfaction. With a pang Heather realized Heloise wasn't going to back down. Once again she was determined to force their hands and try to prove they were lying. Did Heloise think Colt would get so upset about the idea of her marrying another man that he'd blow his cover to stop her? If so, she was dead wrong. Colt was determined to do anything it took to secure the ranch for his brothers.

Heather thought fast. She could make an excuse and put off her wedding to George, but then Heloise would think she had proof she needed. What would she do then?

Raise the stakes, of course. Just like she'd been doing since the day of Melanie's arrival. First there'd been the matter of the rings. Then there'd been this dinner. Now the double wedding. Who knew what Heloise would come up with next?

Heather had to cut her off at the pass before it got completely out of hand.

And she thought she knew how.

"Oh, I don't want to rush things—" Eric began.

"That's a great idea!" Heather blurted. "Heloise, you're a genius. George, honey, don't you think she's a genius?"

Heloise's eyebrows shot skyward. Eric blinked at Heather. This definitely wasn't in the script. Under the table, she pinched him with her free hand. She couldn't let Heloise get the better of them all now.

"Hey! Uh… I mean, hey, that's a terrific idea. Why didn't we think of it?" he sputtered.

"If it's all right with Colt and Melanie, of course." She turned to them and communicated desperately with her eyes that they had to say yes.

"Absolutely n—" Colt started.

"Absolutely!" Melanie said. She gave a little bounce, as if the idea excited her beyond words. "Absolutely! A double wedding sounds fantastic. Doesn't it, Colt?"

"It sounds like—"

"We'd be glad to share our big day with you two. I can't wait!" Melanie interrupted again. "We'll have to call…" She stuttered to a stop and Heather leaped to the rescue.

"Mia. We'll call Mia tomorrow and get it all in hand."

"But—"

Heather cut Colt off before he ruined everything. "Mia is fantastic at sorting out things like this. You and I will meet with her together, okay, Melanie? We'll figure this whole thing out."

"Sounds like I better come along for that meeting," Eric said.

"Me, too." There was no mistaking the anger in Colt's voice.

"Oh, don't worry, we won't spend too much," Heather chirped in attempt to lure Heloise's attention away from that anger.

"You'd better meet with Ellie Donaldson at the bridal shop while you're at it," Heloise said sweetly. "Two brides need two dresses and there isn't time to spare. I expect you'll want to place your orders tomorrow afternoon. And then there are the flowers..."

She was having a fine old time, wasn't she? Heather thought bitterly. Someday Heloise's chickens would come home to roost, though, and then she'd find herself all alone.

Was that it? she wondered. Did Heloise play games in order to get people to pay attention to her? If so, she'd lose her power when she signed away the ranch. She'd be hard pressed to get her nephews' attention then.

It was hard to feel pity for the woman who'd just backed her into marrying a man she didn't want—and who didn't want her, either, judging by the longing looks Eric kept exchanging with Melanie—but somehow she did anyway. Could all of this have been avoided if Colt and his brothers had simply visited Heloise once in a while?

"I know how busy you all are," Heloise said, "so I'll make the appointment at Ellie's myself. Two o'clock tomorrow afternoon."

"If she has an opening," Storm cautioned.

"She'll have an opening," Heloise said darkly and Heather figured Ellie would.

CHAPTER SEVENTEEN

H E WAS GOING to kill Heloise. If he didn't kill Eric first. Colt appreciated his friend's dedication to pulling off the trick, but if Eric nuzzled Heather's neck one more time, he was going to launch himself across the table and strangle the man.

And then his aunt for good measure.

Heloise smiled at him triumphantly. "Aren't Heather and George just the sweetest couple you ever saw?"

"Yeah, sweet," he ground out.

Melanie placed a hand on his arm and it was all he could do not to shrug it off. "I think they'll be very happy together," she said.

"Exactly," Colt said. "Very happy."

He saw a flash of alarm in Eric's eyes. His friend edged away from Heather. Colt relaxed—a bit.

"Regan and Ella, you two outdid yourselves with dinner," Heather said suddenly.

She could try to turn the conversation all she wanted. That didn't change the fact she'd declared her intention to marry Eric. Just how did she think they were going to pull that off? Setting aside for the moment there was no way in hell he'd let her go through with it, there were all sorts of legal implications.

Everyone else chimed in with compliments. Colt was sure the meal was delicious but he couldn't taste it. It was all he could do not to bang a fist on the table and cancel the whole charade right then. But the sharp glances Mason and Austin kept sending his way reminded him exactly why he couldn't do that. Three months, he told himself. He could survive anything for three months.

The meal took forever, and afterwards Heloise sat in the living room for another hour like a queen surrounded by her subjects. Finally, just when he thought he couldn't take it anymore, she rose to leave. "Zane, drive me home. I don't want to call a taxi so late at night. Why you all thought it prudent to keep me out so long past dark, I don't know."

Colt stifled a groan. At least she hadn't asked him to drive her home.

"George? You can walk us out to the car. I have a few more questions for you," Heloise added. "Give that beautiful bride of yours a kiss and come along."

Colt gritted his teeth at the thought of Eric kissing Heather—again. His friend shot him a look and leaned in close to peck Heather's cheek.

"That's not a kiss," Heloise said. "That's barely a how-do-you-do. In my time, men knew how to get a girl all stirred up."

Eric sent Colt another helpless look, and if Colt wasn't mistaken, flashed an unspoken message to Melanie as well. He stepped close to Heather, pulled her into an embrace and kissed her passionately.

Colt's hands balled into fists. When Heather wrapped her arms around Eric's neck and kissed him back, he stepped toward the couple.

"All right, show's over." Zane rushed Heloise from the room in alarm. A moment later they heard the front door open and close. Eric released Heather. "Sorry," he said. "Colt, you know there's no way I—"

"Don't do that again."

"I had to. You heard Heloise."

"I said—"

"Stop it! Just stop it!" Melanie pushed her way between them.

Colt shook off his frustration and held out his hands. "Fine. I'm done here."

"*You're* done?" Eric stepped forward but Melanie caught his arm.

"Enough. We're going upstairs. Colt, get yourself together." She led Eric firmly from the room without another word.

Heather shook her head. "You're an idiot." She followed the others out.

"Wait. Heather!"

Left alone, Colt had to admit she was right.

AT LEAST HER sales were improving, Heather thought when she looked over her accounts at the store the next morning. After all the drama last night, she needed some good news, and the uptick was just what the doctor ordered. Ever since the night of the demonstration she'd noticed more men in the store, too. Tom Hennessey must have passed the word among the other contractors that Renfree's still sold quality goods. She and Susan had worked out a schedule of demonstrations for the next couple of months based on the ideas the customers had come up with. Now she looked forward to seeing the results of Allison's newsletters.

She'd also noticed that the women who attended the laminate flooring event kept coming back into the store as they carried out their renovations. She had a feeling that when they showed their friends what they'd done, she'd get more signups at future demonstrations.

If only the rest of her life was going anywhere near that well. Breakfast had been a strained affair, with Colt and Eric both sullen and angry. In the end, Melanie had snapped at them to grow up and get over it, but neither of them had apologized, or said much of anything. Heather knew she'd screwed up when she blurted out to Heloise her intention to marry Eric, and the men needed to get their acts together if they were going to pull this off. Meanwhile, she needed to get Mia up to speed on this latest twist. She picked up her phone and made the call she'd been dreading all morning.

"Mia? It's Heather. How are you?" she said when Mia answered.

"Forget about me. How are you? Rose told me a crazy story about you and Colt marrying other people. What's going on?"

Heather explained the whole strange sequence of events. "So, Colt's going to marry someone else. And

I'm going to pretend to." They still hadn't actually worked that part out. "We need to schedule a double wedding." As she talked, she started a list on the pad of paper that sat next to her keyboard. *Dress, flowers, invitations, tell Mom about Eric...* She crossed off *Eric* and wrote *George.*

After a long pause, Mia said, "Who are you marrying?"

"A man named Eric Rutherford. Except he'll be George Buckley when we marry." She added, *Get my head examined* to the list.

"Oh, heck. You've dug yourselves a deep hole, haven't you?"

"You've got that right." Heather underlined that last item. "So do you think you can pull it off?"

"A double wedding in less than two weeks with a groom getting married under an assumed name? No problem!" Mia sighed. "Look, send me over all the details. Meanwhile, you and... wait—who's marrying Colt?"

"Melanie Munroe."

"Where do you get these people?"

"You don't want to know." She propped an elbow on the desk and leaned her forehead against her hand.

"Well, you and Melanie need to buy wedding dresses, pronto."

"Already on it. What else?"

"Bring her to our meeting later today. I'll get you both up to speed. How many guests will she want?"

"I'm not sure she'll want any."

"Well, thank God for small miracles." Mia paused. "Sorry, that was mean."

"Don't apologize; we've thrown a wrench in your plans. We're the ones who need to apologize."

"Heather, I can make this happen, but are you sure you want me to?"

She appreciated what Mia was really asking. "I don't want you to, but I need you to. We all do, or we'll lose the ranch."

"Oh, Heloise infuriates me! Who does she think—" Mia got herself under control. "Never mind. I'm sure you've already thought everything I'm about to say."

"And more," Heather agreed. "I have to go. Meet you at three-thirty at Linda's?"

"Sounds good."

Heather entered Ellie's Bridals, a small boutique in the middle of town, at five to two and was greeted by the owner, who held a phone to her ear. Melanie came in a moment later, and when it became clear Ellie was tied up in a call that might take a while, they drifted toward the racks of dresses and began to look through them.

Heather had no idea how to choose a dress in which to marry a man she didn't love. She didn't know how she could stand to watch Melanie pick a dress in which to marry Colt, either. At least they'd be equally miserable. Judging by the looks they'd exchanged over the breakfast table this morning, Melanie and Eric were falling hard and fast for each other, and she knew Melanie didn't relish marrying Colt any more than Heather wanted to watch her do it.

She wandered around the store, averting her eyes from any gown she might have wanted to wear when she married Colt—ones that suited her curves and would make her feel beautiful for the man she loved. Instead she focused on tea-length sheath dresses. Something plain and demure for a fake wedding—if it had to happen at all.

When she'd found four or five she thought might do, she let herself into one of the changing rooms, but when she came back out into the fitting area several minutes later, she nearly bumped into Camila. Ellie followed close behind her. Both women cocked their heads and looked her over.

"If you wear that to your wedding, I will shoot you," Camila said.

"Camila's right, Heather," Ellie said. "It doesn't suit you at all."

"Fine. I'll try something else." Heather walked back into the changing room and picked out another slim, fitted tea-length gown. Struggling out of the first one and into the next, she presented herself to Camila and Ellie again.

"That's the same dress!" Camila was indignant. The phone rang and Ellie bustled off, but from her expression Heather thought she agreed with Camila.

"No, it's not." Heather stepped closer. "And you know why I want something plain, so pipe down." She'd called Camila right after her call to Mia and filled her in on everything that had happened.

"Right. To marry your fake fiancé. You know that's

ridiculous, don't you? I can't believe how complicated this has all gotten."

"You can't believe it? Try living it!"

The bells over the door to the store chimed and they both craned their necks to see who'd entered.

"That's Regan," Heather said, "so just leave it, okay? I refuse to buy anything fancy for this wedding."

Melanie came around the racks of clothes with several dresses draped over her arm. She appraised Heather. "That looks sensible."

Camila smacked a hand to her forehead. "You're not supposed to wear something sensible to your wedding!"

"You are when you're in our circumstances. I've got another one; want to try it?" Heather said to Melanie.

When Regan made her way to the fitting area a few minutes later, she held an armload of dresses. She arrived just as Melanie stepped out of her changing room in a sheath dress similar to the one Heather had on.

"No," Regan said. "No, no, a thousand times no. Get those off right now. Both of you!"

"Told you," Camila said.

"Here." Regan shoved the dresses she carried into Melanie's arms. "Go change. Heather, give me two minutes. I'll find you something, too."

The bells over the door chimed again.

"Regan, I'm not in the mood—"

"I don't care. You're going to try them on anyway." Regan disappeared around a rack of dresses. A moment later they heard her greet Ella and Storm.

Camila leaned in closer. "You have to stop this before it goes any further."

Heather didn't have time to answer before Ella came around a rack and presented a gown. "This one is gorgeous! You have to try it on, Heather."

Storm followed her. "I have one for you, too."

"What are you guys doing here?" Heather asked. Reluctantly, she took the dresses they gave her and let herself back into the changing room.

"We're here to help you find a dress. You're one of us, which means you need to look stunning," Ella declared.

"Can't let the family down, you know," Regan chirped when she appeared again. She passed more dresses over the changing room door to Heather. Heather hung them all on hooks.

"But I'm not marrying Colt yet."

"You will soon enough. We have standards to uphold. There's a manual and everything," Storm added.

"Really?" Heather asked, peeping over the door.

"No, not really." Storm laughed at her. "There should be, though. Maybe we should start writing it." She turned to Regan and Ella.

"Rule number one, we Hall wives stick together no matter what. That includes you, too, Melanie," Regan said. "Come on, ladies, show us some dresses."

Ellie rejoined them, beaming happily at the gathering of women. "This is more like it. I'll bring out some bubbly!" She quickly headed off again. Camila was the only one who held back, her expression grim. Heather knew why and if she'd had any choice she would have left the boutique in a heartbeat, but while her circumstances were less than optimal, she couldn't help but appreciate the way the other women had rallied around her. She needed all the friends she could get.

"Try on ours before she gets back," Regan said to Heather. "Ellie always finds the perfect dress and then you won't want to wear anything else."

For the next twenty minutes Heather managed to forget her circumstances and give herself up to the fun of trying on beautiful gowns. She and Melanie took turns standing on the small raised dais Ellie had positioned in the center of the fitting area and looking at themselves reflected in the many mirrors surrounding them.

Melanie found a gown with a plain bodice and tiered skirt that made her look like a cross between a princess and a ballet dancer. With her lean body and graceful air she looked so elegant it brought tears to Heather's eyes. None of her gowns made her feel quite so beautiful, but she told herself that was okay. Even if the dress she bought now was fancier than she'd planned, she wanted to save the very best one for her wedding to Colt.

Actually, she thought she'd seen the gown she'd wear someday to marry him. It hung by itself in one corner of the store. A corner she studiously avoided.

Once Melanie had chosen her gown, however, Ellie turned her attention to Heather and as if she could read her mind, she made a beeline to the gown and brought it back. "This is the one," she said.

"I don't think so."

"Oh, that's beautiful. Try it on," Ella encouraged.

"She's right; you have to try it," Regan said.

Camila shrugged when Heather turned to her for support. "You might as well."

Heather gave in, even though she knew it was a mistake.

The gown fit like it had been made for her. The bodice showed off her curves, just like she knew it would. The sweetheart neckline revealed a tasteful amount of cleavage and small off-the-shoulder sleeves gave the gown a dashing air. The skirt was full and flounced with a beautiful, lacy underskirt peeking out. When she exited the changing room all conversation stopped.

"Oh, Heather, it's beautiful." Regan looked misty and Storm clasped her hands. Heather stepped up onto the dais and took a look.

The dress was everything she'd hoped for. It transformed her from a practical single mother into a radiant bride. Her gaze met Melanie's and she saw her own anguish reflected there.

"What do you think?"

When Melanie didn't answer, Camila spoke up. "She'll take it," she said to Ellie. "Heather, you have to take it."

Heather nodded slowly. She'd take it. But she refused to wear it to marry Eric. She'd sneak off to Silver Falls or even Billings to find another one.

She would only wear this dress when she married Colt.

CHAPTER EIGHTEEN

"**M**IA CALLED. AUTUMN Cruz is coming with some cakes to try after dinner tonight," Regan was saying to Heather when Colt met up with them at the base of the stairs a few days later. He was surprised to see Heather. Normally she worked at this time of the day. He was glad to hear that Autumn was coming over, though. She was married to Ethan Cruz, whom Colt had known as a child. Together they lived with several other couples on the Cruz ranch where Autumn ran a bed and breakfast. She was a phenomenal cook and was becoming known for her wedding cakes.

If she was bringing samples over for them to try, it meant the fake double wedding was still on. It had been touch and go for a couple of days, with him and Eric circling each other like dogs ready for a fight. He'd finally swallowed his pride and admitted he was out of line, however, after Heather persuaded him it wasn't fair to punish Eric for doing his job well. After that, the tension had eased between them.

"Okay," Heather said to Regan and smiled at Colt wanly. He waited until Regan headed back toward the kitchen.

"Everything all right?" he asked when they were alone.

"Not really. I... have a bit of a headache. I'm going to go lie down. Did Richard make it home from school?"

"He's out in the barn helping with chores."

"Good." She started up the stairs.

Colt followed her. "You sure you're okay?"

"It's nothing. I just need a little rest."

"You're pale."

"I told you; I have a headache." She swallowed. "I don't feel very well."

"Are you going to be sick?"

"I don't think so." She didn't look sure and Colt placed a protective hand on her waist as they walked upstairs.

"Come here." He led her to his room.

"Colt, I said I'm tired."

"You can rest right here." He drew her down onto the bed and a thought struck him. "Is there a chance you're pregnant?"

She shut her eyes a moment. "It's far too early to know that. It's only been a week. I'm just stressed out."

"But it is possible."

When she looked at him again, tears trembled on her lashes. "It's possible, but I better not be. I don't think I could stand it."

He winced.

"You know why." She touched his arm. "Not now. Not when you're marrying Melanie."

"I know. I wish to God I was marrying you."

"Me, too."

He hated how helpless he felt in the face of her misery. All he wanted to do was to spend his life making this woman happy. He couldn't do that yet, but he needed to do something. Colt checked his watch. "I'll be back in half an hour."

"Where are you going?"

"To get a test."

"But it's way too early to tell." She rose with him and followed him to the door.

"If it's too early, then we'll have it on hand for when the time is right."

"I don't think the time will ever be right."

"Don't say that."

"I just—" She broke off. "I'm just tired. Drive safe, okay? There's no rush." She turned toward the stairway that led to the third floor. Colt watched her go and slowly trudged downstairs to the front door. He knew Heather had spent every spare moment this week planning the wedding. It had to be hard to put so much time into the sham marriage, especially since they still didn't know how they'd pull it off. Mason and Zane had begun to look into fake identification for Eric, but no one wanted to take things that far.

For the thousandth time he wondered how things had ever gotten so out of control and wracked his brain for another way to solve their problems. Once again he failed to find one.

At the store he read every box to find a pregnancy

test geared toward early results. By the time he headed for home again, it was fully dark outside and he knew his brothers would wonder where he was. He ran up both flights of stairs the minute he got home, but when he opened Heather's door, she was fast asleep, lying diagonally across her bed.

As much as he wanted to know the answer, he couldn't make himself wake her. Instead, he set the box on the end of the bed and let himself out again quietly. Forcing himself to join his brothers to finish the chores, he tried to take his mind off of it, but with every breath the question remained. Was the woman he loved going to grow his child inside of her while he married someone else?

By the time they finished up, Colt was tight with anxiety, and when Austin bumped into him on their way out of the barn, he snapped, "Watch it!"

His brothers exchanged glances. "Everything all right?" Zane finally asked.

"No. It's not all right. But there's nothing for it, is there?" He strode ahead of the others around the outside of the house so he could leave his wet things in the front hall. There was no sign of Heather, but before he could go upstairs to look for her, Regan called, "Wash up everyone. Dinner's on!"

Sometimes Ella and Austin ate in the bunkhouse where they'd made their home, but most nights they joined the rest of the family in the Hall. Someone had already set the long table, and while Colt hesitated, still eager to go find Heather, Ella spotted him. "Help carry the food in, would you?"

After washing up in the small bathroom at the rear of the house he joined the women in the kitchen and spent the next few minutes ferrying platters of chicken, potatoes, beans and rolls into the dining room. By the time he was done everyone had already sat down.

Except Heather.

"Where's Mom?" Richard asked, grabbing a roll and quickly buttering it.

"I'll go find her." Finally, he'd get the privacy he needed to talk to her. Colt sped toward the stairs and climbed them two at a time.

She met him on the third floor. "I read the directions," she said without preamble. "It's too early to take the test."

Something about the way she said it told him there was more. "But..."

"But I think I might be pregnant. It's just a feeling I have and I could be wrong—I'm probably wrong..."

"But you're not wrong, are you?"

She shook her head once. There were dark smudges under her eyes that he longed to kiss away.

"We should talk."

"Not now. No—" She held up a hand when he began to speak. "I mean it. Autumn is coming over after dinner with some sample cakes. Everyone's going to be there for the tasting. I can't do this until afterward."

"Heather—"

She brushed past him, refusing to catch his eye, and after a moment Colt followed her. She was right. This wasn't the time, but the minute the evening was over, he'd bring her back up here and they'd figure out how to make the next few months possible for everyone to endure. He'd seen how well she and Melanie were getting along and Regan, Ella and Storm had all rallied around Heather and Richard. They could do this as long as everyone pulled together.

When they reached the dining room, Colt noticed Melanie had dark circles under her eyes that rivaled Heather's. Eric looked grim and the rest of the crowd grew subdued when it was clear that both the brides-to-be were struggling to keep their emotions in check tonight. He knew Melanie and Eric were inseparable these days whenever they weren't needed elsewhere. Their relationship had passed simple attraction and he wouldn't be surprised if it grew into something permanent someday.

Regan and Ella did their best to keep the conversation light. Mason joined in with a story about the cattle nearly knocking over one of the fences.

"It'd be cold work to fix a fence today," he said.

"That's for sure." Regan chuckled. "Once is enough, anyway."

They exchanged a smile that Colt felt sure had a story behind it. He knew that Regan had helped Mason fix the pasture fences when they'd first arrived at the ranch last spring.

Still, it was an uncomfortable meal and Colt was glad when they were through. He helped everyone else clear the dishes from the table and they were almost done washing up when the doorbell rang, announcing Autumn's arrival.

"I don't know if I can eat another thing," Melanie murmured to Eric. He gave her a sympathetic smile.

"Know what you mean."

Heather, who had barely touched her dinner, moved among the others like a ghost. Colt couldn't stand to see how drawn her features were. As Autumn breezed in with a pile of cake boxes in her arms, he almost pitied her. He had no doubt Mia had filled her in on the circumstances of the fake weddings, but she had no idea what a pit of despair she'd just stepped into. Regan walked by with a stack of plates and Storm followed with clean silverware.

"Can I spread these out on the table?" Autumn asked.

"Sure," Ella said.

Once more everyone took their places, but this time Autumn's happy patter lightened the mood a little. Even Melanie perked up. Heather, however, drew further into herself as Autumn opened each box and explained the contents.

"I'll give you each a piece of paper listing your choices," Autumn said, passing them out. "Everyone make sure you get a pen, too. Rank the cakes in the order of your preference."

"Thanks for doing this," Melanie said politely. She sat next to Eric who, despite what he'd said earlier, had already bitten into a piece of cake. He whispered something to her and she smiled a little.

"Heather? Which one do you want to try first?" Autumn asked brightly. Colt could tell she was doing her best to act as if the situation was normal. He wondered what she thought about it all privately.

Heather looked around at her choices. "I'm not sure. Any of them," she said dully.

Autumn hesitated, then quickly sliced a piece of the nearest cake. Heather took it, and lifted her fork, but instead of cutting into it, she sat motionless. A tear slid down her cheek and dropped onto her plate.

Autumn made a sound of concern and everyone around the table turned to look. Colt stiffened, his fork halfway to his mouth, as another tear traced the same path down Heather's cheek. At the far end of the table, Richard watched his mother with an expression so wretched it felt like the stab of a knife to Colt's heart, and in a moment of stunning clarity, he saw the next few months unwind before him like a film until he could anticipate the results of every move he'd made so far. The truth took his breath away.

He was going to lose Heather—and Richard too.

Not tonight—not all at once, but in a series of small hurts, misunderstandings and separations.

It would happen when he had to put Melanie first ahead of Heather. When his son watched him touch a woman who wasn't his mother. When he kept his distance while his baby grew in Heather's womb. Bit by bit, wound by wound. Until one day the gulf between them would be too wide to cross.

Nothing was worth that.

Not even the ranch.

Colt stood up slowly, reached across the table and took hold of Heather's plate. He slid it roughly back toward Autumn then reached for Melanie's and Eric's too. "We're done here."

"Hey!" Eric reached to take his back. Autumn lifted a hand to her throat while Heather only watched him, that bleakness still in her eyes.

"Colt, what are you doing?" Austin stood, too.

"Nothing against your cooking, Autumn; the cakes are fine," Colt went on. "But I'm done. Heather's done. It's over."

"Now, wait a minute—" Mason began.

Colt cut him off, his gaze locked with Heather's. He willed her to understand what he was saying. "I won't marry someone I don't love. I won't watch the woman I love marry someone else, either."

Austin leaned forward, but Ella laid a hand on his arm.

Heather blinked as if waking from a dream and swiped her sleeve over her cheeks. "I'm okay. I can do this. I've just had a rough day—"

"No." Colt refused to listen to another word. "You can't. Neither can I. And I'm ashamed I let it go this far. Look at us. Look at what we're doing. We're all lying. Together. To our relatives. To our friends. To our minister. To… God. All because Heloise gets off on making us dance to her tune. I won't do it." He braced his hands on the table and faced Heather. "I love you. I want to marry you right now. Today. I should have done it thirteen years ago." He turned to the rest of them. "As for the ranch, I'm sorry; the last thing I ever wanted was to let you all down again—to let our land be broken apart and sold off. Whatever happens next, I will do everything I can to help each of you set up a new home."

Silence met his declaration and before anyone could breach it, Colt decided to come clean about the rest of it too.

"I've got more to say." He gathered his thoughts. "Austin, I'm not sorry I hooked up with Heather all those years ago. I loved her as much back then as I do now. I am sorry we snuck around and weren't up front about it. That was wrong."

"I—"

Colt cut him off. "And before we move on and talk about what to do next, there's something else I have to say. Something all of you should know. I was there the day that Dad died. I spoke to him minutes before his aneurysm. Hell, seconds maybe."

You could have heard a pin drop in the dining room. A ring of faces waited to hear what he'd have to say next. Autumn had eased herself back from the table to stand near the door, but she was still listening. He knew there were few secrets in this small town. Knew too that Autumn cared for the others at this table nearly as much as he did. She had every right to hear what he said next.

"I was on my way to meet Heather. Dad knew it somehow. He tried to stop me. I refused to talk to him. I ran right on by." His voice went rough and he cleared his throat. "I wish to God I'd listened. I wish I'd stayed—"

Mason stood up. "Nothing you could have done would have saved him. We all have our regrets." He surveyed the rest of them and sighed, bowing his head a moment before he began to speak again. "Colt's right; this is too much to ask of anyone. We had a good run, but the game's up."

Zane nodded slowly. "I'm sure glad I met Storm, but you're right, Colt; Heloise's conditions are ridiculous. And maybe we have been silly to let it get this far."

Colt turned to Austin. "You have every right to be pissed."

"I am pissed," Austin said heavily. "Not at you, though. At me. Back when Heather broke up with me I knew we weren't meant to be together. I didn't want to admit that, though. I wanted to bring a little piece of home with me when I left for the service. That was selfish. I'm sorry, Heather, and Colt—I'm sorry you thought you had to hide your feelings all this time. You two are meant for each other, that's clear to anyone who looks at you."

Colt let out a breath. He'd waited years for his brother's forgiveness and now he had it. It felt good. "How about the rest of you? Aren't you mad?"

"About Dad?" Zane asked. "I wish you'd stayed with him, too. I wish he hadn't died alone. He was a great man—a family man. He didn't deserve that. But his passing was fast and if I got to choose the way I went, I'd want that for myself. At any rate, we don't get to control that, do we? The one thing I know is Dad wouldn't want us to sit around a table sniveling over him." He grinned. "He'd want us to celebrate."

"While we lost the ranch?" Colt couldn't find a way past that part.

"While we found each other. Look at us. After all these years apart here we are, building a life together."

"Dad would like that," Mason agreed.

"I'll miss this, though," Regan said slowly. "I love having everyone around this table."

Ella nodded. "I didn't think I'd like sharing a home at first. That's why I pressured Austin to make the bunkhouse our own place, but I've grown to like sharing meals and chores."

"I love it here," Storm said simply. "I love being with all of you. I'll miss that a lot, too."

"Why don't we just buy another ranch?" Richard piped up from the far end of the table. "All together?"

Colt gazed at his son with affection. Richard looked as worried as any of them, but the anger he'd carried for days was gone, replaced by a hopeful look in his eyes. That alone told Colt he'd done the right thing.

"That's not a bad idea," Mason said after a moment's hesitation.

"It's not the first time the idea's come up, either," Austin put in. "I've got a lot of good memories here. We all do. But we could start fresh."

The others nodded.

"Of course we can," Regan said. "Why couldn't we build a life together somewhere else?"

"I'm in," Storm said. "Zane?"

"Hell, yeah."

"I'm in, too," Ella said. "Heather? Colt? What do you say?"

Colt could barely speak over a throat that had suddenly constricted. "Heather?"

She nodded vigorously, tears sliding down her cheeks again. "Yes, I'd love that."

"Then I'm in, too." He walked around the table, pulled Heather up from her chair and kissed her.

"You all are making me cry," Autumn said, wiping away her own tears. "I know all of us at the Cruz ranch will do whatever we can to help, too. Now stop talking and eat some cake!"

ELLA WAS THE first to pull out her phone and start looking at real estate, but before long Mason and Storm had joined her. The others ate cake and squabbled good-naturedly over which was the best one.

"I guess I can cancel my wedding dress," Melanie said to Heather when they met up in the kitchen to replenish their cups of tea. "For now, at least."

"You and Eric have hit it off, huh?"

"We have." Melanie smiled. "I think I might move to Missoula next so we can give this relationship a chance. Eric wants me to move in with him, but it's too soon for that. I don't want to rush anything. I've decided I want to savor each and every step of the way, you know?"

"I do know. Except I feel the opposite now. I want to marry Colt before something else happens."

"We could fly to Vegas tonight," Colt said, coming into the room. "I've got a credit card."

Heather shook her head. "I want to be married right here in Chance Creek. I wish we could hold the reception at the Hall like all your brothers did, but I'll be happy no matter how it turns out. I'm going to miss this place, though."

"No more tears," Regan said, joining them. "Ella's already got a list of five ranches for us to go see." She filled up her cup of tea and sailed back out of the room.

"Are you all right with this?" Heather asked Colt.

"I'm better than all right. I'm going to marry you. I'm going to be a dad to Richard. We're going to have another baby." He kissed her softly on the cheek. "And this time I'll be there every step of the way."

Heather folded into his embrace. "I could be wrong, you know."

"If you are, we'll get busy and put it right."

"I love you." She rested her cheek against his broad chest and listened to his heartbeat. It was steady and strong, like Colt.

"I love you too."

"Get a room!" Storm said, coming in to grab more napkins. "I'm just teasing. You'd better get back in there, actually. The cake is going fast."

They broke apart and Heather led the way back into the dining room. She laughed when she saw the state of Autumn's beautiful desserts. Most had been almost totally consumed. It relieved her to see how well everyone had rallied after making such a momentous decision. In fact, she didn't think she was the only one who felt like a weight had slid from her shoulders. The atmosphere in the dining room was almost giddy.

When Autumn left, the men went back outside to check the livestock one last time and Heather joined the other women in the kitchen as they did a final clean up. She felt the need to express again how sorry she was that they were going to lose the ranch.

"Don't even say it." Ella held up a hand when Heather opened her mouth to speak her thoughts. "We know you're sorry. Heather, it's not your fault. It's not Colt's fault. Heloise has to take the blame and Colt's right; I'm ashamed I let it go this far, too."

Regan and Storm nodded. "We let her push us around," Regan said. "Not that I minded the outcome when I married Mason."

"I didn't mind marrying Zane either, obviously," Storm said. "But that doesn't make what Heloise did right."

"I know what you mean," Ella said. "On the one hand, if Austin hadn't placed his ad, I never would have met him. On the other, who is she to tell them they have to marry?"

"I'm glad I met Melanie, too," Heather said, smiling at her. "But it isn't fair for Heloise to punish all of you for Colt's actions, either."

"You know, it's strange how much good has come out of Heloise's craziness," Storm said. "But it's time to stop. Colt can't marry Melanie. That's all there is to it."

"I'm worried about the men, though," Heather said. "This ranch is where they grew up and it will be hard for them to leave it. Watching it be developed—that's going to break their hearts."

"They left it once before and they survived," Ella reminded her. "Not only that; they thrived. It's only land—and there's a lot more of it around. Tomorrow we'll go look at new ranches. Who knows? Maybe there'll be an even better one."

Heather appreciated her upbeat view, but she wondered how everyone would feel once they'd all retreated to their bedrooms and reality hit. She had a feeling the transition would be a lot harder than Ella thought.

CHAPTER NINETEEN

"**H**ERE COMES TROUBLE," Heloise said when she let Colt into her room at the assisted-living facility the following morning.

Colt bristled. He'd known what he would face today when he came to tell his aunt the news, but her broadside did nothing to calm him down. He was committed to his plan to marry Heather, but he'd lain awake most of the night sick at heart at the idea of the ranch being divided up and sold off piecemeal. The land had been in their family for generations. It killed him to know that legacy was over. Still, they had no other choice but to give it up. "You're exactly right, Heloise. You're not going to like what I have to say."

"And yet you're going to say it anyway."

"Here's the thing. You don't get to call the shots in my love life anymore. In fact, I can't believe my brothers let you mess around with theirs."

"Your brothers aren't complaining about where they've gotten. Each one of them is in love with his bride."

"Maybe. No thanks to your meddling, though."

"Ha! Absolutely thanks to my meddling. Not one of them would have found his wife without my help. You should know all about that. Now sit down, you're giving my neck a crick."

"I'd prefer to remain standing. I won't be here that long." He took a step closer, liking the advantage his height gave him. "I'm not going to marry Melanie."

"Well, you want that ranch, so I know you're going to marry someone. Who is it?"

He struggled to keep her needling words from getting under his skin. "Heather."

"Which means I was right all along! I can smell a liar like a pig smells truffles. I knew the minute I saw her in your house you two were together."

"Fine. Now we've cleared everything up." He turned and headed toward the door.

"We haven't cleared anything up. I told you I wouldn't stand for a fake wedding." Heloise rose creakily and followed him. "Where do you think you're going?"

"Away from here."

"Colt Hall, you stop right there, you stubborn, stupid—"

"You know what, Heloise? You can take Crescent Hall and shove it up your—" He bit back the rest of his words, yanked the door open and slammed it shut behind him instead. Striding down the hall, he heard the door open again, but he wasn't going to stop for anything now. He thought it would hurt to leave Crescent Hall behind, and it did, but he felt like he could breathe for the first time in almost a year. Ever since the start, this deal with Heloise had pressed down on him. He'd known he would have to pay the piper sooner or later. He'd thought the best ending he could hope for was to be saddled with a wife he didn't love. He'd thought he'd end up with a divorce and the desire to stay away from Crescent Hall—and his brothers—for the rest of his life. Instead he'd found his way back to them, and to Heather—and his son. No matter how hard it might be to say goodbye to his family's home, he'd come out ahead. Far ahead.

The drive to Crescent Hall passed in a blur and when he reached the ranch again, he decided there was one more person he needed to speak to. After parking his truck, he walked toward the nearest pasture and pulled out his phone. It was a bitterly cold day with a wind that crept down the collar of his coat, but he didn't want to make this call inside.

His mother picked up her phone on the third ring and he braced himself for the difficult conversation ahead. "Hey, Mom. It's me. Colt."

"Finally. I've been waiting for you to call. I was so glad to hear you'd made it home all right."

"You know I'm here to stay, right?"

"Yes, I heard that. I want to know the whole story, though."

"I'll tell you about it sometime. Not right now, though." He steadied himself. "I've got some bad news."

"Okay." Her tone was cautious. "I'm listening."

"We're losing the ranch. It's my fault."

"You don't want to marry Heather after all?" Her

disappointment was plain.

He wasn't surprised to find she'd heard all about Heather. "I do, actually. In fact, we're already engaged. I guess you know all about Richard."

"I met him at Zane's wedding. You have a wonderful son, Colt."

"I know that." He pushed on and explained everything that had happened. "But the thing is, since it's clear to Heloise that I was going to fake my marriage, she's going to sell the ranch to developers. They're going to parcel it up and build houses."

There was a long silence. "I'm sorry to hear that," Julie said finally. "But I'm not sorry you're going to marry Heather. Ever since I found out about Richard, I prayed that would happen."

"But it means we can't bring you home like we promised back at the start of all of this. We're going to lose Crescent Hall because of me."

"Honey, I can imagine it feels awful for that to happen, but I've lived more of my life off the ranch than on it. I've had other homes, and I will again. Crescent Hall is special—really special—but it's just a house and a piece of land. At the end of the day, what matters to me is that you're happy."

He struggled to keep the sorrow out of his voice. They were all trying to put a brave face on it, but losing the ranch felt like losing a member of the family. "We're looking for a new place—together."

"I'm happy to hear that. And I can be patient. I've waited this long to come back to Chance Creek. A few more months don't matter."

"I'm glad you feel that way." Colt walked a few paces, the snow crunching beneath his feet.

"Family first. Not ranches, Colt; family. That's what the Halls are all about. Most of us, anyway."

"So you're not mad?" He swallowed against the pain that threatened to block his throat and scanned the landscape, automatically locating the herd of cattle and making sure all was well with them. Satisfied, he leaned against a fence post.

"At you? Of course not! I'm mad as heck at Heloise, though."

"Never mind about Heloise. Will you come to the wedding?"

"Of course. I look forward to getting to know Heather again."

"Thanks, Mom. We'll find a place, you know. We'll build you a home soon. A good home." He'd make it his first priority as soon as they'd bought a spread. He knew how much it would mean to his mother to come back to the town where she'd once been so happy.

"I know. I have the best sons in the world."

"I don't know about that." Colt pushed away from the pasture fence and turned toward the Hall.

"I do."

"Mom, I've got something else to say." This was the hard part. He wished he didn't have to put it into words, but he knew he wouldn't be able to move forward in his new life until he'd cleaned the slate of his old one.

"I'm listening."

"It's about Dad."

"Go ahead, Colt."

"I... I was there the day he died. Just before he... collapsed. He wanted me to stop—to talk. I didn't. I kept on going."

"Oh, Colt." Sorrow thickened her voice. "You know nothing you did had anything to do with his death."

"The aneurysm got him, but I'm the one who stressed him out so bad. It was me—"

Julie's laugh stopped him cold. "You stressed him out? You're joking, right?"

"No, I'm not joking." Stung, he turned around and paced back.

"Colt, you were the least of Aaron's worries at the time of his death."

He stopped in his tracks. "What do you mean?"

"The price of beef nose-dived that year. He was terrified he wouldn't make a profit. Mason was dating that stupid Irene Littlefield. I mean, pardon me for being cruel, but she was dumb as a stump and Aaron was sure Mason would forget to use birth control sooner or later. Then there was Austin all ready to run off and join the Army, when he could barely match his socks in the morning, and let's not forget Zane."

"What about Zane?" Colt was bewildered. He hadn't remembered half of that.

"Zane? Flunking English—a required class for graduation? Aaron was beside himself that Zane wouldn't get a diploma. And that was just the beginning of his worries, Colt. And guess what? None of it killed him.

The aneurysm just happened."

"But—"

"Honey, here's the thing. When you're sixteen you think the world revolves around you. You don't even see other people or notice their problems—or even their triumphs half the time. Your father had concerns. So does every adult. Life is really darn complicated."

"I'm beginning to realize that."

Julie laughed again. "I bet you are. I wish it didn't have to be so complicated for you. All parents wish that for their kids, and yet that doesn't change anything. Don't take too much on yourself. Your father loved you. No, that doesn't begin to describe it. Your father adored you. He would be so proud of you today. He'd want you to be happy. He'd want you to love your wife and son. And he'd want you to hurry up and find another ranch so that I can come and spoil Richard rotten!"

"I'll do that. I swear, Mom. There's more, though."

"More?"

He laughed. "It's good news this time. Heather thinks she might be pregnant again."

"Oh, Colt!" Her happiness rang out through the phone. "Tell her I can't wait. I love you. You know that, right?"

"Yeah, I guess I do."

MEET ME AT *the obstacle course at noon.*

Heather smiled when she read Colt's e-mail. She'd spent the night cradled in his arms after they'd talked for a long time about their wedding, her possible pregnancy, and finding a new ranch. She'd had fallen asleep at some point and woken to find herself alone. She'd known Colt must have gone to do chores several hours earlier. She'd got dressed, saw Richard off to school and headed into work. Now she checked her watch. She still had an hour before her lunch break.

First things first, she had to call Mia. She hoped it wouldn't send the wedding planner over the edge to find out their plans had changed again.

Mia answered the call before the first ring finished. "I've already heard the news. Thank God you all came to your senses!"

"You aren't angry?"

"Angry? Heck, no—I'm thrilled! And before you ask if I can change the wedding again—yes, I can pull it off."

"Actually, I wondered if you could put it off."

"Really? Why?"

She hoped she could express her feelings clearly. "Because I've waited to marry Colt for so long. I want my wedding day to be special. Now that it isn't about Heloise or the ranch anymore, I want it to be about Colt and me. I want to send out invitations I love; not the ones I can order fast. I want to choose each element of the wedding from flowers to catering with the same care I want to put into my marriage. I will never marry again, Mia. Colt's my man. I want my wedding to say that." She hesitated. "I don't know if that's possible."

"Of course it's possible! That's my job, Heather. When do you want to get married?"

Heather thought about Heloise. A wicked smile

tugged at her lips. Heloise had demanded Colt and his brothers marry before April first. She checked the calendar. "April second."

"You've got it. I'll check with Reverend Halpern first thing, since I know he's officiating. Did he ever hear about your double wedding?"

"No. I don't think Colt got around to calling him before we changed our minds."

"Good. Less explaining for me to do. You leave it all up to me. You're going to get the wedding of the century now that I've got some time to plan it."

"Thank you, Mia."

At ten minutes to noon, Heather arrived at the Hall. The sun was peeking out of the clouds into a partially blue sky. Sucking in the crisp air, she made her way toward the obstacle course, taking her time because she was conscious that she wouldn't live on this ranch much longer. She hoped the men would build another obstacle course on their new spread when they bought one. Richard loved the course as much as Colt and his brothers had at his age. And who was she kidding? Colt and the rest of them still loved it.

The course was deserted when she approached, but before long pounding footsteps warned her Colt was coming her way. He must have arrived ahead of her and decided to do a circuit through the obstacles.

He burst out of the woods and slid to a stop in front of her. "There you are." Breathing hard, he checked his watch. "Damn, I'm out of shape."

"You are not." Heather loved his shape. "I'm sorry I

missed seeing you run."

"Oh yeah? You like that?"

"It always got me hot when we were young."

"You don't say." He pulled her close and kissed her. "I can do the course again if you like."

"Hell, yeah."

Colt chuckled. "Call my start." He crouched down and Heather smiled, remembering a hundred other times she'd seen him do the same thing as a teenager.

"On your mark, get set. Go!"

Colt leaped up and grabbed the monkey bars, going hand over hand across them before leaping down again. He raced to the climbing wall and jumped up to grab the top, swinging his legs over it in one fluid motion. It never got old to watch the Hall men run the course, and watching Colt run was a treat. He was still so much himself, but at the same time so different from the boy she used to know.

She moved down the center of the course and enjoyed the show that Colt put on. Because he wore a winter jacket, she couldn't see the ripple of his muscles, but she could imagine it. His body was a thing of beauty.

When he raced to a stop again, he checked his time and walked in a circle to catch his breath. "Better," he said.

"Awesome, you mean."

"If you say so." He wrapped an arm around her, still breathing hard. "Come on."

"Where are we going?"

"It's a surprise."

"I like surprises. Actually, I have one for you, too."

"Oh, yeah? What's that?"

She hoped he wouldn't be upset. "I moved our wedding back so we can have time to plan it right."

He stopped and faced her. "You aren't having second thoughts?"

"Of course not. I love you, Colt. I don't want a shotgun wedding, though. I want the real deal."

"Me, too," he said after a moment. "I guess I can wait a little longer. What's the date?"

"April second."

Colt chuckled. "You really want to stick it to Heloise, don't you?"

"I guess I do."

"You know what? Me, too. April second it is." He took her hand and began to walk again. She went with him happily. Now that nothing stood in the way of their marriage, she could enjoy her time alone with him. As they paced through the snow beneath the trees, she remembered another time years ago when they'd walked this way. On that day, she'd known they were going to make love for the first time. Her whole body had hummed with wanting. She felt like that again today. Just knowing they'd be together tonight made her sensitive to every brush of his arm against hers.

So when they walked out of the woods and she spotted an old Impala parked by the side of the road, she laughed out loud. "That's not my mother's, is it?" She knew it wasn't; Audrey had sold that car years ago.

"No, but it'll do the trick. Come on." He tugged her

toward it.

Amazed, Heather climbed in when he opened the passenger door for her. "Where did you get it?"

"Rented it in town. I have to have it back by five." He got in and started the engine. "Should we find us a deserted road?"

"As fast as possible," she agreed, then laughed again when Colt gunned the engine. Ten minutes later, he pulled the Impala over on a quiet stretch of back road outside of town where they were almost guaranteed privacy. They climbed into the back seat where she was delighted to find several blankets and even a pillow. "This is posh!"

"We're not as young as we used to be."

"Speak for yourself."

Colt unzipped his coat and pulled off his sweater. "Come here."

She took off her jacket too, and tossed it into the front seat. Colt gathered her into his lap and she wrapped her arms around his neck, but when he slid a hand up under her sweater she yelped. "Cold!"

"Sorry." He retreated, rubbed his hands together for warmth and tried again. Soon both of them were warm enough it didn't matter anymore. Heather couldn't get enough of kissing him. Freed from all her worry, she wriggled around until she straddled him and made out with him like her life depended on it.

"Hang on there." Colt came up for air. "We've got time."

"We've got to make up for lost time, you mean."

Heather clung to him. Suddenly she wanted to be sure he never got away again, even for a minute. "I've got so many kisses saved up for you."

"Me, too. But I want to do a whole lot more than kiss you."

He made short work of her sweater and bra and Heather shivered in the cool air while he tugged his shirt off and laid her down on one of the blankets. Pulling another one up to cover them, he bent to brush his mouth over her breast. Heather arched back, no longer caring about the cold. All she cared about was Colt touching her. Kissing her. Laving her sensitive skin with his tongue. As he moved from one breast to the other, she realized that she could share this every night with him for the rest of her life. No more games. No more hiding. Just the two of them, together.

"I want you inside of me."

He pulled back and searched her gaze with his.

"Colt, I need you—now."

He didn't require any more urging. He shucked off his jeans and boxer-briefs and helped her out of her pants. Hooking his thumbs in the band of her panties, he said, "Are you sure? We could wait if you want to."

"Colt!"

He greeted her outburst with a wolfish grin. "Just kidding." He tugged off her panties, moved between her legs and true to his word, he soon nudged against her. It was cramped in the back seat, but Heather didn't care; she wanted Colt close. Sliding into her, he groaned, "That's it. From now on we live right here."

"In the back seat of an Impala?" She could get on board with that.

"Exactly." He pulled out and pushed in again. "Forget ranching. And home décor. From now on we live on love."

"And sex?"

"Lots and lots of sex."

"Where will we put Richard and the baby? Might get a little crowded—"

"Pipe down, woman, I'm making love to you."

Yes, he was. And it was delicious. Heather propped her feet on the door and relished the feel of him moving inside of her. Colt filled her perfectly and the sweet friction of his motions already had her senses reeling off the charts. Lifting her hands over her head, she took hold of the other door and let Colt have his way with her. As he stroked in and out of her, she closed her eyes and gave herself up to each and every sensation.

"You are gorgeous," he whispered. "How did I survive all these years without you?"

"I don't know. I never want to let you go again."

"I love you."

"I love you, too."

"Open your eyes." His request was husky and she opened them to find him watching her. "I want to watch you come."

"I don't know—"

"Yes, you can. I know you can."

Of course she could. This was Colt. She could share anything with him. Letting go of all her worries, she concentrated on feeling the motion of him within her. Filling her up and sliding back out, he satisfied her every longing, and when she let go, her orgasm rolled through her, and she cried out, never tearing her gaze from his. When he came, he bucked against her but never looked away. She could see the love and desire in his eyes and knew that the future held so much that was good. She let his thrusts carry her up and over the edge again and her cries mingled with his until they both collapsed, panting for breath.

Afterward, when she felt Colt tugging at her hand, she didn't know what he was trying to do until he slid her ring off. Propping himself up above her he held it up. "Heather Ward, I'm a single man again. I'm free to marry whoever I want, and I'm here to tell you the only woman I want is the one lying beneath me right now. I want to make love to you every day for the rest of our lives. I want to share my dreams with you, tell you my plans, talk over my troubles with you, raise our children together and begin and end each day with you in my arms. Heather, will you marry me?"

She didn't think she could love a man more than she loved Colt right now. "Yes." She held up her hand and let him put her ring back on, erasing all that had gone before. "What time is it?"

"Are you serious?"

"Just tell me!"

Colt made a face but checked his watch. "About one."

She fished around among their clothes until she

found her phone. Colt raised an eyebrow while she dialed work but when she told Susan she wouldn't be back today, he grinned. She clicked off her phone and tossed it aside.

"That gives us four more hours before you have to take this car back. Come here." She tugged him down to her, and as he wrapped his arms around her she knew she didn't care where they made their home as long as they could be together.

CHAPTER TWENTY

"YOU AGAIN," ROSE said when Colt walked into Thayer's Jewelers the following day.

"Me again," Colt agreed. He handed her a small velvet box. "I need to return this." Melanie had handed him back her ring at breakfast. He had a feeling she'd get another one soon enough, judging by the way Eric looked at her whenever she was near.

"Came to your senses?" Rose asked. She accepted the box and moved to the cash register. He figured Mia had broken the news to Rose already since they worked together, but Rose obviously hadn't forgiven him yet for buying Melanie the ring in the first place.

"Something like that."

"Glad to hear it. Are you in the market for another one? I'll need your credit card to process the return." She took his card, pressed a few keys, opened the cash drawer and shut it again.

"I already bought one for Heather weeks ago, but I do need a ring re-sized." He held out another box, this one containing the wedding band he'd bought for himself alongside Heather's engagement ring back in

Billings.

Rose handed him a receipt, opened the box and pulled out the ring. Holding it up, she looked off into the distance a moment and broke into a dazzling smile.

Colt's heart lifted. "Is it good?"

"It's so good." To his surprise Rose came around the counter and hugged him. "I'm so happy for you and Heather. You've got a terrific future together."

"I know." He did know, but it was good to get confirmation, even from such a strange source. "You'll get your wedding invitation soon."

"Glad to hear it! I'll have the ring ready in plenty of time."

"Sounds good." He turned to go.

"And Colt," she called after him. "Congratulations."

"Thanks."

Colt couldn't wait to get home.

WHEN HEATHER ENTERED Fila's restaurant a few days later, she was surprised to see many of her friends grouped around a central table. She'd thought she was going to meet Mia for an update on wedding plans. Instead, Mia, Camila, Fila, Regan, Ella, Storm, Rose and Autumn all looked up to greet her.

"What's going on?"

"This is an intervention," Camila announced. "A business intervention. I know Renfree's is doing much better than it was just a month ago, but there's a lot more for you to do."

"You need to change the name, for one thing,"

Storm said.

"And redecorate, for heaven's sake," Mia said.

"And expand your online advertising. I like the news-letter you sent out," Autumn said.

"I think you should throw a party after you redeco-rate, too," Storm said.

Heather sat down between Camila and Mia and joined in the conversation. Fila left the table and came back with platters of Afghan nachos and then dug into the food along with the rest of the women.

"What are you going to name the store?" Ella asked.

Heather thought about that. "I'm not sure."

"Heather's!" Camila and Mia said in unison.

"Seriously, it has to be Heather's," Camila said. "You have to stop being afraid to put your stamp on that store."

Regan waved a chip. "Heather's is a place that serves contractors, but also works with people who've never done a reno project before."

"Especially women," Mia put in. "From what I heard, making your demonstration like a party was genius."

"That was all Susan and Allison," Heather said.

"But they had you for a boss and knew you wouldn't shoot down their ideas. That's good management."

Heather smiled at her friends' enthusiasm. "You're right; it is time to roll up my sleeves and get to work. I've got a few ideas."

"COLT, CAN YOU come up here?" Heather called down

the stairs a week later.

Just in from the barn, he heard the urgency in her voice and shucked his outer gear off quickly before taking the steps two at a time.

"Where are you?"

"In here."

He strode down the hall to his bedroom and found Heather pacing inside. She handed him the plastic applicator of a pregnancy test and suddenly he found it difficult to breathe.

"Are you…?"

"Look!"

He did, and whooped a second later when he saw the answer. "We're going to have a baby?"

"Yes!" She laughed when he scooped her up and swung her around in a circle.

"Girl or boy?"

"Colt—we won't know for months!"

"I don't care. I'll take one of each."

"Bite your tongue!"

Colt carried her to his bed, laid her down gently and kissed her all over. "You are amazing."

"All I did was get pregnant," she protested and giggled as he kissed her behind her ear.

"But you did it better than anyone else." He kept on kissing her and soon Heather relaxed with a happy sigh. "You sure you don't want to move the wedding up?"

"I wouldn't dare. Mia would kill me."

"Can't wait for our wedding night."

"Neither can I."

They'd booked a cottage on the California coast near where Storm's family had once lived. Five glorious days alone together. Colt doubted they'd even make it to the beach.

"What's wrong?" Heather asked. "You're staring at me."

"Nothing. I was just wondering what would have happened if you hadn't answered my ad."

"Don't even think about that."

"Thank you for being so brave." He lowered himself down on top of her.

"Thank you for being so horny."

"You know, I'm feeling kind of—"

"...horny again?" she supplied for him. "Why am I not the least bit surprised?"

CHAPTER TWENTY-ONE

"**I**T'S NOT CRESCENT Hall," Colt said several days later. He stood with his brothers on a property twenty minutes to the west of town and surveyed the large, plain clapboard house in front of them.

"No, it's not," Mason said, "but it has nearly the same square footage and we could always add a porch."

"The barn's smaller," Austin pointed out.

"But the stables are bigger," Zane said.

"Not as many acres," Colt said.

"The terrain is more varied, which would be good for my training camps. Not that I expect to have a say," Dan said.

"Your input is welcome." Mason paced around to the side of the house and the rest of them trailed after him. "With ten of us and friends to help, we'd make a home out of this in no time."

"Where would we build the course? No woods close by." Zane scratched his head.

"We could build it out in the open."

No one said anything as they tramped on. Colt knew what they were thinking: out in the open wouldn't be the same.

"The realtor will be here any minute," Zane said, "and if this isn't the place, we'll find one. We have time."

"I'm a little surprised Heloise hasn't kicked us out of the Hall yet," Austin said as Mason stopped again. They took in the main building from the back. Colt wondered if the rest of them were as disappointed with it as he was.

"It isn't April first yet. Maybe she thinks Colt might change his mind."

"No way in hell."

His brothers laughed. "We're just kidding you," Austin said. "No way we'd let you. I figure we've got until April second."

"Until your wedding day," Mason echoed.

They were all quiet as they thought about that.

"Then we'd better keep looking," Colt said.

"YOU LOOK STUNNING," Audrey said nine weeks later.

"Just beautiful," Julie agreed. Colt's mother had flown in the night before for the wedding, and she and Audrey were already fast friends.

"Doesn't she?" Camila agreed. "Like a picture."

Heather smoothed her hands over the fitted bodice and flounced skirts of her gown. The last few weeks had been a blur of activity. Camila and Storm had organized a raucous bachelorette party at the Dancing Boot and a bridal shower hosted at Fila's, complete with fantastic food and silly games. They still hadn't found a ranch to buy, but at the wedding rehearsal dinner the night before, the talk centered on a ranch Austin had spotted north of town that was for sale. The others all planned to go and view it in the days after the wedding. If it was worth seeing, Heather and Colt would take a look when they came back from their honeymoon.

The only thing that bothered Heather was that Heloise hadn't spoken to them since the day Colt broke the news they were getting married. While she hadn't kicked them out of Crescent Hall yet, they knew she could do so at any time and they had begun packing. Colt had refused to invite Heloise to the wedding, which didn't sit well with Heather no matter how much trouble the old woman had caused, but she didn't push him to change his mind. Heloise couldn't expect a warm welcome from the men she'd manipulated for so long.

Since they couldn't hold their reception at the Hall, they'd chosen the Cruz ranch's Big House as the next best thing. With its furniture removed, its huge living room would accommodate their guests. Autumn would cater the affair from the bed and breakfast's stunning kitchen and all their friends had helped decorate the house beautifully.

She tried to release her worries and focus on the present moment. Today was her day. *Their* day. In just a few minutes she'd walk down the aisle on her mother's arm and marry the man she had loved for most of her life. No matter what they faced next, they would face it together.

Mia popped her head in the door. "Everything is all set. Colt's waiting for you at the altar. Are you ready?"

Heather grinned. Was she ever.

"NERVOUS?" MASON ASKED Colt over Richard's head, as he took his place with the rest of his brothers at the end of the aisle in the Chance Creek Reformed Church. Richard had agreed to be Colt's best man, as long as the rest of the Hall men joined him at the altar. Colt had gladly acquiesced.

"Nope." He was lying. He was nervous. Nervous that Heather would change her mind at the last minute. Nervous that he'd mess up during the ceremony somehow. Nervous that they'd never find a ranch, or that he wouldn't be the father his children needed.

"Yeah, you are." Mason grinned at him. Richard smiled, too. Austin and Zane chuckled.

"Shut up."

Behind them, Reverend Halpern cleared his throat. Mason muttered, "In trouble, as usual."

"Bite me."

Halpern cleared his throat again as all of them laughed, but a swell of music from the organist covered it up. Camila appeared in a peach-colored dress followed by Regan, Ella and Storm in similar gowns. Ella's strained over her very pregnant belly, but Regan's accentuated her now svelte form. Julie held her new grandbaby, Aaron, in her arms as she sat in the front row. Colt's gaze slid past all of them to Heather, who'd just appeared on her mother's arm at the head of the aisle.

"You got this." Mason straightened. Colt took a deep breath. Yeah, he had this. At least, he'd do his best, but as Heather progressed toward him he knew he was shaking. He hoped like hell he could be the man she deserved. He never wanted to let her down again.

When Heather reached his side, Colt met her gaze and knew that for all the love that shone in her eyes, more must be shining in his. He would always regret the thirteen years they'd lost, but now they'd spend the rest of their lives together.

"Dearly Beloved," Halpern began and Colt took Heather's hand.

"JUST AS I thought."

Several hours later, Heather nearly tripped and dropped her glass of faux champagne when Heloise walked into the Big House and put her hands on her hips.

"It's a fine how-do-you-do when your nephew gets married and doesn't even invite you!"

"Heloise, this isn't the time." Mason tried to intercept her. She jabbed at him with her cane until he held up his hands in surrender and backed off.

"This is exactly the time. Everyone's here; I won't have to repeat myself."

"Heloise, don't make a scene," Julie said, stepping forward. Heloise waved her cane at her, too.

"I'll make a scene if I want to."

"You actually thought you'd get an invitation to our wedding after what you did?" Colt pushed past the others and faced his aunt.

"I don't see why not, seeing as how I practically arranged it."

"Are you out of your mind? You told me you wouldn't stand for a fake wedding!"

Heather stepped forward, afraid Colt might take a swipe at his aunt. Heloise stood her ground. "Are you saying this is a fake wedding?"

"Of course not!"

"Exactly my point. I wouldn't have stood for it if you'd married that Melanie woman." Heloise raised her chin smugly. Melanie, who stood nearby with Eric, frowned.

Colt sputtered. Heather watched him fight for words. She was eager to say a few choice ones of her own.

"But—"

"As for who's responsible for this wedding, I am— just like I'm responsible for each and every one of your brothers' weddings, too. Not one of you would be married before fifty at the rate you were going. If I hadn't made it a requirement to get your ranch, you all would still be single!"

"Heloise, that's the most ridiculous thing I've ever heard you say," Julie said.

"But it's true, ain't it?"

Nobody seemed to know how to answer that. Finally Colt said, "You know what, Heloise? You've had your say. I think it's time you left."

"Why?"

He stepped closer to her. "Isn't it enough to kick me off my property? You have to ruin my wedding, too?"

"Who's kicking you off your property?"

"You are!"

"Says who?" She put her hands on her hips.

"Says you," Colt bellowed, clearly at the end of his patience. "When I went to tell you I planned to marry Heather, you said you wouldn't stand for a fake wedding—"

"And since all of your weddings have been real," Heloise interrupted, "I'm going to give you this." She thrust the package into his hands.

"What is it, a letter bomb?" Colt held it at arm's length.

"It's a gift. Open it! Imbecile," she muttered.

After a long moment, Colt did. When he'd torn off the small silver bow and the white and silver wrapping paper, he held up a packet of papers. "What is this?"

"It's the deed," Mason said in a shocked tone, coming to stand next to him. "It's the deed, isn't it, Heloise?"

"You all have eyes. Use them." But Heather noticed Heloise watched avidly as Colt, his brothers and their wives crowded around the document.

Colt handed the deed to Mason and came to take Heather into his arms. He lowered his mouth to hers and tightened his arms around her. For a moment Heather forgot everything else and she melted in her husband's embrace. "I love you," Colt whispered into her ear. "No matter if we'd landed in a tent in Siberia, I would still love you."

"Forever?"

"Forever."

"I'm the one who just gave you a ranch. Why don't you sweet-talk me?" Heloise humphed.

"Under all that vinegar you're as sweet as shoe-fly pie, aren't you, Heloise?" Zane pulled her into a bear hug and planted a loud kiss on top of her head.

Heloise whacked him with her cane. "Enough of that!" But Heather glimpsed the smile that flitted across her face.

Chuckling, Zane let her go and swept Storm into his arms.

"Thank you, Heloise," Mason said, still reading the document. Regan clung to his elbow, reading it, too. Austin held Ella, who had buried her face in his neck, her shoulders shaking.

Heather knew how she felt; her relief threatened to overwhelm her, too. They would have made a good life anywhere they went, but Crescent Hall was their home and it meant the world to her to know they could remain there. As Cheyenne and her daughters enveloped Storm and Zane in an embrace, Colt tightened his grip on Heather. "Thank you, Heloise," she managed to call out over Colt's shoulder before he kissed her again.

"That's more like it," Heloise said. "Now, I have some ideas for the place..."

Julie groaned. "Really, Heloise. Don't you think you've—"

"Uh-oh," Ella said. She pulled away from Austin and clutched her belly.

"Honey? What's wrong?"

"I think it's the baby. Oh..." Her focus went inward. Regan sprang into action.

"Zane, pull Austin's truck around close. Mason, call

the hospital and let them know we're on our way. Austin, do you have the number for your doctor?"

Heather stepped back and let the others do what they needed to do, trailing after them when they began to make their way to the front door, Austin half-supporting, half-carrying Ella. Camila, Maya and Stella came to stand near Heather, and she appreciated their unspoken support.

"I'm sorry, Heather," Ella called over her shoulder as Mason threaded her arms into her coat.

"Don't be sorry," Heather exclaimed. "You're having your baby!"

"Are you coming?" Storm asked her excitedly.

Heather laughed. "I think Colt and I better stay and take care of the rest of our guests."

"We'll help," Camila said, and Stella and Maya nodded.

"Good luck, Ella!" Heather added. "Can't wait to meet your baby."

"Bye!"

"Bye!"

Heloise managed to slip out in the rush toward the door, so when Heather and Colt made their way back into the Big House's great room, only a small group of their friends and family remained. Heather noticed an envelope on the refreshment table she hadn't seen before. When she picked it up, she felt something heavy in the bottom.

"What's this?"

Colt shrugged. "Open it."

She did and found a card and an old-fashioned key inside.

This old key hasn't fit a lock at Crescent Hall for fifty years, the card read in a spidery handwriting Heather instinctively knew was Heloise's, *but it opened the original front door and I wanted you to have it. Thank you for helping me to bring the last of my nephews home to Chance Creek. Just in time, too. I'm off to Missouri for a month. My cousin has five granddaughters, and none of them are married yet!*

Heloise hadn't signed the card, but Heather didn't care. She knew she'd treasure it for the rest of her life, just as she'd treasure the memories of how she'd found her way back to Colt again.

"What is it?" Colt asked.

"Just a gift from a friend." She pocketed the key and set the card aside, and took her husband's hand. "Dance with me."

"Any time."

EPILOGUE

Six months later

"**I** LOVED THE Founder's Day celebration last year," Regan said as she packed the last of the food into a picnic basket and reached down to chuck baby Aaron under the chin. "The fireworks were the best part. I can't wait to see them again tonight."

"I can't wait for the live music," Julie remarked, taking the basket when Regan handed it to her. Julie had moved back to Montana only the month before, after her sons had built her a house on the east side of the ranch.

"I'm looking forward to seeing everything." Ella held her baby, Michael, in one arm and a folded blanket in the other. "Ready, Storm?"

"Just about." Storm finished hooking her tiny newborn, Gabriel, into a front-carrying pouch. "Let's go, Sarah. I told Mom and the girls I'd be there by ten."

"I'm coming." Sarah had rejoined them on the ranch in June, when she'd left the Army and married Dan. Now she worked alongside her husband at their extreme training camp, but lately Heather had seen a secret smile dancing on Sarah's lips and she felt sure another baby would arrive at the ranch next winter. "Melanie, how about you?"

"I'm ready, too." Melanie and Eric had driven from Missoula, where they'd settled down together in anticipation of their wedding in November. "Come on, Heather."

"Coming." Heather finished packing cans of pop and beer into a large cooler. "Colt, I need you!"

"Be right there." He came downstairs a moment later, reached around her large belly and gave her a quick kiss. "How's the mama?"

"This is so much harder than I remember," she complained. "I'm as big as a house."

"You're as tiny as a sparrow. Besides, you still have a month to go."

Heather groaned good-naturedly. She was definitely larger this time around, but that was because she was carrying twins.

"Everybody ready? Let's move it out!" Mason called from the front hall. Richard pounded through the house and burst out the front door ahead of them.

"Are you going to be all right today?" Colt asked Heather as he hefted the cooler and followed her to the front of the house.

"Sitting while the parade goes by, sitting while you all check out the fair, sitting while I eat my picnic food, sitting while I watch the historical re-enactments and fireworks later tonight? Yes, I think I'll be all right."

"That's a lot of sitting."

"Maybe I'll walk to the pretzel booth." She craved soft pretzels these days. She liked the big flakes of salt.

"Don't forget we have to dance under the stars."

"I guess I can do that, too. Slowly."

"Mom! Dad! Hurry up!" Richard called through the open front door.

Heather paused when they reached the front porch and watched her family—her large, extended family—load up their trucks and pile in for their day of fun in town. She let her gaze trail over the wide lawn, the pastures in the distance, and the hills far beyond. She turned to look back at the Hall itself.

"What are you thinking?" Colt paused beside her, biceps bulging as he held up the heavy cooler.

"How proud your father would be of what you've done. Look at this place. You've restored it to what it used to be. It's beautiful."

"Yeah. It feels like home again."

"It feels like home to me, too."

THE END

Read on for an excerpt of Volume 1 of the **SEALs of Chance Creek** series – **A SEAL's Oath**. Please note that this novel is not part of the **Heroes of Chance Creek** series.

Visit Cora Seton's website (www.coraseton.com) and sign up for her Newsletter. Find her on Facebook (facebook.com/CoraSeton).

OTHER TITLES BY CORA SETON:

THE SEALS OF CHANCE CREEK

A SEAL's Oath
A SEAL's Vow
A SEAL's Pledge
A SEAL's Consent

THE HEROES OF CHANCE CREEK

The Navy SEAL's E-mail Order Bride (Volume 1)
The Soldier's E-Mail Order Bride (Volume 2)
The Marine's E-Mail Order Bride (Volume 3)
The Navy SEAL's Christmas Bride (Volume 4)

THE COWBOYS OF CHANCE CREEK

The Cowboy Inherits a Bride (Volume 0)
The Cowboy's E-mail Order Bride (Volume 1)
The Cowboy Wins a Bride (Volume 2)
The Cowboy Imports a Bride (Volume 3)
The Cowgirl Ropes a Billionaire (Volume 4)
The Sheriff Catches a Bride (Volume 5)
The Cowboy Lassos a Bride (Volume 6)
The Cowboy Rescues a Bride (Volume 7)
The Cowboy Earns a Bride (Volume 8)

A SEAL'S OATH

BY CORA SETON

W OMEN. WHERE WAS he going to find enough
women?

Staff Sergeant Boone Rudman folded himself into
the narrow seat allotted to him on the small plane he'd
just boarded along with fifty-something other souls
bound for Chance Creek, Montana. He carefully stowed
his battered leather briefcase under the seat in front of
him, handling it with the reverence due to something so
special. His grandfather had given it to him when he
graduated from high school. His own grandfather had
carried it to Yale University back in 1929. It wasn't until
World War II that the Boones had become Navy men.
Ever since there had been two traditions in the family—
serving their country and passing down the briefcase to
the oldest son of each generation.

He tucked it further beneath the seat, turning over
his dilemma in his mind. They'd need several women to
start—maybe even a half-dozen. That number would
need to ramp up over the coming months. Of all the

tasks on the to-do list inside his briefcase, finding those women ranked as the toughest in his mind. It wasn't that Boone had ever found it difficult to attract women. They liked his broad shoulders and the muscles he'd built up during his time in the service. As long as he regaled them with stories about his training days or funny incidents he'd seen along the way, everything was fine. The trouble started when he spoke from the heart about his passions. Hydroponics, geothermal heat, and local resources made their eyes glaze over. When he started on micronutrients, closed system aquaculture and rain gardens, they ran for the hills.

Somewhere there must be women who truly cared about sustainable living.

Boone just hadn't met them yet.

Discontent rippled through him, but Boone refused to let it gain control. He'd been too long without female company. The nature of his work as a Navy SEAL had made finding a partner difficult. The nature of his hobbies and interests made it downright impossible. If sex was all he wanted he could find what he was looking for in any bar, but Boone wanted more than sex. He wanted to find his equal. A passionate, intelligent woman on fire to follow her dreams and build a better life for herself. He wanted to start a family—a carefully planned, population-neutral family of two children they'd raise with all the right ideals.

Boone chuckled at this high-minded portrait of his needs. Who was he kidding? He just wanted someone to fuck who didn't bore him at the breakfast table the following morning.

He glanced down at the worn leather briefcase again. Inside it lay a sheaf of paperwork and maps, along with the laptop he'd used to plan out every element of the community he intended to build when he arrived at Westfield ranch. It was strange to travel without the men he'd served with in the Navy SEALs for so long. Jericho and Clay had watched his back since BUD(s) training. Walker had helped guide their Navy careers and led them through situations they shouldn't have survived.

Now he was on his own. Temporarily. Boone liked to think of himself as an advance party of one. He'd arrive in Chance Creek ahead of the others, scope out the terrain, set up headquarters and prepare for the rest of them to land. Together they'd build a community that could survive a future of climate change and scarce resources. With their combined intelligence, know-how and can-do attitudes they were singularly positioned to succeed in a way other would-be sustainable communities hadn't.

As long as they could find some women.

He greeted the flight attendant with a smile several minutes later when the plane levelled out and it was time for his packet of pretzels and cup of pop. He examined the items she placed on his tray table—the individually wrapped snack, the plastic cup, the soda can whose heavy contents had already travelled miles to get to him—and reminded himself not to lecture the flight attendant on waste. Change started with individuals who cared. First he'd fix his own life. Then he'd helped those around him. He was young, strong and smart. Plenty of time to change the world.

As he sat back and munched his pretzels, Boone relaxed, knowing he couldn't fail. Walker had provided the land. He had the plans and the knowhow. His buddies would soon supply the man power.

All they needed was women.

Boone had no idea where those women would come from, but he felt confident he'd figure it out.

RILEY EATON PULLED the rental moving truck into the gravel area in front of Westfield mansion and sighed with contentment. "There it is. It isn't Pemberley, but it's as close as we'll find in Chance Creek."

"It's beautiful," Savannah Edwards said. "Look at that house!"

Riley bit back a smile. Westfield was beautiful. With its stone exterior it presented a proud façade worthy of Jane Austen's Regency England. She didn't care that it sat on a ranch in Montana. It would do wonderfully.

"It's gorgeous!" Avery Lightfoot said.

"More than gorgeous—three floors! It's stunning, Riley!" Savannah echoed.

"I guess it's nice," Nora Ridgeway pronounced quietly, "but it's so remote."

Riley refused to let her enthusiasm be dampened by Nora's reaction when Avery and Savannah were so thrilled. She couldn't help but smile at the friends who'd stepped out of their lives to join her on this adventure. She wished she could take credit for the idea, but it had been Nora who instigated the decision—albeit accidentally. Classmates at Vassar, they'd scattered after graduation, but they'd kept in touch regularly and six months ago they'd met for their own private five year reunion at the Sanctuary Spa in Santa Fe, New Mexico. During the first couple of days they'd swapped stories of their career triumphs and bemoaned the lack of decent men in the world. Forty-eight hours in, however, they'd begun to speak their minds.

Savannah picked up the dog-eared copy of *Pride and Prejudice* which Nora had found tucked in the dresser in her room and carried with her to the patio where they sat. "Am I the only one who'd trade my life for one of Austen's characters' in a heartbeat?"

Riley remembered the hush that had fallen. They were seated in a flagstone courtyard around a clay chiminea as dusk eased into darkness and the air took on a chill. "You want to live in Regency England?" Nora had asked sharply. "And be some man's property?"

"Of course not. I don't want the class conflict or the snobbery or the outdated rules. But I want the beauty of their lives. I want the music and the literature. I want afternoon visits and balls. Why don't we do those things anymore?"

"Who has time for that?" Riley's job at the ad agency kept her working until all hours. She couldn't remember the last time she'd taken a full day off of work, let alone visited anyone.

"I haven't played the piano in years," Savannah said wistfully. "I mean, I was never any good—"

"Are you kidding? You were fantastic," Avery said.

"I don't think I could stand all those long walks through the countryside," Nora said. "Have you noticed how much time those women spend walking in the movies?"

Riley knew Nora loved city life, but she was as burnt out as the rest of them. As a teacher she felt she should go where she was needed and she taught at in an area of Baltimore that resembled a war zone. She couldn't imagine Nora was happy no matter how much she claimed the work fulfilled her.

"So why don't we do it?" Avery said in the lull that followed Nora's comment.

"Do what?" Savannah asked.

"Create an Austen life. A beautiful life, with time for music and literature and poetry and walks—and maybe even balls."

"How on earth would you do that? And why would you want to?" Nora took a long drink from her mug of herbal tea.

"We'd pool our resources together. We've all saved something, right? We'd buy some big old house on a huge plot of land and start a Jane Austen bed and breakfast. The women who visited would step into Regency times and take a break from their crazy lives, just like we want to do."

"That's… genius," Riley said. "Isn't it genius?"

"It kind of is," Avery said.

"Where would you find the house and land?" Nora asked. Riley noticed that although she was distancing herself from the plan she seemed awfully interested in the answer.

"I might know of a place," Riley said, and they were off and running.

A SEAL's Oath

The Cowboy's
E-Mail Order Bride

BY CORA SETON

"**Y**OU DID WHAT?" Ethan Cruz turned his back on the slate and glass entrance to Chance Creek, Montana's Regional Airport, and jiggled the door handle of Rob Matheson's battered red Chevy truck. Locked. It figured—Rob had to know he'd want to turn tail and head back to town the minute he found out what his friends had done. "Open the damned door, Rob."

"Not a chance. You've got to come in—we're picking up your bride."

"I don't have a bride and no one getting off that plane concerns me. You've had your fun, now open up the door or I'm grabbing a taxi." He faced his friends. Rob, who'd lived on the ranch next door to his their entire lives. Cab Johnson, county sheriff, who was far too level-headed to be part of this mess. And Jamie Lassiter, the best horse trainer west of the Mississippi as long as you could pry him away from the ladies. The four of them had gone to school together, played football together, and spent more Saturday nights at the bar than he could count. How many times had he gotten them out of trouble, drove them home when they'd had one beer to many, listened to them bellyache about their girlfriends or lack thereof when all he really wanted to do was knock back a cold one and play a game of pool? What the hell had he ever done to deserve this?

Unfortunately, he knew exactly what he'd done. He'd played a spectacularly brilliant prank a month or so ago on Rob—a prank that still had the town buzzing—and Rob concocted this nightmare as payback. Rob got him drunk one night and egged him on about his ex-fiancee until he spilled his guts about how much it still bothered him that Lacey Taylor had given him the boot in favor of that rich sonofabitch Carl Whitfield. The name made him want to spit. Dressed like a cowboy when everyone knew he couldn't ride to save his life.

Lacey bailed on him just as life had delivered a walloping one-two punch. First his parents died in a car accident. Then he discovered the ranch was mortgaged to the hilt. As soon as Lacey learned there would be some hard times ahead, she took off like a runaway horse. Didn't even have the decency to break up with him face to face. Before he knew it Carl was flying Lacey all over creation in his private plane. Las Vegas. San Francisco. Houston. He never had a chance to get her back.

He should have kept his thoughts bottled up where they belonged—would have kept them bottled up if Rob hadn't kept putting those shots into his hand—but no, after he got done swearing and railing at Lacey's bad taste in men, he apparently decided to lecture his friends on the merits of a real woman. The kind of woman a cowboy should marry.

And Rob—good ol' Rob—captured the whole thing with his cell phone.

When he showed it to him the following day, Ethan made short work of the asinine gadget, but it was too late. Rob had already emailed the video to Cab and Jamie, and the three of them spent the next several days making his life damn miserable over it.

If only they'd left it there.

The other two would have, but Rob was still sore about that old practical joke, so he took things even further. He decided there must be a woman out there somewhere who met all of the requirements Ethan expounded on during his drunken rant. To find her, he did what any rational man would do. He edited Ethan's rant into a video advertisement for a damned mail order bride.

And posted it on YouTube.

Rob showed him the video on the ride over to the airport. There he was for all the world to see, sounding like a jack-ass—hell, looking like one, too. Rob's fancy editing made his rant sound like a proposition. "What I want," he heard himself say, "is a traditional bride. A bride for a cowboy. 18—25 years old, willing to work hard, beautiful, quiet, sweet, good cook, ready for children. I'm willing to give her a trial. One month'll tell me all I need to know." Then the image cut out to a screen full of text, telling women how to submit their video applications.

Unbelievable. This was low—real low—even for Rob.

Ready for children?

"You all are cracked in the head. I'm not going in there."

"Come on, Ethan," Cab said. The big man stood with his legs spread, his arms folded over his barrel chest, ready to stop him if he tried to run. "The girl's come all the way from New York. You're not even going to say hello? What kind of a fiance are you?"

He clenched his fists. "No kind at all. And there isn't any girl in there. You know it. I know it. So stop wasting my time. There isn't any girl dumb enough to answer something like that!"

The other men exchanged a look.

"Actually," Jamie said, leaning against the Chevy and rubbing the stubble on his chin with the back of his hand. "We got nearly 200 answers to that video. Took us hours to get through them all." He grinned. "Who can resist a cowboy, right?"

As far as Ethan was concerned, plenty of women could. Lacey certainly had resisted him. Hence his bachelor status. "So you picked the ugliest, dumbest girl and tricked her into buying a plane ticket. Terrific."

Rob looked pained. "No, we found one that's both hot and smart. And we chipped in and bought the ticket—round trip, because we figured you wouldn't know a good thing when it kicked you in the butt, so we'd have to send her back. Have a little faith in your friends. You think we'd steer you wrong?"

Hell, yes. Ethan took a deep breath and squared his shoulders. The guys wouldn't admit they were joking until he'd gone into the airport and hung around the gate looking foolish for a suitable amount of time. And if they were stupid enough to actually fly a girl out here, he couldn't trust them to put her back on a plane home. So now instead of finishing his chores before supper, he'd lose the rest of the afternoon sorting out this mess.

"Fine. Let's get this over with," he said, striding toward the front door. Inside, he didn't bother to look at the television screen which showed incoming and outgoing flights. Chance Creek Regional had all of four gates. He'd just follow the hall as far as homeland security allowed him and wait until some lost soul deplaned.

"Look—it's on time." Rob grabbed his arm and tried to hurry him along. Ethan dug in the heels of his well worn boots and proceeded at his own pace.

Jamie pulled a cardboard sign out from under his jacket and flashed it at Ethan before holding it up above his head. It read, Autumn Leeds. Jamie shrugged at Ethan's expression. "I know—the name's brutal."

"Want to see her?" Cab pulled out a gadget and handed it over. Ethan held it gingerly. The laptop he bought on the advice of his accountant still sat untouched in his tiny office back at the ranch. He hated these miniature things that ran on swoops and swipes and taps on buttons that weren't really there. Cab reached over and pressed something and it came to life, showing a pretty young woman in a cotton dress in a kitchen preparing what appeared to be a pot roast.

"Hi, I'm Autumn," she said, looking straight at him. "Autumn Leeds. As you can see, I love cooking..."

Rob whooped and pointed. "Look—there she is! I told you she'd come!"

Ethan raised his gaze from the gadget to see the woman herself walking toward them down the carpeted hall. Long black hair, startling blue eyes, porcelain-white skin, she was thin and haunted and luminous all at the same time. She, too, held a cell phone and seemed to be consulting it, her gaze glancing down then sweeping the crowd. As their eyes met, hers widened with recognition. He groaned inwardly when he realized this pretty woman had probably watched Rob's stupid video multiple times. She might be looking at his picture now.

As the crowd of passengers and relatives split around their party, she walked straight up to them and held out her hand. "Ethan Cruz?" Her voice was low and husky, her fingers cool and her handshake firm. He found himself wanting to linger over it. Instead he nodded. "I'm Autumn Leeds. Your bride."

AUTUMN HAD NEVER BEEN more terrified in her life. In her short career as a columnist for CityPretty Magazine, she'd interviewed models, society women, CEO's and politicians, but all of them were urbanites, and she'd never had to leave New York to get the job done. As soon as her plane departed LaGuardia she knew she'd made a mistake. As the city skyline fell away and the countryside below her emptied into farmland, she clutched the arms of her seat as if she was heading for the moon rather than Montana. Now, hours later, she felt off-kilter and fuzzy, and the four men before her looked like extras in a Western flick. Large, muscled, rough men who all exuded a distinct odor of sweat she realized probably came from an honest afternoon's work. Entirely out of her comfort zone, she wondered for the millionth time if she'd done the right thing. It's the only way to get my contract renewed, she reminded herself. She had to write a story different from all the other articles in CityPretty. In these tough economic times, the magazine was downsizing—again. If she didn't want to find herself out on the street, she had to produce—fast.

And what better story to write than the tale of a Montana cowboy using YouTube to search for an email-order bride?

Ethan Cruz looked back at her, seemingly at a loss for words. Well, that was to be expected with a cowboy, right? The ones in movies said about one word every ten minutes or so. That's why his video said she needed to be quiet. Well, she could be quiet. She didn't trust herself to speak, anyway.

She'd never been so near a cowboy before. Her best friend, Becka, helped shoot her video response, and they'd spent a hilarious day creating a pseudo-Autumn guaranteed to warm the cockles of a cowboy's heart. Together, they'd decided to pitch her as desperate to escape the dirty city and unleash her inner farm wife on Ethan's Montana ranch. They hinted she loved garden-ing, canning, and all the domestic arts. They played up both her toughness (she played first base in high school baseball) and her femininity (she loved quilting—*what an outright lie*). She had six costume changes in the three minute video.

Over her vehement protests, Becka forced her to end the video with a close-up of her face while she uttered the words, "I often fall asleep imagining the family I'll someday have." Autumn's cheeks warmed as she recalled the depth of the deception. She wasn't a country girl pining to be a wife; she was a career girl who didn't intend to have kids for at least another decade. Right?

Of course.

Except somehow, when she watched the final video, the life the false Autumn said she wanted sounded far more compelling than the life the real Autumn lived. Especially the part about wanting a family.

It wasn't that she didn't want a career. She just wanted a different one—a different life. She hated how hectic and shallow everything seemed now. She remembered her childhood, back when she had two parents—a successful investment banker father and a stay-at-home mother who made the best cookies in New York City. Back then, her mom, Teresa, loved to take Autumn and her sister, Lily, to visit museums, see movies and plays, walk in Central Park and shop in the ethnic groceries that surrounded their home. On Sundays, they cooked fabulous feasts together and her mother's laugh rang out loud and often. Friends and relatives stopped by to eat and talk, and Autumn played with the other children while the grownups clustered around the kitchen table.

All that changed when she turned nine and her father left them for a travel agent. Her parents' divorce was horrible. The fight wasn't over custody; her father was all too eager to leave child-rearing to her mother while he toured Brazil with his new wife. The fight was over money—over the bulk of the savings her father had transferred to offshore accounts in the weeks before the breakup, and refused to return.

Broke, single and humiliated, her mother took up the threads of the life she'd put aside to marry and raise a family. A graduate of an elite liberal arts college, with several years of medical school already under her belt, she moved them into a tiny apartment on the edge of a barely-decent neighborhood and returned to her studies. Those were lean, lonely years when everyone had to pitch in. Autumn's older sister watched over her after school, and Teresa expected them to take on any and all chores they could possibly handle. As Autumn grew, she took over the cooking and shopping and finally the family's accounts. Teresa had no time for cultural excursions, let alone entertaining friends, but by the time Autumn was ready to go to college herself, she ran a successful OB-GYN practice that catered to wealthy women who'd left childbearing until the last possible moment, and she didn't even have to take out a loan to fund her education.

Determined her daughters would never face the same challenges she had, Teresa raised them with three guiding precepts:

Every woman must be self-supporting.

Marriage is a trap set by men for women.

Parenthood must be postponed until one reaches the pinnacle of her career.

Autumn's sister, Lily, was a shining example of this guide to life. She was single, ran her own physical therapy clinic, and didn't plan to marry or have children any time soon. Next to her, Autumn felt like a black sheep. She couldn't seem to accept work was all there was to life. Couldn't forget the joy of laying a table for a host of guests. She still missed those happy, crowded Sunday afternoons so much it hurt her to think about them.

She forced her thoughts back to the present. The man before her was ten times more handsome than he was in his video, and that was saying a lot. Dark hair, blue eyes, a chiseled jaw with just a trace of manly stubble. His shoulders were broad and his stance radiated a determination she found more than compelling. This was a man you could lean on, a man who could take care of the bad guys, wrangle the cattle, and still sweep you off your feet.

"Ethan, aren't you going to say hello to your fiancee?" One of the other men stuck out his hand. "I'm Rob Matheson. This is Cab Johnson and Jamie Lassiter. Ethan here needed some backup."

Rob was blonde, about Ethan's size, but not nearly so serious. In fact, she bet he was a real cut-up. That shit-eating grin probably never left his face. Cab was larger than the others—six foot four maybe, powerfully built. He wore a sheriff's uniform. Jamie was lean but muscular, with dark brown hair that fell into his eyes. They had the easy camaraderie that spoke of a long acquaintance. They probably knew each other as kids, and would take turns being best man at each other's weddings.

Her wedding.

No—she'd be long gone before the month was up. She had three weeks to turn in the story; maybe four, if it was really juicy. She'd pitched it to the editor of CityPretty as soon as the idea occurred to her. Margaret's uncertain approval told her she was probably allowing her one last hurrah before CityPretty let her go.

Still, just for one moment she imagined herself standing side by side Ethan at the altar of some country church, pledging her love to him. What would it be like to marry a near stranger and try to forge a life with him?

Insane, that's what.

So why did the idea send tendrils of warmth into all the right places?

She glanced up at Ethan to find him glancing down, and the warm feeling curved around her insides again. Surely New York men couldn't be shorter than this crew, or any less manly, but she couldn't remember the last time she'd been around so much blatant testosterone. She must be ovulating. Why else would she react like this to a perfect stranger?

Ethan touched her arm. "This way." She followed him down the hall, the others falling into place behind them like a cowboy entourage. She stifled a sudden laugh at the absurdity of it all, slipped her hand into her purse and grabbed her digital camera, capturing the scene with a few clicks. Had this man—this…*cowboy*—sat down and planned out the video he'd made? She tried to picture Ethan bending over a desk and carefully writing out "Sweet. Good cook. Ready for children."

She blew out a breath and wondered if she was the only one stifling in this sudden heat. Ready for children? Hardly. Still…if she was going to make babies with anyone…

Shaking her head to dispel that dangerous image, she found herself at the airport's single baggage carousel. It was just shuddering to life and within moments she pointed out first one, then another sleek, black suitcase. Ethan took them both, began to move toward the door and then faltered to a stop. He avoided her gaze, focusing on something far beyond her shoulder. "It's just…I wasn't…."

Oh God, Autumn thought, a sudden chill racing down her spine. Her stomach lurched and she raised a hand as if to ward off his words. She hadn't even considered this.

He'd taken one look and decided to send her back.

ETHAN STARED INTO THE STRICKEN EYES of the most beautiful woman he'd ever met. He had to confess to her right now the extent of the joke she'd been led into thinking was real. It'd been bad enough when he thought Rob and the rest of them had simply hauled him to the airport for a chance to laugh their asses off at him, but now there was a woman involved, a real, beautiful, fragile woman. He had to stop this before it went any further.

When she raised her clear blue gaze to his, he saw panic, horror, and an awful recognition he instantly realized meant she thought she'd been judged and found wanting. He knew he'd do anything to make that look go away. Judged wanting. As if. The girl was as beautiful as a harvest moon shining on frost-flecked fields in late November. He itched to touch her, take her hand, pull her hard against him and...

Whoa—that thought couldn't go any farther.

He swallowed hard and tried again. "I...it's just my place...something came up and I didn't get a chance to fix it like I meant to." She relaxed a fraction and he rushed on. "It's a good house—built by my great granddaddy in 1889 for the hired help. Solid. Just needs a little attention."

"A woman's touch," Rob threw in.

Ethan restrained himself, barely. He'd get back at all of his friends soon enough. "I just hope you'll be comfortable."

A snigger behind him made him clench his fists.

"I don't mind if it's rough," Autumn said, eliciting a bark of laughter from the peanut gallery. She blushed and Ethan couldn't take his eyes off her face, although he wished she hadn't caught the joke. She'd look like that in bed, after...

Enough.

"Give me the keys," he said to Rob. When his friend hesitated, he held out a hand. "Now."

Rob handed them over with a raised eyebrow, but

Ethan just led the way outside and threw Autumn's suitcases in the bed of the truck. He opened the passenger side door.

"Thank you," she said, putting first one foot, then the other on the running board and scrambling somewhat ungracefully into the seat. City girl. At least her hesitation gave him a long moment to enjoy the view.

Rob made as if to open the door to the back bench seat, but Ethan shoved him aside, pressed down the lock and closed the passenger door. He was halfway around the truck before Rob could react.

"Hey, what are you doing?"

"Taking a ride with my fiancee. You all find your own way home." He was in the driver's side with the ignition turning over before any of them moved a muscle. Stupid fools. They'd made their beds and they could sleep in them.

He glanced at the ethereal princess sitting less than two feet away. Meanwhile, he'd sleep in his own comfortable bed tonight. Maybe with a little company for once.

The Cowboy's E-mail Order Bride (Volume 1)

ABOUT THE AUTHOR

Cora Seton loves cowboys, country life, gardening, bike-riding, and lazing around with a good book. Mother of four, wife to a computer programmer/eco-farmer, she ditched her California lifestyle nine years ago and moved to a remote logging town in northwestern British Columbia.

Like the characters in her novels, Cora enjoys old-fashioned pursuits and modern technology, spending mornings transforming an ordinary one-acre lot into a paradise of orchards, berry bushes and market gardens, and afternoons writing the latest Chance Creek romance novel on her iPad mini. Visit www.coraseton.com to read about new releases, locate your favorite characters on the Chance Creek map, and learn about contests and other cool events!

Blog:

www.coraseton.com

Facebook:

www.facebook.com/coraseton

Twitter:

www.twitter.com/coraseton

Newsletter:

eepurl.com/xhLRf

Made in the USA
Middletown, DE
16 September 2017